FLEET OF KNIVES

Also by Gareth L. Powell
and available from Titan Books

Embers of War
Fleet of Knives
Light of Impossible Stars (February 2020)

GARETH L.
POWELL
FLEET OF KNIVES

AN EMBERS OF WAR NOVEL

TITAN BOOKS

Fleet of Knives: An Embers of War Novel
Mass market edition ISBN: 9781785655234
E-book edition ISBN: 9781785655227

Published by Titan Books
A division of Titan Publishing Group Ltd
144 Southwark Street, London SE1 0UP

First mass market edition: January 2020
10 9 8 7 6 5 4 3 2 1

A CIP catalogue record for this title is available from the British Library.

Printed and bound in the United States.

Did you enjoy this book?
Please email us at: readerfeedback@titanemail.com
To receive advance information, news, competitions, and exclusive
offers online, please sign up for the Titan newsletter on our website:

TITAN BOOKS.COM

To Edith and Winter

"There would be no dance, and there is only the dance."

T.S. ELIOT

PROLOGUE

SAL KONSTANZ

"I'm almost at the top."

I'd been climbing since first light. The high desert wind's thin fingers kept snatching at my cape. I had a scarf wrapped across my mouth and nose to keep out the swirling sand and ash, and wore dark goggles to protect my eyes from the glare.

"I know." The *Trouble Dog*'s voice came via an implant in my right ear. "I'm monitoring your position, and your vital signs." She sounded impatient, but I didn't have the breath to respond. The Temples of the High Country stood on an imposing mesa, high above an arid wasteland, and the only way to reach them was via steps carved into the side of the mesa's rust-coloured cliffs.

"I still think it would have been quicker for me to drop you at the top," she said.

"You know that's forbidden." The steps had been smoothed to a shine by the millennial action of wind and sand, and the tread of countless feet—both human and otherwise. My lungs and thighs burned from the ascent. I spoke between laboured breaths. "And besides, it's kind of missing the point. Climbing the steps is part of the experience."

Altogether, it had taken me three hours. I had camped at the foot of the cliffs and set out in the chilly pre-dawn light, determined to reach the summit before the midday heat made such effort even more arduous.

"If you say so."

The Temples of the High Country were some of the oldest alien ruins known to mankind. They were a spiritual and archaeological treasure beyond value—but I hadn't climbed all this way just to look at a few crumbling sandstone walls. I unslung my pack and let it drop to my feet. Set against the antediluvian backdrop of these ruins, my own problems seemed minor and ephemeral, my own worries petty and futile. I crouched beside the pack and withdrew a black long-stemmed rose from a side pocket. Its silk petals fluttered in the wind.

"A couple of paces to the left," the *Trouble Dog* said. Although she was currently languishing in a parking orbit, forty thousand kilometres above this desert, her sensors could still resolve and locate surface features to within a micron.

I shuffled position. "Here?" I looked at the ground between my feet. Fifteen years ago, at the outbreak of the Archipelago War, Gunnery Sergeant Greta Nowak had died defending the top of this great stone staircase. "Are you sure?" The tactical computers overseeing the battle had logged her exact position at the moment of her death—but now, a decade and a half later, nothing remained to mark the spot, not even a stain on the exposed, wind-scoured rock.

"I am."

"Okay, then."

From my pocket, I pulled an antique silver frame containing a photograph of George Walker, the *Trouble Dog*'s former medical officer. He had been killed while we were trying to rescue the crew of a ditched scout ship. I'd neglected to order a risk assessment of the local fauna, and he'd paid with his life.

I rubbed the glass with my sleeve, wiping away dust and finger smudges. The frame was solid silver, and hopefully heavy enough not to be blown from this site by the high desert winds. The picture had been taken in the *Trouble Dog*'s infirmary during the Archipelago War, before the ship resigned its commission and declared its allegiance to the House of Reclamation. In it, George wore the bright orange jumpsuit of a naval medic. He looked younger than I remembered him. His hair wasn't completely grey, his face not as deeply lined. And yet, there could be no mistaking that smile. I knelt down and leant the frame against the powdery red stone of the nearest wall, angled so that, each morning, the first rays of the rising sun would strike it and illuminate his face. I ran a fingertip across the glass, tracing the line of his cheek. A dry wind tugged at the hem of my cape. To the west, three of the planet's five moons were still visible, lingering like pale onlookers.

"Sorry, George." It was all I could think of to say. I raised the rose to my covered lips, and then laid it in front of the frame, its stem weighed down with a fist-sized rock. I had nothing to say to Greta Nowak. I hadn't known her. She had fallen here, and her recovered-but-unclaimed body had been harvested for its organs and stem cells. Although shrapnel had peppered her heart and lungs, her kidneys, liver and spleen had helped save the lives of three wounded comrades. Meanwhile, her stem cells had been forwarded to a naval facility a dozen light years distant where, a year later, they were used to grow organic processors—brains—for a pack of six Carnivore-class warships. And those six had been the *Trouble Dog* and her siblings.

The rose was the *Dog*'s way of acknowledging this, just as the photograph was my way of saying goodbye to George.

•

As noon approached, I lay in the shadow of the temple wall, with my head resting on my arm. The rocks beneath me were hard and awkward, stripped of sand by the desert wind. Unable to find a comfortable position, I watched shimmers of heat rising from the stones at the plateau's edge.

"So, what now?" The *Trouble Dog* sounded bored. "Are you going to climb all the way back down?"

"First I need to wait for it to get cooler."

"And when will that be?"

"In a couple of hours."

"Are you quite sure you don't want me to come and pick you up?"

I smiled behind the scarf. "I'm very sure, thank you." We both knew the ruins lay at the centre of a dome-shaped no-fly zone. And, to tell the truth, I was rather enjoying the solitude. After what we'd been through in the Gallery, we were due some time away from our duties.

In fact, that was the point of this shakedown cruise.

Following the battle, we had been placed in quarantine until the doctors satisfied themselves we weren't unwittingly carrying any alien pathogens. Even the *Dog* had what

14

it called "a check-up from the deck up." Then, when they were quite certain we posed no medical threat, the House elders subjected us to an extensive debriefing. Our testimonies, and the ship's records of events, were pored over in exhaustive detail, from the initial distress call sent by the *Geest van Amsterdam* to the emergence of the million-strong Marble Armada, and my reluctant assassination of a Conglomeration admiral on the bridge of his flagship.

Throughout its history, the House of Reclamation had been an apolitical organisation, dedicated simply to the preservation of life and the rescue of stranded spacefarers. So it came as no surprise that the House elders were less than thrilled to find themselves suddenly thrust into the centre of the biggest military and political shake-up since the Archipelago War.

We spent weeks being cross-examined, physically examined, and subjected to every test they could think to run upon us. The *Trouble Dog* had emerged from that distant mausoleum at the head of an alien armada large enough to outnumber the combined forces of every government in the Human Generality—and the elders were under a lot of external pressure to discover how much influence the *Dog* and its crew might have on the forthcoming actions and intentions of that armada.

We answered all their questions to the best of our abilities. And when the *Dog* finally declared she was flat-out leaving, they at least had the good sense not to argue.

Carnivore-class heavy cruisers can be headstrong beasts, and this one had recently been betrayed by—and forced to kill—one of her siblings.

Sometimes, it was easy to forget that a human mind lurked at the heart of the ship. At a hundred and seventy-two metres in length and displacing ten thousand tons, she was a formidable creature conditioned for battle. But behind the missile racks, torpedo tubes and sensor blisters, she was becoming increasingly capable of genuine emotion. Even though three quarters of her thoughts ran on artificial processors, no amount of silicon could fully mask the storm of grief and guilt now swirling in that cloned cortex.

She had killed her sister. It had been in self-defence, but that didn't make the fact of it any easier for her to deal with.

And me?

I'd ordered the death of another human being. I'd done it to save his crew from a fight they couldn't possibly hope to win, but I still felt like a murderer.

We both needed time to come to terms with what we'd done, and we needed to say goodbye to our fallen comrades.

The elders of the House had, extremely reluctantly, granted us a sabbatical. And frankly, we'd earned it.

Lying there, in the shadow of the ruined wall, I stared into the sky and thought about George, about the war, and about the people we'd lost. About how life accumulates its hurts upon us the same way asteroids find themselves weathered and pocked by cold barrages of interplanetary dust.

•

What is honour?

While commanding a medical frigate during the war, I had the opportunity to talk to a lot of wounded soldiers— both men and women. Some were struggling with mortal wounds. Sightless, jaws clenching against the pain, they would grip my hand and ask if I thought they'd acquitted themselves with honour. They seemed to equate honour with bravery; to have been wounded while acting with honour meant they had faced the enemy without fear, that they were more than just shredded cannon fodder—that they had behaved in such a way that their families could draw comfort from their conduct, knowing they had upheld the values for which they fought.

But to me, honour has always meant something else. Something nobler and more personal. My great-great-grandmother defined it when she wrote in the founding documents of the House that, "Courage is making the choice to forgive, even when every nerve in your body cries out for vengeance."

For me, honour is having that courage, and the strength to do the right thing, even though it might run counter to my own interests. And by that token, the Conglomeration commanders dishonoured themselves at the Battle of Pelapatarn. Faced with a choice between losing the war and destroying an ancient, irreplaceable world filled with billions of arboreal intelligences, they chose the latter. They chose the wrong path because it suited their short-term needs. But those trees had been there for untold millennia, growing and dying, each with a lifespan greater than many human civilisations. Destroying them was a desecration. It was a genocide of staggering short-sightedness. And, as far as I was concerned, they all shared the blame, from the generals who'd given the order to the commander of the Conglomeration Fleet, who in turn passed it along to the captains of the ships that finally prosecuted the atrocity. I held complicit everyone in the chain of command, from Captain Deal down to the individual, anonymous ships in her strike force. If they had possessed a scrap of honour, they would have laid down their own lives rather than participate in such barbarity.

I had been in the system when the crime took place, but my frigate had been ordered to hold position with the other support ships, in orbit around the larger of Pelapatarn's two moons. We could only watch in horror as the pictures came in—pictures of a world aflame, and death on an unimaginable scale.

I'd joined the Outward Navy when my parents died. I'd done it because I wanted to escape the shadow of my family, and especially my great-great-grandmother. But in the aftermath of Pelapatarn, I knew I could no longer serve an organisation dedicated to violence, however righteous or justified—or *honourable*—that violence might be. And so I resigned. I turned the medical frigate over to my second-in-command, and transmitted an application to the House of Reclamation.

And when I pinned on that sixteen-pointed yellow star, and read the emblazoned motto, Life Above All, I knew with certainty that I had found a place where I could serve the remainder of my days with real honour— the kind that comes from compassion and forgiveness rather than cruelty and expedience.

•

I awoke two hours later, stiff from lying on such a hard surface, and surprised to have slept so long. The climb up the side of the mesa must have tired me more than I'd realised.

"Welcome back." The sound of the *Trouble Dog*'s voice filled me with an unexpected pang of desolation. Why was I out here, lying on a desert rock a hundred light years from where I'd been born? A hundred light years from the graves of my parents, and who knew how much further from the frozen husk of the only man I'd ever loved.

"Did you sleep well?" she asked.

I rubbed my eyes and levered myself up on my elbows. The wind still felt warm, but it had lost the furnace-like breath of midday.

"As well as can be expected." I sat up. Something clicked in my lower back, and I suppressed a groan.

"Why didn't you wake me?"

"I thought you might appreciate the rest."

I blinked in surprise. "That's unusually considerate of you. If I didn't know better, I might suspect you were maturing."

I packed away my things and walked back towards the head of the steps. As I approached, I saw a small knot of tourists cresting the edge of the plateau on donkeys. They had ridden up during the heat of the day, and were all red-faced and panting beneath their wide-brimmed hats. When they caught sight of me, their smiles were filled with the comradeship of mountaineers passing each other on a high peak. As they dismounted from their rides, we passed a few pleasantries about the heat, the steepness of the climb and lack of safety rails.

Then one of the men asked, "Are you a member of the House?" He had a thick moustache and a military bearing. I looked down at my loose clothes, wondering how he could have guessed. Then I remembered the badge I'd used as a clasp for my cape: a relief image of the House of Reclamation's sixteen-pointed star, rendered in bronze. I brushed it with my fingers.

"Yes."

"We saw your cruiser in orbit." He jerked a thumb at the implacable desert sky, and I had to resist the urge to glance upward in response.

"Yes," I said, "she's with me."

He nodded, seemingly understanding the complex relationship I had with the offensive heavy cruiser I called both home and sister.

"She's a Carnivore, isn't she?"

"Decommissioned."

"I thought so." He tapped his barrel-like chest. "I spent eighteen years in the Conglomeration Navy. Saw action around Charlotte's World during the war."

He seemed so proud, so pleased with himself, that I couldn't help saying, "I was at Pelapatarn."

For an instant, some of his bluster dropped away.

"You *fought* at Pelapatarn?"

"I commanded a medical frigate."

"Really?" He leaned forward, clearly impressed despite himself. "Was it as bad as they say? The battle, I mean."

"Worse." I couldn't bring myself to elaborate. Some things can't be put into words, and the defeat of the Outward forces at Pelapatarn was an atrocity I had no way to articulate. Luckily, he seemed to understand this as well. We both looked at the dust between us, lost for a moment in our own experiences of the war.

The rest of the tour group moved off, towards the temple ruins. The moustachioed man forced a smile.

"Well, it was a pleasure to meet you, Captain." He saluted. "And it's good to see some ships still have human crews."

I returned the salute, feeling faintly ridiculous. I was getting impatient to begin my descent. I felt sticky and in need of a shower and a cold drink. But his last remark puzzled me.

"Human crews?" All ships carried human personnel, except… "You're talking about the Marble Armada?"

His smile collapsed into a scowl. He hawked phlegm and spat it into the dust.

"Fucking invasion fleet, if you ask me."

"Really?" He obviously had no idea of the part I'd played in rousing the Armada from their millennial slumber. "They don't seem to have done anything hostile." As far as I knew, the Armada had taken station on the edge of the Camrose System, and was currently locked in discussion with the elders of the House, trying to figure out how best to accomplish their mission, which was the prevention of another conflict on the scale of the Archipelago War. I said as much, but my new friend was not to be so easily placated.

"What do we really know about them," he insisted, flushed and sweating, "except they survived the death of the race that built them, and now they're here, offering to help us in turn?"

The Conglomeration had always been introspective and suspicious of other species. It was an attitude that, as a former member of the Outward, I'd always found deeply irritating.

"They don't seem hostile," I said.

He shook his head, disappointed by my naivety. Then he jabbed his thumb against his chest.

"Well, *I* don't trust them," he said, "and neither should you."

PART ONE

LUCY'S GHOST

———————

The universe has an almost infinite capacity to charm and appal.

Sofia Nikitas

CHAPTER ONE

JOHNNY SCHULTZ

The attack came while we were in the higher dimensional void, and it came without warning. I'd had a late-night card session with Santos and Kelly, and was making my way up the companionway to the bridge, eyes still bleary with sleep, when the *Lucy's Ghost* slammed sideways, smacking me hard against the bulkhead.

I ended up on my back at the foot of the ladder. My left shoulder felt battered, and I'd scraped my right shin. I'd been carrying my antique leather pilot's jacket in one hand, and had dropped it when I hit the wall; and somehow, I'd cut my forehead. When I put my hand to it, the fingertips came away red and sticky with blood.

"Hey!" I yelled up the companionway. "What the fuck was that?"

I could feel the artificial gravity flickering as it tried to recalibrate, having been unable to compensate for the savagery of the lurch.

Above me, Vito Accardi's face appeared at the hatch.

"Something hit us, chief."

Keeping one hand over the cut on my head, I scooped up my jacket and scrambled to my feet.

"Yeah, no shit?" I held onto the wall for support. With the gravity skittish, I didn't want to get caught off guard by a second impact. "What was it? Are we being shot at?"

Looking down at me with wide eyes, Vito shook his head.

"I don't know. But you'd better get up here."

•

The *Lucy's Ghost* was a medium-sized trader, licensed to carry a hundred and sixty tons of cargo between the various worlds of the Generality. She was three hundred metres in length and a hundred and fifty across her beam. In profile, she was a blocky, industrial-looking three-sided chisel, with a blunt nose at the front, and chunky propulsion units at the rear. She'd had many owners in her time, and had travelled the length and breadth of the Generality, all the way from Earth to the Rim Stars and the Trailing Edge. In cross-section, she resembled a triangle with rounded points, split into three levels. The cargo area filled most of the large lower deck, with the remainder taken up by fuel containment and engines. The middle deck housed crew quarters, passenger staterooms, a cramped galley, maintenance shops and equipment storage. The smaller upper deck had been given over almost entirely to the bridge, but also housed the main passenger airlock and a small communal lounge area that sported a picture window, torn and scuffed leather seats and a variety of brown brittle-leafed spider plants.

The story around the ports—a rumour I'd done my

best to encourage—was that at the age of seventeen, as a young dock rat, I'd won her in a game of cards. It wasn't true, but it helped my reputation.

I had actually bought her with a combination of money inherited from a childless uncle and a large mortgage from the bank—a mortgage I was still paying off in monthly instalments. Now, ten years and around a thousand light years later, I'd been playing the part of "Lucky" Johnny Schultz for so long, even I sometimes found it hard to remember which version of the story was real and which was made up.

I pulled myself up the ladder and through the hatch, onto the bridge. The main display screen showed an external view of the grey mist that surrounded the ship. A second, smaller screen held a computer-generated image of the *Lucy*'s crew interface: a young girl with bright, playful eyes and hair the colour of starlight.

I dumped my leather jacket across the back of the captain's chair, and strapped myself in, wiping blood-sticky fingers on my thigh.

"What do we know?"

"Not much," Vito said. "The ship didn't see anything."

I looked at the *Lucy*. "Nothing?"

On the screen, she pursed her virtual lips. "Sensor readings remain normal, dearie."

Even after all this time, it still felt strange to hear an old woman's phrasing coming from someone so young-looking; but while the avatar's image had remained frozen since the ship's inception, her mind had aged over the decades she'd been plying the cargo circuits of the Generality.

"No readings of heat, mass, anything like that?"

"Just the void, same as ever it was."

Carefully, I flexed my shoulder. It was already beginning to stiffen.

"Vito?"

The pilot shrugged. He looked rattled. "*Something* hit us."

"But you didn't see what it was?"

"It didn't come from the front." I could see beads of sweat like jewels on his upper lip. "And the ship didn't see it…"

"Are you sure it was an impact? Could it have been explosive decompression?" I thought maybe something had blown internally, causing a hull rupture.

The *Lucy* answered, "All internal compartments read as still pressurised, dearie. But I'm detecting serious damage to the starboard hull plates. Whatever hit us definitely came from outside."

That ruled out accident, malfunction or sabotage.

Vito rubbed his lips with a nervous hand.

"Pirates?"

"In the void?" I shook my head. "It's not possible. You can't track another ship through the hypervoid. And besides, even if there were another ship out here, the *Lucy* would have seen it."

"Then what hit us?" He seemed on the verge of giggling. "A hypervoid monster?"

"Don't be stupid." Faced with the abyssal emptiness of the void, the human brain—with its evolved ability to spot camouflaged predators lurking in the long grass—tended to impose patterns and threats where none existed. Men and women who stared into the shifting mists of the higher dimensions sometimes saw shadows moving in their peripheral vision, and imagined strange, impossible beasts skulking at the limits of visibility, like wolves circling the glow of a campfire.

Vito's laugh had a nervy edge. "Well, what else do you think it was, chief? A chunk of rock? An old beer bottle chucked from somebody's airlock?"

"Not likely." You needed an engine to stay in the hypervoid. Anything without power would quickly drop back down through the dimensions, into the normal, everyday universe. So the chances of us having hit some piece of random debris were infinitesimally small. I pulled up feeds from all the external cameras on the hull, but saw nothing more than the usual shifting emptiness.

"Nothing on your sensors?" I asked the *Lucy* again.

"Not a sausage, dearie."

"Hmm…" Keeping one eye on the external screens, I called down to the crew lounge. Riley Addison answered. Twenty-five years old, with long auburn hair and a gold stud in her right eyebrow, she was the ship's loadmaster, in charge of the loading and unloading of cargo, and keeper of the ship's stores.

"What's going on?" she asked.

"We hit a bump." I could see her frowning at the blood smeared across my forehead. "Is everybody else okay?"

"Mostly just a few cuts and bruises." She had a red mark on her cheek, as if she'd taken a glancing blow from something small and heavy, like a loose coffee mug or screwdriver. "Although Chet was down in engineering when it happened. It got thrown around pretty bad."

"How is it?"

"It looks like it might've busted a couple of ribs." Chet was the ship's Druff engineer. It had shiny scales, six limbs, and six hands that also doubled as faces.

"Shit."

"Any idea what hit us?"

"I'm working on it. Have you heard from Abe?" Abe Santos was the ship's cook. He would have been in the galley, preparing the midday meal.

"He dropped a saucepan on his foot."

"Is he okay?"

"It's swelling up and he's in a lot of pain. Looks like a nasty break, coupled with some scalding. Though to be honest, he seems more annoyed about the ruined spaghetti than anything else."

I smiled. "Well, that can't be helped. Any word from Jansen and Monk?"

"I haven't been able to reach them."

"Keep trying." I reached for the button that would end the call. "Get Dalton to do what he can for the others, and then make sure you're all strapped in. I don't want any more injuries."

Addison threw a half-assed salute. "Yes, sir!"

I returned my full attention to the outside view. I'd never been particularly bothered by the emptiness of the hypervoid. Perhaps it was because I'd been crewing ships since I was fifteen years old, and had become accustomed to the swirling, tenuous mists. Maybe I was braver than most. Or maybe I simply lacked the imagination to conjure up horrors from nothingness. Whatever the reason, I wasn't frightened of staring into the abyss.

"Coming up on target in five minutes," Vito said. He activated the intercom and his voice rang through the ship. "All hands, prepare to drop back into reality. Four minutes forty-five, and counting."

Although he was the pilot, the *Lucy's Ghost* carried out the vast majority of navigational calculations. An unaided human brain simply couldn't crunch the kind of numbers necessary to plot a course through the higher dimensions—and hurling yourself into the hypervoid without doing the math was a good way to disappear and never be heard from again.

Nothing had changed on the external screens, so I asked the *Lucy* to keep monitoring them while I took a final look at the details of our target.

We were planning to intercept an old Nymtoq generation vessel called *The Restless Itch for Foreign Soil*. It had been constructed from a hollowed-out asteroid in the days before the Nymtoq discovered higher dimensional travel, and had been in flight now for almost ten thousand years. The society within fell apart and died out long before it reached its intended destination, and so the Nymtoq had been maintaining the old ship as a memorial, placing it on a looping course that took it back and forth through their territories, endlessly plying the dark spaces between the stars, at speeds that ensured it only came close to the light of inhabited systems once every few centuries.

Our plan was to pull alongside, cut our way in, and strip out as much saleable tech as we could carry. The battles of the Archipelago War had left wrecked human ships in a dozen systems across the Generality. Over the past couple of years, we'd scraped a living salvaging materiel and spare parts from them, but now the good finds were drying up, and we needed an alternate source of income—even one that was technically illegal, and likely to land us in a world of trouble if the Nymtoq ever discovered what we'd done. They would consider what we were planning an act of piracy, but I preferred to think of it as salvage. The *Restless Itch* had been adrift for centuries with its crew gone and systems dormant, while the rest of the universe zipped past it in the hypervoid, covering similar distances in days rather than decades. It was a monument, a flying tomb. And we were archaeologists, come to case it for valuable antiquities.

At least, that's what I told myself. The truth was, we were simply going to break in and lift anything that took our fancy. We didn't have the time or inclination for finesse.

Vito cleared his throat. "Four minutes fifteen." He began to throttle back the engines, preparing for a gradual transition back into normal space. If the *Lucy*'s calculations were correct—and the coordinates I'd bought worth the money I'd paid for them—we'd emerge into empty space a few tens of kilometres from the massive, drifting bulk of the *Restless Itch*.

"Four ten."

I gripped the arms of my couch and offered a silent prayer to any gods that might be listening. If we failed here, I wouldn't be able to afford to pay the crew, let alone fuel and provision the ship for another flight. Yes, we were risking the ire of an alien species, and the wrath of human customs officials, but if we couldn't secure a decent cargo, and bring it safely to market, we'd all be grounded and out of a job.

"Three fifty."

I double-checked my harness. The transition to normal space could occasionally be rough, and I'd been thrown around enough for one day. I tested the fastenings and adjusted the straps to make them more comfortable. My heart had begun to pound with the excitement and anticipation of the coming raid.

Only another three minutes…

I was still looking at the countdown when I caught movement in my peripheral vision: an impression of something black slipping between wisps of mist. By the time I turned my eyes to the screen it was gone.

"Ship, what was that?"

"What was what, dearie?"

I indicated the display in question. "There was something on the starboard screen, just for a second."

"My sensors aren't registering anything."

"There it is again!" This time the image was on the forward screen: a lithe black shape twisting through the murk, maybe two hundred metres from the *Lucy*'s prow.

"Where?"

"There!" I jabbed my finger at the picture, but the thing had already disappeared back into the mist.

I turned to the pilot. "You saw it, didn't you?"

Vito's eyes were wild. His fingers gripped the edge of his console. He tried to speak, but nothing came out. I saw him swallow hard, and he gave a tight, fearful nod. I wasn't hallucinating; he had seen it too, which meant it had to be real. And yet, still the *Lucy*'s avatar frowned.

"I'm afraid I'm still not detecting anything," she said.

"Are all your sensors working?"

"I checked them twice." She sounded vaguely indignant. "And all the diagnostics came back green."

"Then use landing radar, infrared. Turn on everything we've got." I could feel my pulse thumping in my chest. My stomach fluttered. I glanced at Vito.

"Two minutes to dropout." He'd found his voice. I gave him a thumbs-up, and returned to the screen.

And there it was!

Space twisted and split, and from the distortion a creature leapt. A huge, impossible creature that fell with the speed of a striking hawk, its lacy black wings folded

33

back against its body, its mouth open and fangs gleaming in the starlight. I had the impression of a gaping jaw filled with jewelled teeth. Then the screen blanked, and the ship wrenched itself sideways.

For a moment, we were being shaken in those titanic jaws. Then we were tumbling free as the creature swirled away like smoke, circling around for another strike.

"Drop us out!" I called to Vito, as alarms filled the bridge. "We can't wait for it to hit us again. Drop us out, now!"

His hand jerked the controls, and the *Lucy's Ghost* fell. Without finesse, she battered her way through the transitional zone between dimensions and spilled out into normal space, wounded and toppling, gas venting from holes in her starboard side. The stars whirled sickeningly around us for a couple of seconds—and then we slammed into the rocky flank of the *Restless Itch* like a hang-glider into the side of a mountain.

CHAPTER TWO

ONA SUDAK

From the window of my cell, I watched the sky grow pale. Somewhere, beyond the prison walls, birds were singing. Below me, in the flagstone courtyard that occupied the centre of the prison, half a dozen uniformed soldiers stood loading and inspecting their rifles in the thin, predawn light. Their voices were soft and low and, in the frosty morning air, their exhalations came as little ephemeral wisps of cloud. Between them and the rearmost wall, a pockmarked wooden stake marked the spot where, in a few short moments, I was scheduled to die.

Four years ago, under my real name of Annelida Deal, I had led the fleet that sterilised Pelapatarn. It was an action that brought the grinding attrition of the Archipelago War to an abrupt, horrific end, at the cost of a few thousand human lives and the destruction of a billion-year-old sentient jungle. And even though I had been acting under orders when I allowed my ships to commit that atrocity, the courts—under growing pressure from a populace appalled at the lengths to which its military had gone on its behalf—held me responsible for the destruction and loss of life, and sentenced me to be put to death here in this prison, on the anniversary of the armistice.

In my head, the two sides of my personality were at war. The part of me that had once pretended to be a poet named Ona Sudak railed against the injustice of it all—against dying here in this squalid little prison after everything I had done and seen—while the side of me that was Annelida Deal and had lived through the war laughed, and asked, *Why not? What makes you so special? Did you think you had a destiny? That the universe had a purpose in sparing you thus far? Well, guess what? So did every casualty on every battlefield throughout history: every serf murdered by an unjust lord; every peasant that starved in their hovel; every victim of accident, disease or random violence… They all thought the world had a plan for them, and they were all wrong. And they died shitty, untimely and disillusioned deaths because of it— because individual life means nothing in the cascade of history, and the gods have better things to worry about than your survival.*

I watched one of the soldiers clip a fresh magazine into his carbine. The rifles they were using were the same model I'd used in basic training: a robust firearm with few moving parts, designed primarily for ruggedness and simplicity of use.

In the cell behind me, the military chaplain coughed.

"If you wish to unburden yourself, now would seem to be the time."

I turned away from contemplation of my soon-to-be executioners.

"No, thank you."

The Reverend Thomas Berwick was an avuncular man with a round face and wide, sympathetic brown eyes. He wore the black robes of the Church, and clutched in his lap a thick, leather-bound holy book.

"This might be your last chance to confess," he said, "and make peace with your gods."

I felt my fists clench. "Why? So I can salve the consciences of those who condemned me?"

He gave a sympathetic half-smile, and spread his hands. "No, my daughter. For the sake of your soul."

My *soul*? If I'd had the energy, I might almost have laughed. "Have you ever seen a man die, padre? And I don't mean here," I jerked my head at the window, "where it's relatively quick and clean. I mean on the battlefield, when they're hit by an artillery shell and reduced to a splatter of slurry, and all that's left's a stinking mess of blood and shit and gristle? Or in a naval battle, when their section depressurises and the blood boils in their lungs? Or when they step on a mine and it blows their leg off up to the waist, and their innards are spilling out into the dust and they don't die quickly, and they most certainly don't die quietly?"

The chaplain's Adam's apple bobbed as he swallowed back his distaste.

"No, I can't say that I have."

"Well I've been there." I lowered my voice. "I've seen men and women die in ways so brutal and horrific that you probably can't even begin to imagine them, and I'll tell you this: I've seen nothing to convince me we're anything more than meat and bone and sinew." I tapped the side of my head. "We live in here, beneath this cap of bone, and there's nothing else. No emergency escape hatch that whisks us to heaven. No undying ghost that leaps from our mouth when the bullets enter our cranium." I turned back to the window with an angry shrug. "When you're dead, you're dead. There's no afterlife, no mystical white light, just darkness, oblivion, and an endless eternity of nonexistence."

Berwick was silent for a moment. Then he said, "That's a very negative point of view."

I shook my head. Below the window, the soldiers were practising their stances.

"It's not a point of view, padre, it's a fact. And as for being negative, well, I'm about to be shot, so you'll have to forgive me if I lack my usual cheery temperament."

Far beyond the prison walls, a dark speck appeared. Low and moving fast against the backdrop of the dawn, it skimmed the crests of the distant hills that had for the past six months marked the furthest boundaries of my visible horizon. I watched for a couple of seconds, and then lost sight of it as it dropped below the level of the wall.

I heard chair legs scrape the stone floor as the chaplain pushed himself laboriously to his feet.

"We only have a couple of minutes," he puffed. "They'll be coming for you soon. Do you at least have any final words? Any messages of comfort you'd like me to convey to your friends or family?"

I looked down at my hands.

"Tell them I followed orders. Tell them I respected the chain of command. And, ultimately, I did what I thought was for the best."

"You believe you did what was right?"

I pictured six Carnivore-class heavy cruisers entering the atmosphere of Pelapatarn and sweeping across its single continent in an arrowhead formation. I pictured their fusion warheads blossoming over the jungles, igniting firestorms that would choke the atmosphere for months, and I pictured the wrecked ships in orbit, the smouldering tree stumps and cremated animals on the ground. I imagined the terror of the soldiers from both sides as they saw the bombardment—an almost solid curtain of nuclear fire—sweeping across the treetops towards them, knowing there could be no escape, nowhere to hide. Had they appreciated the sacrifice they were making, in those last few instants before they were vaporised? Could they possibly have understood that their deaths would bring an almost immediate end to the war—and if so, could they have found it in their hearts to forgive me?

"No." The word came out hoarse. "That's not what I said. My exact words were, 'I did what I thought was for the best.' There's an important distinction."

"I see…"

I looked around at him. "You'll tell them that?"

"I will convey your words verbatim."

"Thank you."

I turned back to the window, just in time to see a flyer—obviously the black speck I had seen a moment before—rise from behind the prison wall, hover in the air for an instant, and then settle into the courtyard.

"Ah," Berwick said over the whine of its engines, "it seems we have visitors." He craned to see past my shoulder. "And that looks like a naval flyer. Were you expecting anyone?"

I turned back into the room with a shrug. Since being returned to the Conglomeration for trial, I'd had precious little contact with my former employers.

"Who knows?" I walked over to the wooden table, decanted a glass of stale water from the ceramic pitcher and took a drink. "There are plenty of people who want to see me dead, not least the admiralty."

"You think they've come to watch?"

"The vultures are circling."

I replaced the glass on the table and tugged the hem of my coarse prison shirt. Then I smoothed back my hair and fastened my collar. I hadn't been allowed to wear naval uniform for the execution, but that didn't mean I couldn't take pride in my appearance. If those bastards from the admiralty had come to watch my final moments, I wanted to be prepared. I wanted to walk out of this cell with my chin high and my back straight, and meet the bullets sent my way with dignity and poise, just to deny them the satisfaction of seeing me broken and humbled—and if they had come anticipating a final, pleading apology, they would be profoundly disappointed.

"How do I look?"

The chaplain glanced down at my prison clothes. His eyes were damp, and glittered wetly in the light of the cell's solitary bulb. "As elegant as can be expected, I suppose."

"Then I'm ready."

I tugged each cuff into place and set my jaw. I heard boots approaching in the corridor outside. Swallowing back my trepidation, I gave Berwick a final nod, and then turned to face the door.

Keys clanked and rattled in the lock, and the chipped and flaking cell door opened on noisy hinges. Two men stood on the threshold, filling the space. I had been expecting uniformed prison guards, come to escort me to my execution. Instead, these men wore black fatigues and mirrored goggles, and carried automatic pistols.

"Who's this?" one of them demanded, pointing his weapon at the chaplain.

Berwick threw up his hands in surprise. "I'm the chaplain," he said. "I'm here to offer comfort to the condemned. Why, what's happening? Who are you?"

"That's not your concern."

The gun snapped twice and Berwick clutched his chest. The holy book fell from his hands.

The second newcomer reached for me. "Come on," he said. "You're coming with us."

The pistol cracked a third time. The shot took the chaplain in the cheek. His head snapped sideways with the force of the impact, and he collapsed. A strangled moan came from him. His heels drummed the stone floor. He seemed to be trying to squirm away from his attacker.

The fourth shot was to the back of his head, where the spinal column joined the skull. After that, he lay still.

A hand closed on my upper arm, and I didn't resist. I allowed myself to be led from the room and into the corridor. The shooter followed us, pausing at each of the cell doors we passed to fire a couple of shots through the bean slot—the narrow aperture through which our daily meals were supplied.

"What's he doing?" I asked.

The man leading me increased his grip on my arm. "Neutralising witnesses," he said.

We carried on to the end of the corridor, and then down the echoing stone steps to the ground floor. Two uniformed prison guards lay dead inside the doors that led out to the courtyard. In the courtyard itself, the firing squad I'd watched clean and load their weapons now lay sprawled and scattered in the morning light. Their bright red blood ran along the grooves between the flagstones, towards the gutters that edged the courtyard. Stepping over their twitching, cooling bodies, my captor pulled me towards the flyer I'd seen land. Through its waiting hatch, I could see other men and women in black clothing and silver lenses, cradling pistols with fat silencers. Were these friends or assassins? I didn't have the opportunity to enquire. Rough hands seized my arms and hauled me aboard. And then, even as they were strapping me into a seat, we were airborne and wheeling up above the craggy prison walls, into the clear skies I'd been looking at since my incarceration six months previously.

CHAPTER THREE

TROUBLE DOG

I kept watch as Captain Konstanz picked her way down the perilously slippery temple steps. But while part of my view was focused on her, other parts of my attention saw larger pictures. From just over a tenth of a light second above her head, I could see not only the equatorial desert, but also the dusty smattering of ice at either of the planet's poles. I was also keeping track of every moving object in the system—every splinter of ice, every chunk of rock, and all four of the slow-witted tourist ships currently pottering their way to and from the spaceport on the edge of the desert—and it was gratifying to realise I was by far the largest and most heavily armed vessel in the locality, boasting as I did a full suite of upgraded defence screens, including three additional batteries of anti-missile cannon, and strengthened hull plating. My engines had been tuned, my internal systems overhauled, and I'd even been allowed to keep some of the offensive modifications I'd made while tooling up to fight my siblings in the remote mausoleum known as the Gallery. Of course, the elders of the House of Reclamation hadn't allowed me to reinstall the full range of ordnance I'd carried as a naval cruiser. I had no apocalypse-class antimatter warheads, for instance; no quantum suppressors or strong-force nullifiers, and definitely no chemical or biological payloads whatsoever, not even a lousy rat bomb. However, they had let me repair and reinstall six turret-mounted rail guns, one spinal maser, and seven fully stocked torpedo tubes armed with fission warheads. I might have lost the killing bite of my military days, but I had regained some of my claws, and they were sharp and tough enough to seriously maul anything that endangered the safety and wellbeing of my crew.

My crew.

As a heavy cruiser and ship of the line, I had been bred to value and protect my crew, but not at the expense of operational success. I had loved them, but not mourned them when they were lost in battle. The implanted aggression and pack loyalty of a wolf ensured my affections and allegiance remained with my fellow ships—the five Carnivore-class heavy cruisers I considered my brothers and sisters. Three of those had been lost during the war; the other two attacked me during the battle of the Gallery, and I had been forced to destroy one in self-defence, breaking a bond that went right the way back to the laboratory in which we'd both been grown. And it had been this act of violence that had brought Captain Konstanz and me closer. We had become sisters in misfortune and regret, having both faced down overwhelmingly superior odds, and been forced to take lives in order to preserve our own. And, quite unexpectedly, I found my loyalties attaching themselves to her, and to the other members of my crew: the former marine, Alva Clay; the medical student, Preston Menderes; and the alien engineer, Nod. Turned on by my former siblings, I broke my conditioning and found myself a new pack, and a new set of priorities.

And now I itched for something to do—for some action to break up the monotony of this shakedown cruise. I wanted to fly as far and fast as my engines could take me, to blaze across the galactic disc and hurl myself through the higher dimensions like a javelin.

Starlight prickled my hull. A gas giant lay three light minutes out, hanging like an ochre fruit against the blackness of space. I could hear its magnetic fields singing, and taste the tenuous wisps of hydrogen and methane that had made it out this far—stray molecules ripped from the gargantuan planet's upper atmosphere by the tidal action of its rings and moons.

It was right that we had come here to honour George. It was something the captain needed to do. She needed closure. But I felt little beyond passing regret. I missed George, but he had died while my former conditioning remained in force, so I felt unable to muster anything approaching true grief at his passing.

I was curious about the woman soldier who had died at the top of the temple steps a decade and a half before, thereby providing the stem cells from which my organic components had been grown. In some senses, she had been me, and I wanted to honour that bond. I knew her name and face—indeed, I had gained access to her complete military records—and yet when I looked down at the mesa where she had died, I saw only a dusty rock.

As an engine of war, I hadn't been designed to ponder mortality—only enforce it.

CHAPTER FOUR

SAL KONSTANZ

By the time I reached the desert floor at the bottom of the temple steps, the afternoon sky had turned the colour of lightly poached salmon, and my legs had taken on all the consistency and strength of steamed asparagus. Luckily, I didn't have to walk far to reach my hired dustboat, which was still parked in the mesa's shadow, exactly where I had left it. I threw my pack into the cargo hopper at the back. Then I settled into the front seat and savoured the relief of no longer being on my hot, aching feet. The spaceport lay a hundred kilometres to the west, in the direction of the setting sun and, after a day spent beneath the seemingly endless, wide-open desert skies, all I really wanted now was to get back to the *Trouble Dog* and the enclosing familiarity of her cabins and gangways.

I closed my eyes for a moment.

I had come so close to losing her. George's death had been my fault. If I hadn't just prevented the outbreak of another war, and come limping home from battle at the head of a million-strong armada, I think they would have taken my captaincy—and I wouldn't have blamed them in the slightest.

Thinking of the Marble Armada reminded me of the tourist I'd met at the top of the steps, and his distrust of them. Although his words had surprised me, I found I could sympathise with his point of view. To me, surrounded and outnumbered as I had been, their sudden intervention in the Gallery had seemed a miracle—but I could see how the appearance of such a vast alien fleet might unnerve someone who hadn't been present at that crucial moment, especially someone who'd fought in the Archipelago War, in which even the largest and bloodiest naval engagements involved fleets only a fraction of the size of this new armada.

"Shall I meet you at the port?" the *Trouble Dog* asked via my implant, her voice breaking into my thoughts.

"Okay." I unfastened and removed my hiking boots, unpeeled my socks, and threw them all into the hopper with my pack. "But you'd better give me a couple of hours to reach town." I stretched out my toes, savouring the relative freshness of the air in the shadow of the mesa.

"Preston and Nod are aboard. Shall I contact Alva?"

"No." With a touch of the joystick, I brought the vehicle's blunt nose around to face the horizon. "I need to speak to her first."

"I can put you in touch with her now?"

"No, thank you. I think I'd better talk to her in person."

"Do you think she's still angry with you?" The question was asked without tone or inflection. The dustboat's cockpit was open to the elements, so I made sure the silk scarf was securely tied across my mouth and nose, straightened my protective goggles, and clipped the safety harness into place.

"Let's just say we need to clear the air."

Alva Clay and I had barely spoken since leaving Camrose Station. She had testified against me during the inquest into George's death. She hadn't wanted to see me thrown out of the House, but George had been her friend and colleague a lot longer than she had been mine, and she still carried a lot of anger at the way he'd been killed—dragged below the ocean by a razor-tentacled monstrosity before any of us could react.

The brake and accelerator pedals felt pleasantly cool against the bare soles of my feet. I engaged the propellers, pressed down on the accelerator, and the boat surged forwards in response, its fans throwing up a cockerel's tail of sand and grit.

•

As I skimmed across the badlands between the mesa and the port, I thought back to the moment I'd been told I wouldn't face disciplinary charges for George's loss.

I had been in Ambassador Odom's office on Camrose Station, and all was apparently as it had been the last time I'd sat across the desk from him, immediately prior to my departure for the Gallery and the events that had transpired in that remote, eldritch system.

Here in the office, the same jellyfish lived out their thoughtless, gossamer existences in the corner fish tank. The framed pictures on the spotlessly white walls portrayed the same antique, bullet-shaped ships. Even Odom himself seemed every bit as tweedy and precise as he had been the last time we'd talked. For now, the status quo on Camrose Station had been preserved, and it was only me that had changed.

"How are you feeling?" Odom asked.

"Okay."

"You don't sound very sure."

"I'll be fine." I'd spent the past fortnight confined to quarters with nothing to do but brood. Knowing this, Odom frowned. He was plainly unconvinced by my answer.

"You know, no one's blaming you for what happened in the Gallery," he said, smoothing down the ends of his moustache with forefinger and thumb. "It was a difficult situation. You did what you had to."

"I killed a man."

Odom sighed. "You had no choice."

I shook my head. "That doesn't make it right."

"Neither does it make it entirely wrong." He sat forward and placed his efficiently manicured hands on the desk. "Are you ready to come back to work?" The directness of his question surprised me.

"I still have my commission?"

Odom looked serious. "Good captains are in short supply. Especially captains with firsthand experience of working with our new allies."

He was, of course, talking of the Marble Armada. I glanced down at my short, bitten fingernails. "What do you want me to do?"

"The *Trouble Dog*'s been repaired," he said. "I want you to take her out on a shakedown cruise. Check everything's working as it should be."

"And George Walker?"

"What about him?"

I felt butterflies rise in my chest. "He died on my watch, remember? Before any of this started, you were going to court martial me for negligence." I had to struggle to keep my voice level.

Odom sucked his greying moustache.

"Given everything that's happened, the elders of the House felt you should be given a second chance."

"That's uncharacteristically generous of them."

Odom ignored my sarcasm. "We'll hold a memorial service for him, and for the others who lost their lives in the Gallery. And there'll be a permanent black mark against your record."

"Is that all?" A good man had died because I'd been remiss in my duty. I deserved some sort of punishment.

Odom narrowed his eyes. "Do you want to resign your commission?"

I could feel my pulse in my ears. I could hardly breathe.

"No."

George wouldn't have wanted me to resign, to take the coward's way out. But surely I deserved more than a slap on the wrist?

Odom spread his hands. "Then I suggest you find a way to put the past behind you."

I felt my fingers contract into fists. "Is that an order?"

"Does it have to be?" He activated the screen inlaid into the surface of his desk. "As I said, the *Trouble Dog*'s been repaired and refitted. Why don't you take her out and put her through her paces? Take a couple of weeks if you need to, and we'll talk again when you get back."

"Yes, sir." I couldn't seem to catch my breath. My arms and legs felt shaky. Moving clumsily, I rose to leave.

"And, Sally?"

I paused at the door, feeling my heart pounding in my chest. "What?"

Odom looked at me for a couple of seconds, then let his gaze drop back to the screen inlaid in his desk.

"You take care of yourself, okay?"

•

Darkness had fallen by the time I pulled into town. According to the *Trouble Dog*, Clay was in a disreputable drinking establishment close to the docks. I returned the dustboat to the hire shop, and set out on foot through the narrow streets. The buildings here were low and sturdy, like sandstone bunkers. The bar was at the bottom of a flight of stairs in the basement of a disused hardware store. Clay was sitting on a barstool at the far end of the zinc-topped counter, drinking alone. The lights in the place were low and the clientele inclined to privacy. In places like this, the ability to mind your own business counted as a survival trait. Nevertheless, I felt eyes on me as I walked the length of the room.

Clay glanced up as I approached.

"You're back, then?" The ends of her words were slurred.

"I am." I unhooked the scarf from my face, and pushed the goggles up onto the top of my head. Clay drained her glass and slid it across the counter. The smell of barracuda weed coming from some of the surrounding booths helped mask the pervasive stink of garlic and stale beer.

"How were the temples?"

"Good." I brushed dust from my chest and arms. "I think George would have liked them."

"No doubt." She signalled the bartender for another drink. The tattoos on her arm glistened like oil in the dim light, depicting burning trees and a flame-wrapped globe.

Struck by them, I asked, "What was it like in the jungle?"

"On Pelapatarn?"

"Before the bombs fell. What was it like?" Busy commanding a medical frigate, I had only seen the planet from high altitude. As a marine, Alva Clay had been down on the surface.

She frowned, as if making an effort to recall.

"Honestly, it was kind of beautiful," she said after a moment or two. "When it wasn't just horrifying and gross." A fresh drink arrived, and she swirled it in its glass, so the light glimmered through its ochre depths. "The humidity was a bitch, of course. The air hardly moved under that canopy. So thick, it was like breathing soup. Like being trapped in God's armpit on a summer's day. But the trees…" She huffed out her cheeks. "The trees were something else. You really should have seen them. The biggest were at least half a kilometre tall, and thick as skyscrapers, too. Some of them were a billion years old."

"Impressive, then?"

She gave me a blank look, as if I'd misunderstood. "The scale was all wrong. We were like ants." She wiped her lower lip on the back of her hand. "And we could hear the trees talking to each other. Sort of sighing, you know. Whispering. But we could never tell what they were saying. We couldn't even tell if they knew we were there. They just kept murmuring away, day and night, until you weren't sure whether their voices were real or just in your head."

"But you said it was beautiful?"

For a moment, I thought she hadn't heard me. She looked down at her boots. When she started speaking again, I had to strain to hear her.

"I remember the evenings," she said. "We dug foxholes between the roots of the trees. The air didn't get any cooler, but the light softened, you know? The jungle stink got more intense. Almost overpowering. Dirt and rotting leaves, and the reek of your own sweat mixed with gun oil and the smell of beans on a portable stove." She made a face. "And some nights, there'd be lines of orange tracer flickering between the trunks. Lighting the place up. Stealth drones taking each other out in the higher branches. Maybe the rumble of a transport plane high above the canopy, where we couldn't see it. It was just fucking…"

She tailed off and her head remained bowed. I thought she was going to continue, but then she seemed to remember where she was. She shook herself, as if dispelling the images she'd conjured, and then looked up at me and frowned.

"But why the fuck am I telling you all this?" Her voice was suddenly angry. "How could you understand? You weren't there. You were safe in the sky."

The bar fell silent, the other clientele sensing confrontation. Keeping my voice low and deliberately calm, I said, "I saw enough."

Clay snorted. "You didn't see dick."

"Whatever." I slid from the stool and stood with one hand resting on the bar. "But if it hadn't been for me, you'd have died down there."

Clay scowled. She knew I was right. "Is that all you came here to say?"

"No." I tapped my fingernails against the countertop. "We're moving on. Leaving tonight. Do you still want to come?"

She leant back on her stool and tried to focus on me.

"You know I testified against you, right? About George?"

"I know."

"And there are no hard feelings?" Her breath smelled like a distillery.

I shrugged. "You're still part of the crew, if you want to be."

Clay considered this. "Are we going anywhere specific?" she asked eventually. "Or are we just running?"

The bartender pushed two shot glasses of clear spirit across the counter. Clay took one; I ignored the other.

"I'm not running from anything," I said.

Clay frowned as she tried to raise the glass to her lips without spilling its contents. "We're all running from something, Sal." She took a noisy sip. "People like you and me don't belong anywhere. Wherever we are, we've always got one eye on the exit, one foot out the door." She finished her drink and the legs of her stool scraped against the floor as she stood. "We're like sharks," she said. "We have to keep moving, or we suffocate."

CHAPTER FIVE

JOHNNY SCHULTZ

The *Lucy's Ghost* crashed against the rocky flank of the ancient Nymtoq ship and the impact cracked her hull. Her spine buckled, her heat shield tore apart, and she fell from the larger vessel like a bug falling from a windshield. On the bridge, the virtual screens flared and died; part of the ceiling collapsed; sparks flew from crippled instrument panels and burning plastic fumes filled the air.

I sagged against the crash webbing in my couch. My neck hurt. With most of the external cameras gone I was blind and disorientated, unable to tell where we were or in what state the ship was. The only functioning screens showed empty space, distant stars.

I looked around for Vito. Caught up in the confusion of the attack, the pilot had forgotten to fasten his harness. Without straps to restrain him, he had been catapulted forward and smashed against an instrument panel. There was blood in his hair and his head lay at an awkward angle. I unbuckled myself and crawled over to him with some thought of administering first aid, only to find upon reaching him that he was already dead. I didn't want to leave him where he was, so I hauled him back into his chair and clipped him in place. His head flopped sickeningly on the end of a broken neck, but there was little I could do about that, save gently push it back against the headrest.

I touched his cheek.

"Ship!"

"Yes, dearie?" The screen had cracked, but her young features were still visible, if distorted.

"Damage report."

"You won't like it."

"Can we manoeuvre?"

"No."

"What about the air?"

A deck plan appeared behind her shoulder. Several compartments flashed red. "We're venting atmosphere in a dozen places. I've tried to isolate the affected sections, but we're still losing more than I'd like."

"Casualties?"

"Unfortunately, we've lost three, including Mr Accardi there."

"Who are the other two?"

"Jansen and Monk. They were still in the cargo bay when we hit. They weren't strapped in."

"Fuck." I rubbed my face with my hands. "What about the *Restless Itch*?"

"Surface damage only. We crushed a few rocks. Nothing it's even going to notice."

I let out a shuddering breath. How had everything unravelled so quickly?

"What's the bottom line? Can we fly?"

"That depends on your definition of flight."

My mind flashed a picture of the creature that attacked us—skin black as space, teeth bright as stars. I didn't want to go up against that again, especially in a damaged ship. Yet what other option was there?

"Can we make a run for home?" If we turned around now and made a dash for civilisation, maybe we'd be okay. We'd lost three crewmates, but the rest would be saved.

"No, dearie. The hull's too unstable. If we try to manoeuvre, it'll come apart."

I slumped in my chair, feeling suddenly tired beyond words. My neck still hurt and the bruises I'd gained falling down the companionway were sore.

"What are we going to do?"

The *Lucy's Ghost* raised an eyebrow. "Are you being rhetorical, dear, or seriously asking for my recommendations?"

I let out a long, hopeless breath, feeling suddenly like a kid caught out of his depth.

"Seriously asking."

The avatar on the screen raised her chin. "Then it's simple, Johnny. Get the crew into pressure suits and evacuate."

I blinked at the sudden change in her tone.

"Where will we go?"

Her kindly little sister persona had given way to that of a firm schoolmistress.

"When we struck," she said, "we weren't coming straight on. We came in at a steep angle and hit a glancing blow." An animation appeared on the screen beside her. "We bounced away after the impact, but now we're travelling in more or less the same direction as the *Restless Itch*. Our courses *are* gradually diverging, but for the next three or four hours, the gap between us should be small

59

enough for you to cross using manoeuvring packs."

"You mean we stick to the original plan? We jump across and cut our way in?"

"In essence, yes. Although the Nymtoq won't like it."

"They don't like anything, but it's not like we have a choice, right?"

The *Lucy's Ghost* smiled mysteriously. "Maybe you do."

"What do you mean?"

Behind her shoulder, the animation's scale increased until other stars began to appear at the edges of the picture.

"At this point in its journey, the *Restless Itch* is within a light year of the Generality." A dotted red line indicated the nominal border of human space.

"Yes, that's why it made such a good target. But we can't travel a light year in pressure suits."

"You won't have to. Out here, borders are permeable. Jurisdictions overlap."

Jurisdictions...

Suddenly I thought I saw what she'd been hinting at. "We could call the House of Reclamation!"

"It has to be worth a try."

"They'll certainly be more sympathetic than the Nymtoq." I felt a weight lift from my shoulders. "Thank you, ship. Please, send the distress call." Racing through the higher dimensions, a hypervoid distress call would reach the nearest human worlds in a few hours. After that, it would be just a matter of waiting for a rescue ship to reach us—a couple of days if we were lucky, a couple of weeks if we weren't.

"Already done, dearie." The avatar frowned. "But things are deteriorating quickly. Structural failure appears imminent. You'd better hustle."

•

The intercom wasn't working. I said goodbye to Vito and, pausing only to retrieve my leather jacket, made my way aft to the crew lounge on shaky legs.

Addison met me at the door.

"Hell's teeth," she said, "you look like shit."

I wanted to tell her about Vito, Monk and Jansen, but I didn't have the words. Instead I looked past her, to the dining area where Dalton was ministering to Santos.

"How's the foot, chef?"

Santos glowered at me from beneath darkened brows.

"The lunch is ruined, *compañero*."

I walked over to the table. It was bolted in place, but knives and forks lay scattered all across the floor.

"Can you walk?" My voice was hoarse. "We need to leave."

Dalton looked up. At sixty-two years of age he was the oldest of us all, and had been crewing merchant ships longer than I'd been alive.

"We're evacuating?" He looked concerned. He knew the dangers of abandoning ship so far from home, and knew how attached I was to the *Lucy's Ghost*. However, he also realised we'd been attacked, and might be attacked again at any moment.

"I don't think we have a fucking choice." The walls gave an ominous groan. "We're running out of air, and the hull's about to buckle. Get yourselves up. Help Santos if he needs it. And get down to the lock. I want everybody suited in five minutes."

I turned to Addison. "Where are the others?"

"Kelly's down in the hold with Henri," she said. "Chet's still in engineering." She glanced around. "Did you have any luck getting hold of Jansen or Monk?"

I shook my head. "They're not coming."

"What about Vito?"

"He didn't make it, either."

"Bloody hell."

"Yeah." I looked at Dalton and Santos. "Okay, you two. Take a communicator and get down to the airlock. See if you can collect Kelly and Henri on your way. Riley, you're with me."

"Where are we going?" Addison asked.

I clipped a communicator to my wrist, and pulled on the jacket.

"To get Chet."

CHAPTER SIX

ONA SUDAK

The flyer took us north, across salt marshes and low hills, to the coast, where cold, grassy mudflats ran down to thick, cement-coloured water.

With the side hatch open, the noise of the air rushing past was too loud to permit unaided speech. Unable to communicate with the armed men and women around me, I tried to relax and control my breathing. For the moment, I had been spared death. If my new captors wanted to kill me, they could simply have shot me in my cell, as they had with poor Berwick, or thrown me from the flyer's open hatch as soon as we achieved enough height to ensure a fatal fall. Instead, they were keeping me alive for some further purpose, and I could only pray it wasn't going to involve anything more unpleasant than the prospect of a firing squad. The way these people had calmly executed the staff and inmates at the prison spoke of a ruthlessness that left me in no doubt of my fate should my usefulness to them come to an end.

I thought of Adam, the young paramour I'd lost in

the Gallery. The young man who'd sacrificed his life for mine. What would he think of all this? What would he think of me?

Fresh sea air swirled through the compartment and my nostrils twitched. Somehow, it smelled of freedom, and that was enough to ignite a tiny ember of hope in my chest. Whatever happened now, I had outlived the sentence handed to me by the court. The soldiers charged with my execution were themselves dead; every breath I took now was a victory in itself, and every second I spent in this flyer took me further from the cell in which I'd endured the past twenty-four miserable, lonely weeks.

My court martial had been conducted in the full glare of the public spotlight. The admirals responsible for issuing the order to raze Pelapatarn were all now living in unobtrusive retirement, and had contrived to place the blame for that atrocity squarely at my feet. No trace of the original order had endured, no shard of evidence to suggest it had originated anywhere but with me. I had been in command of the fleet at the crucial instant, and so the culpability was mine.

Capital punishment wasn't illegal in the Conglomeration, but it was frowned upon and seldom enacted. Rather than get blood on their hands, the authorities considered transportation a more humane option. Why execute a person, they argued, when you could ship them out to a frontier planet and use them as slave labour in the construction of a new civilian settlement? Murderers, rapists and child molesters were crammed into leaky transport ships and despatched to the margins of Conglomeration space. But some crimes were considered too gigantic in scope, and too appalling to be solved by mere banishment. I had been charged with the destruction of an entire biosphere, the murder of nineteen thousand soldiers and four hundred thousand human non-combatants, and the genocide of fifteen billion sentient trees.

Proceedings lasted just over an hour. After a recitation of the charges and evidence, it took the board of seven officers and warrant officers presiding only five minutes to pronounce me guilty on all counts. The fact I had fled the scene of the battle and spent the next three years in hiding did little to dissuade them of my responsibility for the outrage.

After that, it was just a case of waiting for them to decide how exactly they wanted me to die.

I watched the shallows give way to deeper waters. While in the Gallery, I had been stuck for two days inside a flying box, at the mercy of five-thousand-year-old alien technologies. I knew the virtue of patience, and the prudence of using the time I had now to physically and intellectually prepare myself for whatever might ensue.

My heart was racing. Turning my head from the wavelets rushing beneath the flyer, I closed my eyes and willed my shoulders to relax. My breathing slowed and my fists unclenched. I had been a captain in the Conglomeration Navy. This morning, I had been prepared to face death by firing squad, and I would now face whatever lay at the end of this journey with the same dignity and composure.

•

When I opened my eyes again, the four men and women in the compartment with me were pulling on breathing masks. When they had them in place, the woman opposite leaned over and strapped one over my mouth and nose. Then she pulled a pair of goggles down over my eyes. I tried to ask her what she was doing. Flyers like these were strictly for low-level use, with operational ceilings well below the point at which we might require oxygen. I don't think she could have heard me, muffled as I was behind the rubber mask, but she jabbed her thumb downwards, at the slate-grey waters beyond the open hatch. She then sat back and strapped herself into her seat. I couldn't read her expression behind her silver goggles. Around us, the others were also strapping themselves into position, and I experienced a queasy flutter of unease.

As soon as everyone was in place, the flyer tipped to starboard, and we began to shed height in a long, wide turn. I could see the waves rising to meet us. Up front, I could see the pilot leaning into the turn. His actions seemed calm and deliberate.

A flyer like this wouldn't float. Was he actually going to try and land on the water?

I began to struggle against my restraints.

"You're insane!" I called, but the others just looked at me, their silver eyes blank and disconcerting.

The wind tore at us.

The engines howled.

And the ocean rushed up to slap us.

CHAPTER SEVEN

SAL KONSTANZ

Alva Clay was beside me as we left the bar and started walking in the direction of the main port. Although the sun had long since gone down and hard desert stars were glittering overhead, we could still feel the day's heat radiating from the sandstone walls and the packed earth beneath our feet. We didn't talk. We didn't have much to say to each other. Things between us were still brittle and tenuous, like broken eggshells. Instead, we moved in wary but companionable silence, content for now to be headed in the same direction.

Stalls on either side of the narrow street offered food, souvenirs and desert hiking gear to the thin trickle of pilgrims and tourists en route to the Temples of the High Country. The air carried the greasy scent of frying onions, the entreaties of hawkers and the chatter of stallholders. Lanterns burned. Music played from speakers hanging from awnings. The awnings flapped like indolent sails, stirred by the dry evening wind that crept furtively off the desert.

When we were halfway along the street, a shuttle rose

from the port, howling like an unquiet spirit. Clay stopped to watch the blue candle flame of its exhaust.

"I'm sorry I gave you a hard time," she said. "You caught me on a bad day."

"That's okay."

"No, you don't understand." The shuttle was little more than a bright speck now, but she kept her face turned upwards. "Today would have been my daughter's eighth birthday."

"I didn't know you had a daughter."

"I don't anymore."

She seemed so matter-of-fact, I hardly knew how to respond.

"What happened?"

"She was killed in the early years of the war." She shrugged. "Her father took her out shopping, and neither of them came back."

"Is that why you're—"

"Grumpy?"

"Actually I was going to ask if that's why you're such a hard ass all the time, but I guess it amounts to the same thing."

She turned to me, mouth half open in indignation, fists clenched.

"I know what it's like to lose your family," I said.

"You have no idea."

"I lost my parents. I was just a kid."

Clay snorted. "She was my *daughter*. Do you have the first fucking clue what that means? How that felt?"

"No, I don't suppose I do."

She turned away. "No, you *don't*."

"But I'm here for you if you want to talk about it."

She hunched her shoulders. "Fuck off."

"I mean it."

"I don't think talking's going to do any good."

"Nevertheless, I'm here. I'll always be here, if you want me."

Her chin dropped to her chest, and she sighed. After a moment, she looked around. "You're serious, aren't you?"

"I saved your life, Alva. That means I'm responsible for you."

She seemed to mull this over. "I guess you do have your redeeming qualities."

I offered her my hand. "Friends again?"

She looked down at my open palm. "Don't push it."

She gave a wry half-smile, and I felt a wave of almost debilitating relief. We might never be as close as sisters, but for now, I could believe we were going to be okay.

"You do know we're being followed, right?"

I glanced behind me. "Where?"

Clay kept her eyes on me. "About four stalls back. Thin guy. Dressed like a local but moves like a spook."

"The guy with the dark glasses? I saw him. Couldn't miss him, really. Who wears dark glasses at night?"

"I've seen him too many times for it to be coincidence."

The man in question appeared to be browsing through jewellery, but he kept his head angled our way, tracking us in his peripheral vision. I looked away, trying to make it appear I was simply glancing around in embarrassment after our emotional outburst.

"Do you think he's alone?"

"I doubt it."

"What do you think he wants?"

Clay started walking, keeping her pace leisurely and her demeanour casual. "He's keeping an eye on us."

"Why?"

"Hell's teeth, Cap. Why do you think?"

I slouched along beside her, hands in pockets—just a couple of bored spacers looking for something to do. "Who do you think he's working for?"

Clay shrugged. "Could be Conglomeration. Could be Outward. Could be somebody else entirely."

I frowned. We had brought the Marble Armada out of retirement, and there were those who suspected the *Trouble Dog* of having more influence than she did over those legions of white, knife-like ships.

"Should we confront him?"

"You're the captain."

I bit my lip. A year ago, I would have hurried back to the ship and secured the airlock. I hadn't been very good at handling confrontation back then. These days...

"Are you armed?"

Clay raised an eyebrow. With her back to the man following us, she pulled up her vest to expose the glistening brown skin of her belly, and the black metal grip of an Archipelago pistol tucked securely into the waistband of her combat trousers.

"I never leave home without it."

"Then let's say hello."

•

We led our new friend away from the light and activity of the market, into the narrow tangle of passageways that ran between the darkened warehouses on the edge of the port. Above us, the brightening constellations were unfamiliar patterns in an unfamiliar sky.

I touched my ear and spoke to the *Trouble Dog*.

"How close are you?"

"About an hour out."

"Are you still tracking us?"

"One moment... Yes, I have you."

"Do you see the guy tailing us?"

"I have him tagged. Are you in danger?"

I smiled at the concern in her voice. "Not right now, but keep an eye on us, okay? If things get weird, we might need you to come in hot."

I signed off. Beside me, Alva Clay shook her dreadlocked head. "We won't need the big guns."

I glanced down at the bulge beneath her vest. "Look who's talking."

To either side, the warehouses were dark and locked. Corrugated metal shutters covered their doors. Refrigeration units hummed. Steam rose from rooftop vents, orange in the light from the port. Discarded packaging spilled from overflowing dumpsters.

I kept my hands in my pockets, my shoulders hunched. We were three quarters of the way along the passage. At the end, another alley crossed it at right angles.

We turned left, and then stopped. Clay drew her weapon. When the man in dark glasses came around the corner, he found himself staring into its barrel.

For a second, he gaped at us. Then he flinched away and started to run back along the passage. Muttering curses, Clay stepped around the corner and fired a warning shot over his head. In the confined space, the crack of the pistol hurt my ears. The noise of it was like a punch in the chest.

"Run again," Clay called, "and the next one goes through your ass."

The man had already stopped. He turned to face us, hands held in front of him.

"Okay," he said. "You got me."

"Who are you?" Clay walked towards him, keeping her gun levelled at his forehead. Now that I had time to get a proper look at him, I could see she had been right about him not being a local. He wore the same loose linen clothing, but his face was ruddy and flushed, and the sunburn on his nose and cheeks spoke of how unaccustomed he was to this climate.

"I'm nobody." He was out of breath. "Just a pickpocket scouting for marks."

"Bullshit."

"You can't prove otherwise."

"I don't have to prove shit." Clay waggled the Archipelago pistol. "I'm the one holding the gun, remember?"

The man seemed to deflate slightly.

"All right," he said. "I'm not a pickpocket."

I stepped up level with Clay and looked him up and down.

"What are you," I asked, "Conglomeration Intelligence?"

He smiled and shook his head.

"Guess again."

"Outward?"

"Bingo."

I let my arms fold across my chest. "What's your name?"

"Wilkes."

"Is that your first or last name?"

"Does it matter?"

"I guess not." I reached forward and gently pulled his glasses from his face, revealing augmented eyes that glimmered in the alley's gloom with a faint emerald luminescence. "Tell me, Mr Wilkes, if you'd be so kind, why the Outward government has an agent trailing us."

He blinked at me, and I saw the lenses of his eyes rotate as they focused on my face.

"Don't you know?"

I turned his glasses over in my hands.

"I'm guessing it has something to do with the Marble Armada."

He shrugged. "Of course."

"But why?" A warm wind blew up the alley, disturbing piles of paper and sand. Wilkes shuffled his feet, moving his weight from one hip to another.

"You can't blame us for being curious." Beneath the redness, his face was entirely hairless—no trace of stubble, no lashes or eyebrows.

"But Clay and I, we're both Outwarders," I said. "We both fought for the Outward during the war."

"You *were* Outwarders." He looked apologetic. "You gave up your citizenship when you joined the House, remember?"

I felt my cheeks redden. "That doesn't change who we are."

"Doesn't it?" He pursed his lips, as if weighing up the evidence. "Let's see. You voluntarily left the Outward, and now you ride around in a former Conglomeration Navy cruiser. You rescued a known Conglomeration war criminal from the Gallery, and came home at the head of the largest fleet anyone's ever seen—a fleet that seems to have taken your aforementioned ship as its role model."

"So?"

"So the powers that be want to know exactly how much influence the *Trouble Dog* has over that fleet." He raised his chin. "And given the fact the *Trouble Dog* takes its orders from you…"

"You think I'm in command of the Armada?"

"Aren't you?"

"No!"

"And why should we take your word for that?"

Beside me, Alva Clay cleared her throat. "Maybe," she said, "because I'm standing next to her with an Archipelago pistol, and all you've got are two handfuls of sky."

Wilkes's artificial eyes swivelled towards her.

"You *do* know that gun's illegal on most planets of the Generality, don't you?"

"Bite me."

We stood looking at each other. Finally, Wilkes said, "So, what happens now? You can't shoot me."

Clay raised her eyebrows. "Why not?"

"Because." Wilkes tapped the side of his head. "These eyes are relaying everything that happens. If you gun me down, my superiors will have video evidence, and you'll be fugitives."

Events were threatening to spiral out of control. Before Wilkes and Clay could further escalate tempers, I stepped between them.

"Nobody's shooting anybody." I motioned to Clay, who reluctantly lowered her weapon. "You're free to go, Mr Wilkes. Just do me one favour?"

The man lowered his arms to his sides.

"And what would that be?"

"Please tell your masters that it's true the Marble Armada followed the *Trouble Dog* out of the Gallery, but that's only because they'd been waiting five thousand years for someone to lead them and tell them what to do.

As soon as we got back to Camrose we turned them over to the House, and we've had no contact with them since. So, don't ask me who's in charge of them, ask the House."

Wilkes bowed his head and stepped backwards. "Oh," he said, "we intend to."

He gave Alva Clay a polite nod, turned smartly on his heel, and strode briskly back in the direction of the marketplace.

When he'd vanished from our sight, I belatedly realised I still held his sunglasses in my hands. I dithered for a moment, then closed them up and slipped them into my pocket.

"Come on," I said. "Let's get back to the ship."

CHAPTER EIGHT

JOHNNY SCHULTZ

As the others made for the airlock, Riley Addison and I picked our way down through the broken ship. We couldn't take a direct route as most of the starboard bow section had been crushed, concertinaed bulkheads blocked a number of key corridors, and the forward cargo holds had been breached and were now open to vacuum. Instead, we would have to work our way down to the rear cargo hold, and then use a maintenance duct to access the engine room.

As we clambered down the companionways between decks, I was glad of Addison's company. She had a reassuring, unflappable quality that I really needed to be around. Everything had come apart so quickly, I'd barely had time to draw breath, let alone process the losses we'd suffered.

It took us almost fifteen minutes, but we managed to reach the maintenance duct without incident. Addison unscrewed the fastenings holding the duct's hatch in place while I signalled Gil Dalton on the wrist communicator.

"We're all here," he reported. "All suited and ready to go."

"Excellent. We're just about to crawl through to the engine room. I'll update you when we've located Chet."

"Understood." Patched through to the ship's network from his helmet mike, his voice sounded echoic and flat. "Just one question."

Addison unscrewed the final fastening and pulled the hatch aside, revealing a long, dark tunnel.

"Be quick."

"We're all ready to abandon ship."

"Yes."

"Where are we going? Aren't we in the middle of deep space?"

It was a good question. In all the flurry of the crash, I'd forgotten to actually brief the survivors.

"We're within range of the *Restless Itch*," I told him. "We can jump over there and cut our way in as planned, and then wait there for a rescue ship."

Dalton said something, but static overwhelmed his reply.

"Sorry, I didn't get that."

More static.

"No, you're breaking up. If you can hear me, sit tight and wait for our signal."

Addison eyed the hold's creaking walls nervously. "If we're going through, we should go now," she said.

I cut the connection. The deck trembled beneath my feet.

"Okay." I motioned towards the hole. "After you."

Addison shook her head. "No way, José. You're Lucky Johnny Schultz, you go first."

I made a face, and then crouched down to peer into the duct. It was roughly the width of a steel coffin. Along its length, some of the access panels were hanging open, trailing intestinal loops of wire and cable.

With every instinct screaming at me to flee the ship before it fell apart, the last thing I wanted was to wedge myself in a confined space. Especially one with loose wiring and cracked steam pipes threatening to electrocute and scald me. If the ship's structure collapsed, I'd be trapped or crushed, and if the bulkhead between here and the forward hold gave way, I'd most likely suffocate before having time to crawl free. If I'd been on my own, I might have turned back there and then. As it was, I could feel Addison's eyes on me.

I zipped up my jacket and smoothed back my hair. I rubbed my palms together and cleared my throat.

"All right, then."

With a sigh, I pushed my head and shoulders into the duct. With my arms stretched in front of me and the jacket riding up around my neck and shoulders, it seemed far more cramped in there than I had supposed. Still, I couldn't quit now. I tried bracing my hands against the wall in order to pull myself forward, but couldn't get sufficient traction. Instead, I was reduced to squirming my way along on my elbows.

After I'd gone a few metres, I heard Addison follow me.

"Mind the grating on the wall here," I called back. "It's fucking hot."

"Don't mind me," she replied. "Just concentrate on moving. There's only so long I can spend staring at the soles of your boots."

•

We emerged headfirst into the engine room. Chet lay in its nest, its six limbs curled protectively beneath it. I crawled over and laid my hand on its iridescent scales.

"Chet?" The flesh cringed beneath my touch, so I knew it was still alive. "Chet, it's me, Johnny. I've got Riley with me. We're here to help you."

One of the limbs uncurled like a roused serpent, raising its hand-face to mine. The fingers uncurled to reveal eyes like small black pearls, and a small mouth lined with prehensile tentacles.

"Johnny?"

"Come on, pal. The ship's going to fall apart around us. It's time to go."

I put my arms around it and tried to encourage it to stand, but it was too heavy for me to move alone.

"Chet stay."

I looked back at Addison and jerked my chin, telling her to come over and help me.

"Chet stay."

"Chet can't stay." I was panting with effort. "If Chet stays, ship go boom and Chet dies."

The little black eyes regarded me with impassivity.

"Chet already dying. Leaking inside. Sleep soon."

"No." I gave one last heave, and then fell onto my backside, defeated. "We can help you. But first we have to get you off the ship."

"Chet not moving. Can't move. Too much damage inside. Can't fix."

"But—"

Another limb uncurled, and its fingers clamped onto my forearm.

"I go to rejoin World Tree. Work done, now rest." The pressure on my wrist increased. "But you take message."

I tried not to squirm out of its grip. "What message?"

"Message for other Druff." The body in the nest

sagged lower. The scales seemed to have lost some of their lustre. "Tell them, Chet dead."

"We will," Addison said.

Chet's raised face swivelled to look at her, like a cobra eyeing up a second intruder.

"This important. Tell them white ships are cousins."

"What?" Addison looked confused.

"Cousins," Chet insisted. "Very important you tell." A tremor seized it. Somewhere on one of the upper decks, something collapsed with enough force to crack the ceiling above our heads.

"I'm not leaving you here," I said. "I don't care if you're dying, I can't just walk away and leave you."

The force of its grip eased, and the arm withdrew beneath it again. Only the one hand-face remained visible, and it was swaying on the end of its arm.

"You will tell them?"

"Yes, of course. But what about you?"

"I am content." The fingers around the edge of its face began to close, like the petals of a dying rose. "Have nest. Good nest. Work done. All work done. Now sleep. Sleep, and dream of World Tree."

Its face scrunched into a loose fist, and withdrew into the depths of the nest. I looked at Addison, and it was clear she had no more idea what to do than I did.

Overhead, the crack in the ceiling began to widen. Dust and lumps of debris pattered down onto the deck like the first grains in an overturned hourglass. Some fell onto Chet's back, rattling against its scales, but it didn't react. Beneath my palm, the rise and fall of its breathing had slowed. The pause between each inhalation stretched longer than the last, until the ragged wheeze began to feel

81

like the last weary gasps of an expiring steam engine.

And then it was gone.

I tried to swallow back the distress that welled up, hot and solid in my throat.

Addison put her hand on my shoulder. "Has it…?"

"Yes."

I removed my hand from its cooling back, and wiped my eyes on my sleeve. Overhead, the ceiling gave another long, grinding creak, and part of it began to bow as if buckling beneath an immense weight. Addison regarded it apprehensively.

"We can't stay here," she said.

CHAPTER NINE

ONA SUDAK

As the flyer hit the waves, the impact threw me against my restraints with a force that left me stunned and disorientated. For a few seconds I didn't know where I was, or what was happening. Then the cabin started to fill with seawater, and I came to with a terrified start. We were sinking, and the men and women around me were making no attempt to escape. I tried to shout at them, but couldn't make myself heard through the breathing mask and the rush of incoming water.

We were way out in the ocean, far beyond the continental shallows. If we slipped beneath the waves now, the weight of the flyer would carry us all the way to the bottom—and even with breathing masks, we wouldn't be able to endure the mounting pressure of that long, crushing fall.

I gasped as the flyer lurched to the side and water slopped against me, soaking the legs of my prison uniform. Seconds later, we were completely submerged. I held my breath by reflex. My ears were filled with a surging roar. Through the goggles covering my eyes, I could see the others still motionless in their seats. What was wrong with them?

My stomach went light as we began to fall. It was like being trapped in a flooded elevator, falling down a deep, unlit shaft. In the gathering darkness, I started rocking back and forth, trying to loosen the straps pinning me to my seat. If I could only get free long enough to escape the open hatch and kick for the surface…

A shadow fell across us, and my heart seemed to stutter in my chest. We were being swallowed, falling into the blackened maw of some vast undersea monstrosity. I saw the lip of the opening pass us. We fell for a few seconds in pitch darkness, and then came to rest with a grinding crash.

Lights came on around us, illuminating the interior of the cabin. We were on our side, hanging from our straps with our heads lower than our feet. Through the hatch, I could see we'd fetched up against a flat surface. I heard the clank and grumble of pumps, and the water level started to subside. My legs were the first part of me to be exposed, then my hips and hands. I could feel my skin prickling with the cold.

Finally, my head was clear. The people around me were unstrapping and worming their way out through the hatch, where welcoming hands pulled them from the wreck.

One of the women who had been sitting opposite came to loosen my straps and ease me down from my chair.

"Quite a ride, huh?"

She pushed me towards the hatch and I crawled out on hands and knees—onto familiar-looking deck plates.

An officer was waiting for me, dressed in the uniform of a commodore in the Conglomeration Navy. As I rose unsteadily to my feet, he threw me a crisp salute.

"Welcome aboard," he said. "My name is Commodore Wronski. Do you know where you are?"

I glanced up at the walls surrounding us.

"At a guess, I'd say we were in the dorsal shuttle bay of a Hyena-class frigate."

He gave an approving nod. "Very good, Captain. Exactly correct."

The members of the squad responsible for my escape from prison were peeling off their masks and goggles. Conglomeration marines were guarding the hatch that led from this bay to the rest of the ship.

"But, what are you doing down here?" My hands had started to shake with delayed shock and the effects of decaying adrenalin. "Why the hell is there a Hyena-class frigate submerged in the middle of the ocean? And why the *fuck* did we have to crash to reach you?"

Wronski lowered his head.

"I apologise for the lack of finesse," he said. "We were working to a very tight, and very literal, deadline. As soon as they scheduled your execution, we knew we had to get you out."

I squeezed my fists to stop them trembling. Seawater dripped from my knuckles.

"You didn't have to shoot the priest."

"What priest?"

"The military chaplain who was in the cell with me." I pictured the poor man spinning around with the force of the shot that took him down. "You didn't have to kill him."

Wronski frowned. "We couldn't leave witnesses. But if it makes you feel any better, your chaplain died in the line of duty, for the greater good of the Conglomeration. I'm sure his gods will receive him kindly. As for you, history will record that you died during an unsuccessful escape attempt. Your flyer crashed into the sea. If anyone comes looking, they will be able to locate the crashed vehicle on the seabed, but your body—and those of your accomplices—will be assumed lost to the currents."

He gave a nod to one of the marines, who stepped forwards and draped a towel around my shoulders.

"Now, let me show you below," he said. "And let's find you some dry clothes."

•

Two marines led me into the innards of the ship. Hyenas aren't large craft, and the walkways and cabins were much smaller than I had been used to aboard the Scimitar I had commanded during the latter stages of the war. Nevertheless, it felt good to be back aboard a naval vessel. The uniforms and equipment were familiar, and even the air carried the same pervasive and unmistakable tang of hot metal, fresh paint, boot polish and sweat.

They led me to a stateroom, where they left me to take a shower and change into the crisp captain's uniform and pair of boots that had been left on the bunk. I hadn't worn a captain's uniform since I fled the bridge of the *Righteous Fury* in the aftermath of the Pelapatarn incident (they certainly hadn't let me wear one during my trial, at which I'd appeared in the dowdy threads of my prison uniform), and the roughness of the material, the stiffness of the collar and the weight of the insignia recalled incidents I'd been trying to ignore and disown for nearly four years.

When I had fully attired myself, I examined my likeness in the mirror on the back of the stateroom's door, but instead of seeing again the self I had discarded at the end of the war—the younger self I still could not quite bring myself to absolve—I saw my new face, the face of a poet, looking uncomfortable and out of place in such a uniform.

As I stared at this partial stranger, another face appeared in the corner of the mirror. Gold-skinned, androgynous and strikingly sensual, with full lips and half-lidded eyes, it regarded me with the arrogance of a teenaged god.

"Hello," I said. "What's your name?"

The figure smiled.

"I am the Conglomeration frigate *Entanglement*. Please allow me to welcome you aboard."

"Thank you." I ran a finger around the inside of my collar, trying to make it sit more naturally. "I assume you already know my name?"

"Of course." The avatar gave the barest suggestion of a nod. "But how would you prefer me to address you?"

It was a good question. As far as the world was concerned, the war criminal Annelida Deal had just died in a crash.

I met my own gaze in the mirror.

"Can I still be Ona Sudak?"

"I see no reason why not."

"Good." It was a name I had chosen for myself, and an identity I had assumed for the three years between the Battle of Pelapatarn and the time I gave myself over to Conglomeration authorities.

"Then I shall refer to you as Captain Sudak."

"Thank you." I tugged at the hem of my tunic, straightening it.

"You'll have to forgive me," I said, "but I don't recall an *Entanglement*. Did you serve in the war?"

"I spent the conflict seconded to Intelligence." The golden avatar waved a languid hand. "But I'm not allowed to talk about it."

"And are you still operating in that capacity? Working for Conglomeration Intelligence, I mean?"

Those luscious lips spread into a mischievous smile.

"I think you've already figured that one out, haven't you?"

•

The marines were waiting in the corridor. When they saw the uniform they snapped to attention, and I returned their salutes.

"Take me to the Commodore," I ordered.

CHAPTER TEN

SAL KONSTANZ

We arrived at the port as the *Trouble Dog* aligned for her final approach.

"Looking good," I told her as she loomed over the perimeter fence.

Lit from below by the runway lights, the heavy cruiser resembled nothing so much as a vast bronze bullet, albeit a bullet whose smooth lines had been distorted by the blisters that housed her primary and secondary sensor arrays and weapon systems. And with a displacement of ten thousand tons, she dwarfed the civilian traffic scurrying from her path.

"Good? What do you mean, good?" Grav-units whining, she lowered herself slowly towards the concrete apron. "I'll have you know I look *magnificent*."

When she came within a few metres of the surface, she lowered a cargo pallet. Alva Clay and I walked across the tarmac, shading our eyes from the dust and loose chippings her grav-units were kicking up, and stepped aboard.

A crowd had gathered at the edge of the landing field,

drawn by the *Trouble Dog*'s size. The liners and traders that brought tourists and cargo to this system were larger, but they seldom entered the atmosphere, preferring instead to ferry their charges to the surface using ground-to-orbit shuttles. The sight of something as massive as a Carnivore-class heavy cruiser hanging over the port must have been a novelty for the locals, and an unexpected bonus for the tourists.

I waved.

Clay gave them the finger.

And then we were inside the ship, and I could finally relax. For three days I had been feeling exposed and anxious in the dust and heat of the desert. Now that I was back in the *Trouble Dog*'s human quarters, I felt that tension ease like a fist unclenching.

Clay walked off in the direction of her cabin, muttering something about getting some well-deserved rack time. When she'd gone, I stripped off the grime-infused rags I'd been wearing, threw aside my goggles and headscarf, and walked back to my room naked, glorying in the feel of cool, conditioned air against my skin.

Later, having dressed in my comfortable old ship fatigues and habitual baseball cap, I ventured into the galley to find Preston Menderes eating cereal, hunched over the glow of a digital textbook.

"Welcome back, Captain," he said.

Preston had replaced George as the *Trouble Dog*'s medic. Unfortunately, he had lied his way through the application process, and possessed little in the way of actual experience or qualification. The only reason he was still aboard my vessel was that he'd agreed to study hard in order to bring his knowledge up to the required standard. That, and the fact I'd grown to feel responsible for him since being forced to put a cannon shell through his old man's head in order to prevent further loss of life at the Gallery.

I walked over to the counter and helped myself to a cup of coffee.

"I think it's about time you got to know the ship a little better," I said.

Preston looked puzzled. "I think I know my way around…"

The coffee was hot and strong, and better than anything I'd been offered on the planet below. "That's not what I'm talking about."

I took him around the torus of cabins that ringed the *Trouble Dog*'s waist, until we came to a little-used companionway leading "up" into the ship's interior.

"What's up here?"

"Wait and see."

I led him up the metal rungs, into what had once been storage space for the ship's complement of marines, but which she had now repurposed for her own use. As we reached the top of the ladder the lights came on, illuminating a large, airy space. Plinths ringed the white-painted walls and formed a double line down the centre of the room, and each plinth held an artefact.

Preston turned around, taking it all in. "What is this?"

"It's the *Trouble Dog*'s trophy room."

"Trophy room?"

A screen lit on the far wall, displaying the ship's avatar. This morning she was in full goddess mode, with lustrous brown skin, a single long, jewelled earring, and golden threads woven into her dark, tied-back curls.

"I wouldn't call it that," she said.

Preston examined the contents of the nearest plinth. "What's this?"

The object was a jagged splinter of smoke-blackened glass, displayed on a purple silk cushion beneath a clear plastic case.

"That," the *Trouble Dog* said, "once formed part of a great stained-glass window in a cathedral on Morag's Haven."

Preston frowned.

"Morag's Haven? Wasn't that bombed during the early days of the war?"

"It was the first combat mission I flew."

"And this one?" He was looking at the next plinth, which held a seemingly haphazard mound of bright silver dog tags.

"I was a troop transport at the Battle of Traitor's Gate."

"And these are all…?"

"These belonged to the marines that were lost."

Preston considered the rest of the room. From where we stood we could see plinths holding unexploded grenades, old shell casings, a rusted cutlass, a child's stuffed rabbit, a powered gauntlet with an inbuilt flamethrower, and several other objects that weren't immediately identifiable.

"And these other pieces?" he asked. "They're all souvenirs from your career?"

The *Trouble Dog* lowered her gaze. "No, not souvenirs."

"Then what?"

"Commemorations, reminders."

"I don't see the difference."

The *Trouble Dog*'s avatar clasped her hands together. "Do you see the penultimate plinth?"

"The one with the plant?"

"It is a tree sapling, and it is alive. In another few years I will need to transplant it to a larger container."

I had seen the contents of this room before, and was aware of the symbolic weight carried by each of the objects on display. Now I tried to see the sapling through Preston's eyes: a pink and blue stalk about the size of a tulip, with a closed bud at the tip. Fine, quivering hairs ran down its length, and it was encased in a simple glass terrarium to protect it from the dryness of the ship's recycled air.

"What does this represent?" he asked.

"You're looking," the *Trouble Dog* told him, "at one of the last remaining samples of life from the jungles of Pelapatarn."

Preston's eyes bugged. "That's a sentient tree? I thought they were extinct."

"Thanks to my sisters and I, they almost are."

"Then this whole room…"

"This room is a monument to my shame. It contains all the reasons I renounced my commission in the Conglomeration Navy."

There was one final plinth—a new one. It held a tiny speck of silver mounted in a transparent glass cube.

"And this one?"

"I'd rather not say."

"But—"

"I don't think you're ready."

Preston's cheeks coloured. "Ready for what? I'm not a child."

"Nevertheless, I think it would be unwise for you to insist on knowing where that speck came from."

The boy's face was red now, with a mixture of indignation and embarrassment. He turned to me for support, but I simply shrugged.

"It's your decision," I said.

The *Trouble Dog* scowled at me from the wall. "I wish you'd thought to ask before bringing him here," she said.

I shrugged again. "It had to happen sooner or later."

"Later would have been preferable."

"No, I think we need to confront this."

Preston had been listening with barely concealed impatience. "Confront what?" he asked. "What is it you won't tell me?"

On the screen, the *Trouble Dog* rolled her beautiful eyes. "Oh, for heaven's sake," she said. "Preston, that fleck of silver paint came from the skin of your father's Scimitar. It was knocked from the hull while we were drilling our way in, in order to assassinate him by firing a single cannon shell into the top of his head."

Everything went still. Preston blinked twice. He opened his mouth, and then closed it again. At his sides, his fingers flexed. He tried to speak but the words caught in his throat.

My own pulse was racing. I said, "It's been months and we've not talked about it."

All I got in return was a horrified look. I tried reaching out to touch his shoulder, but he flinched away.

"Preston—"

He turned and clattered his way down the companionway's metal steps.

When he had gone, the *Trouble Dog* sighed. "I think," she said, "that makes us even."

Now it was my turn to feel surprised. "What could he possibly have done to justify being treated like that?"

"Don't you remember?" She raised her chin. "The first time he came aboard, on Camrose Station. He called me an antique."

I put a hand to my forehead. "That was a year ago."

"He still shouldn't have said it."

I measured the weight of the glass cube in my hands. "You can be a real jerk sometimes, you know that?"

The *Trouble Dog* remained unrepentant. "He started it," she said sulkily.

I picked up the cube containing the silver scrap. "You could have broken it to him a little more gently. I wanted to talk about what happened, to make sure he was okay. But no, you had to rub his nose in it."

The ship's avatar raised her eyebrows. "Are you saying this is my fault?"

"You could have been a bit less blunt."

"I'm a warship, Captain. I don't do 'less blunt'." She arranged her face into a defiant pout. "Now, can you please put my cube back down?"

"Oh, I'm going to put it down, all right."

"What does that mean?"

"It means I'm going to throw it out of the airlock. The last thing Preston needs now is to know it's on board."

I strode to the top of the companionway ladder. Behind me, the *Trouble Dog* said, "Wait!"

"I don't want to argue about this anymore."

"Neither do I." Her tone and posture had changed, becoming more businesslike. "I'm picking up a signal from Camrose."

I felt my heart sink. Over the past couple of weeks I'd become too used to deciding my own itinerary, and taking the ship wherever I saw fit. Now, a communication from home could only mean a curtailment of that freedom, and a return to active duty.

My anger forgotten, I placed the cube back on its plinth. "Patch it through."

CHAPTER ELEVEN

JOHNNY SCHULTZ

I hated leaving Chet, but we had no choice. Addison was right: the ship's shattered hull might disintegrate at any moment, and then we'd all be screwed. We needed to get back to the others and get into our pressure suits while we still had air to breathe.

I let her lead the way. She knew this ship as well as I did, and she had the ability to make decisions under pressure, and act upon them without hesitation. If we were going to find an escape route, she'd be the one to find it. If I'd tried to lead, we'd still be dithering around in the engine room. Under normal circumstances, I might have described myself as a decisive person; but these circumstances were far from normal, and the losses—first Vito, then Jansen and Monk, then Chet; even the ship itself—had come too quickly, cut too deeply for me to trust my own judgement right now. I needed time to absorb the shock of our situation.

We scrambled up broken ladders and wormed our way around fallen machinery. And all the while, the ship moaned and trembled around us. I felt like crying. *Lucy's Ghost* deserved better than this. Chet and the others had deserved better. But there was nothing I could do to help them. No way for me to reset the clock and save them. All I could do was keep taking one step after another, keep my body falling forwards, until we reached the airlock.

Everybody else had his or her suit on, and there wasn't much room left for us. Our suits hung inside the locker like the skins of flayed ghosts. We dragged them out into the corridor and helped each other dress. With great reluctance I said goodbye to my jacket, leaving it folded on the deck. Then we rejoined our comrades and closed the inner lock door.

"Communications test," I said into my helmet mike. "Can everybody hear me?"

Five voices answered in the affirmative. I could see their frightened eyes behind their curved faceplates. Each of their suits was of a different make. As security officer, Kelly's was an army surplus model, with armour plating on the torso and limbs; Dalton's was the standard orange that denoted a medic; and Santos's was a bulky blue, heavily patched specimen that looked older than he was. If he'd told me it was a family heirloom, I'd have believed him. Only the accountant, Henri Bernard, had a new-looking suit, conspicuously lacking the grime and scuffs acquired by the rest.

"Where are the others?" Henri asked.

I couldn't trust myself to speak.

"We're all that's left," Addison said. "Now, have we got the manoeuvring packs?"

Kelly and Dalton gave the thumbs-up. Each had a skeletal frame strapped to their backs, with gas jet nozzles fixed to each corner. Usually, I would have taken one of the packs, but Dalton needed it to help the injured Santos make the jump. The rest of us would use lines to clip ourselves to Kelly, and she would pull us across to the *Restless Itch*.

"What about the cutting equipment?" I asked.

Santos was leaning against the airlock wall, resting his damaged foot. He patted a cylindrical kit bag.

"I have it here, chief."

"And weapons?"

"I have them." Kelly held up a canvas bag. "All the rifles, plus as much ammunition as would fit."

"Thanks."

I reached over and took the bag filled with cutting torches from Santos. There was no way he could carry it while limping.

As I straightened up, I noticed Dalton regarding Kelly with sceptical eyes.

"Do you really think we'll need all those guns?" he asked. "I mean, it's a derelict ship. Are we really expecting resistance?"

Lena Kelly gave him a look that could have chilled beer.

"You stick to your duties, Gil," she said, "and let me attend to mine."

Beneath us, the deck juddered.

"We'd better get that outer door open," Addison said.

I instructed Bernard and Addison to clip their lines onto Kelly, and Santos clipped his onto Dalton, then I turned to the controls and punched the override. The atmosphere drained from the chamber, and the hatch slid aside to reveal a wash of hard, bright stars. Dressed in our mismatching suits and lashed together in two groups, we tumbled out into the universe.

For a minute or so, all I could hear was the sound of my breathing. Then I managed to steady myself. Addison, Bernard and I were clipped to Kelly, and she was working the thrusters of her manoeuvring pack, trying to tug us into alignment. A few dozen metres away, I could see Dalton carefully towing Santos.

I glanced back at the *Lucy's Ghost*. The collision with the larger ship had crushed the entire starboard side of her bow, and cracked her spine in half a dozen places. Whole sections of her hull had buckled and split, wreathing the wreck in glittering clouds of frozen air and shards of splintered debris. Just seeing her in such a state filled me with sadness and shame. She'd been my home, my livelihood and my friend, and I had failed her.

Pulled around by a tug on my line, I faced the *Restless Itch*. In the unreal clarity of the vacuum, her charcoal-coloured flank seemed to fill half the sky, and I could see every crag and outcrop on her surface. Dim lights burned in the depths of her craters. The melted-looking domes and antennae protruding from her surface looked like cancerous growths.

How could I have been arrogant enough to contemplate an assault on such a structure? The size of it alone was enough to paralyse. From here, it looked as big as a moon. And it had been travelling for centuries, hauling its way doggedly through the void at speeds far less than that of light. How could I ever have hoped to storm such a leviathan with a handful of crew and a few cutting torches? If we'd tried to explore it without a reliable map of the interior, it could have taken us weeks just to traverse its length, from bow to stern. Just finding the bridge would have necessitated a major expedition. Casing the entire asteroid for valuable artefacts would have taken months.

"Holy shit!" The voice came over the open channel. It sounded like Addison. I swivelled around on the end of my tether until I could see her.

"What is it?"

I couldn't see her face behind her visor, but her gloved hand pointed back in the direction of the *Lucy's Ghost*.

"Look," she said.

With difficulty, I turned until the ship came back into view. And, as I looked at the broken, tumbling ruin, I felt cold fingers close on my gut. Addison was pointing to a spot just forward of the *Lucy's* stern, where something had torn a ragged hole in the ship's flank.

"What's that?" She sounded puzzled. My mind flashed back to the moments before the crash, to the sinuous black shape I'd thought I'd seen in the mist, and the final strike, when I'd fancied I'd glimpsed a gaping mouth filled with teeth.

I said, "I think we were attacked."

Addison's helmet had a lamp. She directed the beam into the wound.

"It doesn't look like a torpedo strike," she said.

"I don't think it is."

"This section hasn't been pushed in by an impact, it's been scooped out. It's almost as if something took a bite out of us."

"Something did."

"You can't be serious."

"I saw it. So did Vito, before he… before…"

She turned and I caught a glimpse of her face inside

101

her helmet, lit from beneath by readouts and displays.

"You're saying a *creature* did this?" Her eyes were wide with concern and disbelief. Too late, I realised we were still on the open channel, and the rest of the crew would be listening in to our every word.

"Yes," I said, not caring if they believed me or not. "A big fucking creature with teeth sharp enough to pierce hull plate."

CHAPTER TWELVE

ONA SUDAK

Buried at the exact centre of the vessel, the Hyena's bridge was the most secure room on the ship. When I arrived, Commodore Wronski rose from his command chair and saluted.

"Welcome, Captain Sudak."

For a second, I frowned. Then I realised the *Entanglement* would have passed on my preference. The ship hadn't asked which name I preferred solely for its own benefit, but on behalf of everyone else as well.

"Thank you, sir."

The bridge was circular, with workstations arranged around a central data pillar. Tactical screens covered the walls and dome-shaped ceiling. Wronski's chair was one of three positioned close to the door, with a view of the entire room.

"Please," he said, indicating the empty chair next to his. "Won't you join me?"

We sat, and watched the bridge crew hurry about their assigned tasks. From the main screen, I could see we were still underwater, but now we were moving.

"We've been putting some distance between ourselves and the crash site," Wronski explained. "When we're clear, we'll break surface and make for orbit."

"And until then, what's my status?" I sat straight. "Am I a prisoner?"

To my annoyance, Wronski smiled. "Gods above, no." He took a square of embroidered cloth from his pocket and dabbed his forehead. "Quite the opposite in fact."

On the main screen, the frigate's lights cut through the murky water. Shoals of brightly coloured fish scattered from its path.

"Then please, would you mind explaining what I'm doing here?" I tried to keep my voice level and my tone reasonable, but evidently failed to banish all traces of the frustration I felt, for Wronski looked at me as if I'd snapped at him.

"Of course," he said, sounding a little taken aback. He pocketed the handkerchief, rubbed his hands on his thighs, and stood. "If you'll follow me, I'll endeavour to explain everything."

With a nod to his second-in-command, he led me to the briefing room adjoining the bridge.

The briefing room had chairs for the frigate's senior officers, arranged around a wooden meeting table. Wronski parked himself at the head of the table, and indicated I should sit to his right. I shook my head. I just wanted answers.

"All right," he said, still sounding a little put out. "I'll tell you what I know."

He tapped the tabletop and a hologram appeared in the centre of the room.

"This is one of the alien ships you helped bring back from the Gallery," he said. The ship in question resembled a dagger made of porcelain or marble. "Right now, there are a million of them parked around Camrose Station."

I sighed. "I've already told the navy everything I know about the Marble Armada."

"Yes." Wronski placed his hands on the table, one resting on top of the other. "I've read the transcription of your debriefing."

"Then I don't know what else you want from me." While marooned in the Gallery, I'd spent some time in the company of a creature that spoke on behalf of the white ships, but I'd told my interrogators everything I could recall of our conversations.

"It's not what *I* want," Wronski said crossly. "It's what the ships want."

"The ships?"

"Some weeks ago, we received a request from the Armada." He moistened his lips. "From what I've been told, it seems they need a human representative to accompany them, to have the final say on certain moral questions."

"They need a leader?" I was surprised. "I thought they had the *Trouble Dog*?"

Wronski shook his head. "The *Trouble Dog* gave them a purpose, but she's not their leader." He adjusted the controls and the hologram changed. The scale expanded until we were looking at a veritable cloud of white ships. "The impression I get is that now they have their purpose, they require a biological entity to sanction the actions necessary to implement it."

"What actions?"

"I don't know."

"And where do I come in?"

Wronski leant back in his chair. All traces of resentment

were gone from his face, replaced by an expression that might have been curiosity, and might have been pity.

"You're the biological entity."

"Me?" I waved the suggestion away. "Don't be absurd. I've already been judged by the Armada, and declared unworthy."

"Nevertheless. To have one of our own aboard, helping direct their activities—you can see how that might be a great advantage for the Conglomeration."

"Yes, but—"

Wronski rose to his feet. "You realise now why we had to snatch you from that prison?"

I held up my hands to stop him from talking.

"I'm sorry, Commodore. I think you've got the wrong person. The Armada's avatar accompanied me to the *Trouble Dog*, but then lost interest. It wanted me to stand trial for what I did at Pelapatarn. Beyond that, I don't think it had any use for me."

Wronski tapped his fingers against his chin. "I'm afraid that's where you're wrong, Captain Sudak. You see, when they contacted us, they asked for you personally."

CHAPTER THIRTEEN

SAL KONSTANZ

The signal was from Ambassador Odom and had been relayed from Camrose via a higher dimensional transmitter. The sound quality was passable, but the picture kept freezing. Random bursts of pixels came and went, and the ambassador's speech kept drifting out of sync with the movements of his mouth.

"There's a ship in distress," he said. "I'd like you to go after it."

I felt my smile stiffen. "Does this mean you're returning us to active duty?"

Odom glanced away. "As it turns out, you're significantly closer than any of our other vessels."

"That doesn't answer my question."

Static hissed across the screen. Through it, Odom said, "I would have preferred you to have had more time to iron out any issues arising from the *Trouble Dog*'s refit. But I don't see I have any choice here. You can get to the site a week earlier than anything else we've got in the area."

I felt a flush of excitement. I'd been enjoying our

freedom, and thought I'd be reluctant to give it up, but now the call had come, I realised it would be good to have a purpose again. We'd recuperated from our injuries and paid our respects to those we'd lost. Now we needed something to stop us wallowing in our regrets. It was time to move on, and start looking ahead again, rather than astern.

"I'm sending through the coordinates and a copy of the signal," Odom said. "It's from a privateer called *Lucy's Ghost*, operating out of Tusker Quay with a crew of ten."

I glanced at the specs. The ship seemed to be a fairly standard freighter. Maybe she was a little on the elderly side, but nothing really out of the ordinary. I removed my baseball cap and ran a hand through my hair.

"She's pretty far out."

"Right on the border with the Nymtoq territories."

"Any idea what she's doing out there?"

Odom shrugged. "None, I'm afraid. But the Nymtoq have been a little touchy of late, especially since the brouhaha in the Gallery." He chewed his lower lip for a moment. "Please make sure you don't do anything to antagonise them."

I grinned at him.

"Who, us?"

"Yes, you."

"We'll do our best."

Odom clasped his hands together. "Thank you, Sally. I know you won't let me down."

I made a face.

"Don't jinx it. We're not there yet."

•

I asked the others to meet me in the galley.

Alva Clay turned up barefoot and hung-over, wrapped in a blanket and rubbing sleep from puffy eyes. Preston lingered at the door, refusing to look directly at me. Only the Druff engineer, Nod, seemed fully awake and attentive. It lowered itself to the floor in the middle of the room, and turned four of its six faces in my direction.

The *Trouble Dog* joined us via a projection of her avatar on the wall screen. Now we were back on active service, she'd dropped her earlier finery for a simple white tunic, coloured her lips black, and shortened her hair into a severe, businesslike crop.

Standing at the front of the room, I tipped back the brim of my cap.

"Okay, listen up. We've got a job. There's a crashed freighter about fifteen lights from here, with a crew of ten."

Clay stifled a yawn. "And the House wants us to go?"

"We're the nearest."

She rubbed her eyes. Her dreadlocks were tied back in a thick bunch at the back of her head. "I thought we were on sabbatical?"

I shrugged. "We've been recalled."

"And you got me out of bed for this?"

I opened my mouth. I had expected excitement at the prospect of a new adventure.

"I wanted to make sure we were all in agreement," I said.

Clay rose to her feet with an irritated huff. "You're the *captain*, you don't need our agreement. If you say that's where we're going, that's where we're going." She pulled the blanket more tightly around her shoulders. "Now, if you'll excuse me, I haven't slept in three days."

We stood looking at each other. After a moment, it

dawned on me that she was waiting for my permission to leave.

"Okay, fine." I waved her away. "You're excused."

She smiled. "Thank you. Just wake me when we get there."

She turned to the door, and Preston moved aside to make way for her. When she had gone, he looked directly at me for the first time.

"How long until we reach the crash site?"

"About a day and a half."

"Then I'd better go and check our infirmary." He pointed vaguely towards the corridor, shifting his weight from one foot to the other. "Make sure everything's shipshape and ready for any casualties."

"Fine." I turned to Nod. "And I suppose you want to scurry back down to engineering, to check on the engines?"

The Druff regarded me with four sets of coal-black eyes. Two of its faces tilted to the side.

"Much work," it said, using all four of its uncovered mouths. "Always work. No rest."

I held up my hands.

"Okay." Knowing I was beaten, I waved them away. "Go on, get out of here."

I waited until they'd gone, then helped myself to another cup of coffee.

What kind of crew were we if we couldn't bear to be in the same room as each other for more than a couple of minutes? Clay seemed to be trying to prove something, but I was unsure what or to whom; Preston seemed to have regressed into a resentful adolescent; and Nod remained just as inscrutable and grumpy as ever. I closed my eyes and inhaled steam from the cup. When I opened them, I saw the *Trouble Dog* watching me from her screen.

"I'm sorry," I said. "I'm sure you've had better commanding officers. Ones who knew how to inspire a crew."

The avatar shrugged a white-clad shoulder.

"I've had worse. Once," she continued, "I had one so awful the crew tried to mutiny."

"Really?" I hadn't heard that story. Despite allowing me access to her museum, the *Dog* could be surprisingly reticent about her military service. "What happened?"

Another shrug.

"I removed all the oxygen from the mutineers' quarters." She said it so matter-of-factly it took me a moment to process the implications.

"You *killed* them?"

"Oh no." I caught a flash of gleaming incisors. "I only did it for thirty seconds, and they were all successfully revived afterwards."

"That's horrible."

"Effective, though."

A three-dimensional display appeared in the air before me. It showed our destination in relation to our current position. Nearby stars were shown as softly glowing points of rubicund fire linked in a web of clean blue lines. I considered the numbers floating beside the line linking our current system with our target.

"Can we get there and back in one hop?" I asked her.

"Easily."

"No need to refuel en route?"

"Not since the refit." Her old drives had been upgraded, giving her increased efficiency, greater range and additional fuel capacity. "We've got enough for a thirty-six-hour jump to the crash site, and then two days back to Camrose."

"So there's nothing keeping us here?"

The *Trouble Dog* gave a smile that showed her teeth. "I'm ready to fly, Captain. Just give me the word."

•

Carrying my coffee, I left the galley and strolled around the circular corridor at the *Trouble Dog*'s waist, passing empty offices, mothballed gymnasiums and unused barracks. Eventually, I reached one of the companionway ladders that led up to the bridge at the heart of the ship. The climb was tricky with one hand, so I took the rim of the plastic cup in my teeth, and ascended carefully, so as not to slop scalding coffee on my upper lip.

Once on the bridge, I placed the coffee on top of my command console, next to the potted spider plant I kept there, and settled into my chair. The bridge was like a scuffed and comfortable cave, lined with readouts and display screens. The rest of the crew seldom ventured up here, and I had come to regard it as something of a personal fiefdom—a sanctuary free from the vicissitudes of planetary climate and human society.

Right now the main screen showed a view of the port, from the dusty, sand-blown runway to the perimeter fence and the desert stretching beyond. Heat shimmered from the tarmac.

I doffed my cap, hooked it over the arm of the chair, and raked my fingers through my hair. It had been evening when the ship had picked Alva and me up from the planet, and I badly needed to eat and sleep.

"Okay. Are we ready?"

The *Trouble Dog*'s avatar appeared on one of the smaller screens.

"All systems powering up," she reported.

"Do we have launch clearance from the port?"

She arched an eyebrow. "Do we need it?"

"It's always polite to ask."

"One moment." Her image froze for a couple of seconds. When she came back, she said, "Flight clearance approved. They're emptying the sky for us. There shouldn't be any traffic between here and orbit."

"Crew secure?"

"All strapped down."

"Then sound the acceleration warning, and take us up."

"Aye-aye, Captain."

The landing field dropped away like a weight loosened from a balloon, and I watched it dwindle to a grey smudge on the orange sand. By the time we were four kilometres up, I could just about make out, looming on the far horizon, the mesa supporting the Temples of the High Country. And I wondered if there were any tourists standing there beside George's photograph, looking back at us—and whether they saw us as anything more than a distant bright spark rising into the interminable blue of an endless sky.

CHAPTER FOURTEEN

TROUBLE DOG

Since resigning my commission, I have spent much of my time trying to better understand humanity. To this end, I have studied their philosophies and religions, their irrational beliefs and their most cherished ideals. I browsed works by great thinkers, pondered holy texts drawn from a dozen cultures and traditions, from Mesopotamia to the present day, and immersed myself in the sea of their literature and poetry, trying to get a handle on the slippery notion of a "human condition".

I particularly enjoyed looking back through their various scientific explanations for the workings of the universe, from the classic Aristotelian model of a nested cosmos, through to Newton's laws and Einstein's general relativity.

One of my favourites was the slightly daft notion that faster-than-light travel violates the laws of causality. This was once considered a viable scientific theory. Now, of course, my very existence proves how erroneous it was.

Imagine you aim a missile at a planet one light year away. Through your telescope, the target appears as it was twelve months ago. You fire the missile, and let's say for the sake of argument that it travels at twice the speed of light. That missile takes six months to reach the planet, and the light from its detonation takes a year to crawl its way back to you. Eighteen months pass between pulling the trigger and seeing the result. Cause and effect are clearly delineated.

Ah yes, the theory argues, but what about the people standing on the target world? To them, the image of you firing your warhead arrives six months *after* the missile falls on them. Therefore they are seeing the cause of their calamity half a year after experiencing its effects.

It's a ridiculous argument. You fired your missile, and six months later it hit its target. Nothing is changed by the fact that the light of your action takes such a long time to schlep its way across the intervening space—just as nothing is changed by the fact you see lightning before you hear thunder. The event that produced both happened according to the laws of the universe; it just takes a while for all its effects to reach you. Does the bullet that hits you before you hear the shot violate causality? No it doesn't, and neither does the bullet that hits you before you *see* the shot. As far as the bullet is concerned, its effects (hitting you) follow on from its cause (being fired from a gun); it's only your perceptions that say otherwise.

At least, that's how it was explained to me.

That was the trouble with faster-than-light travel through the higher dimensions. It really threw a monkey wrench in humanity's understanding of physics.

Me, I couldn't care less. Does a falling bomb care a jot how gravity works? Does a prowling hawk give aught for the physical complexities that keep her aloft?

CHAPTER FIFTEEN

JOHNNY SCHULTZ

The surface of the Nymtoq sleeper vessel towered before us like a cliff face, as pitted and cragged as any asteroid, every detail sharp and clear without air and haze to obscure the view.

We were aiming for a cargo hatch recessed in a small crater a half-kilometre forward from the stern. By the time we reached it, the *Lucy* looked no larger than a broken toy. For a moment, I watched her ravaged, slowly tumbling hulk fall away behind us, taking with it the bodies of our fallen crewmates, and swore a silent oath to come back for them one day, to recover their remains and give them a decent burial.

"We're ready to cut, boss." Lena Kelly had the vacuum torch fired up. I waved my gloved hand at the hatch.

"Do it." The sooner we were inside, the better.

"Wait!" Addison had braced herself in the corner of the hatchway. "There's a panel here. I think I can get it open."

"You speak Nymtoq now?"

"No, but there's only one button. So I guess it'll be

one press to open the door, and another to close it again."

I caught a scowl behind Kelly's faceplate and smiled to myself.

"Okay, smartass," I said to Addison. "Why don't you push it?"

"I just did."

At first, there was no response. Then the hatch moved. It jerked up half a centimetre, and rolled silently aside, disappearing into a slot in the wall. Behind it, we found a large cylindrical cavity with another door at the far end.

"This ship was supposed to last generations," Addison said, hauling herself inside. "They would have kept the important controls simple."

One by one we followed her, until only I was left clinging to the surface. I turned my head and shoulders to get one final look at the *Lucy*. I'd left four members of my crew back there—five if you included the ship herself. But I had no time for grief or self-recrimination. No time to think they'd have all still been alive if they hadn't followed me on my damn fool quest. The five remaining members of my crew were still breathing, and counting on me to keep them that way. I told my suit to log the *Lucy*'s position and trajectory for future reference, and then turned my back on her. The dead could wait.

Feeling simultaneously determined and terrified, I clambered into the airlock. As I cleared the hatch, Addison hit a control on the wall, and the outer door rolled back into place, sealing us off from the comforting light of the stars.

•

They started calling me "Lucky" Johnny Schultz around the time I bought the *Lucy*. Being an insufferably cocky seventeen-year-old, I'd put it about that I'd won her in a card game, and people had believed me. Traders can be a superstitious lot, and soon any success I had—any deal that paid off, any cargo that fetched a decent price—was ascribed to my "luck", rather than any innate business acumen I might possess. But that's the thing about luck— it doesn't really exist unless you're looking for it. And once you start believing in it, you start seeing it everywhere.

If we managed to stay alive long enough to be rescued, it would only bolster my reputation. Never mind the fact I'd lost five members of my crew and wrecked my ship. My survival alone would be enough to convince the port rats I was still fortune's favoured child.

•

The interior of the *Restless Itch* was pressurised, but dark. Once we were through the airlock's inner door, Kelly and Dalton abandoned their manoeuvring harnesses. Dragging additional loads had almost exhausted the propellant in their tiny thrusters, and they were too bulky to carry. While they were doing that, Addison used her suit's sensors to check the composition of the air, and then removed her helmet.

Beside her, the accountant, Henri Bernard, hesitated. "Is it safe?"

Addison shrugged in the beam from his helmet lamp. We were standing in a black-walled corridor that seemed to recede into infinity in both directions. Our shadows danced along the walls, where strangely organic-looking vents and pipes bulged. Some vented steam and other vapours, which glistened in our lights.

"Nothing that'll kill you quickly."

"What's that supposed to mean?"

"It means we're fine for now, but I wouldn't want to stay here more than a few days."

Bernard turned and stomped a few paces down the echoing corridor, and then stopped with his back to the rest of us. Over the radio, I could hear him muttering under his breath. Ignoring him, I cracked the seal on my own helmet. The air in the corridor was cool and carried a stale, chemical smell, like a long-forgotten swimming pool. I wondered how long it had been since anyone—or anything—had breathed it.

As I looked around, I saw Kelly had already unsheathed one of the guns, and was keeping watch on the corridor, fulfilling her role as security chief even as her captain stood around sniffing his surroundings.

Okay, I thought. Time to be decisive. Time to act like a captain and live up to the image of Lucky Johnny Schultz.

"Okay, Bernard, get back here and help Santos with the provisions." I clipped my helmet to my belt. "I'll take one of the guns. Kelly and I will be on point. Dalton, you've got the medkit. Addison, you take a weapon and bring up the rear."

"Where are we going, boss?" Kelly asked.

"We need somewhere to hole up. Not too far from the surface, but somewhere secure where we can make ourselves comfortable for a few days."

Kelly seemed to understand. "A defensible position within detection range of potential rescuers?"

"Yeah, that sort of thing. And access to the communications array would be a bonus, if we can get it working."

"On it." She threw a crisp salute, and started walking, gun swinging from side to side as she scanned the corridor ahead for potential threats. I followed a few paces behind, my own weapon held with the barrel facing the floor. I'd had to remove my gloves to fit my finger through the trigger guard. As I walked, with the others shambling along behind me, I ran the fingers of my free hand along the corridor walls behind the tangle of pipes. They were as smooth and cold as obsidian. They had been hacked from the living rock thousands of years before humans discovered spaceflight, and for most of that time these internal spaces had been empty and unused, their former inhabitants having killed themselves off in a desperate, anarchic fit barely a third of the way into their millennial voyage. In the flickering torchlight, I could feel the weight of those centuries settling into my bones. The eight long decades of the *Lucy's* career seemed like a snap of the fingers in comparison.

CHAPTER SIXTEEN
ONA SUDAK

As we took a circuitous route to avoid revealing our point of origin, the journey to Camrose Station took two days. I spent most of that time ensconced in my cabin learning all I could about the ongoing talks between the Marble Armada and the House of Reclamation, who were acting in this matter as representatives for the entire Human Generality. So far, there was little enough to go on. Having been abandoned by its creators five millenniums ago, the Armada had slept away the intervening centuries in a pocket universe, locked in the heart of a gaudily carved planet. They had been waiting for an entity worthy of their loyalty, one who could provide for them a purpose; and they had found such a creature in the Reclamation Vessel *Trouble Dog*.

I spent the rest of my time doing as little thinking as possible. Perhaps one day I would write about my experiences as a condemned woman, and resume the career of Ona Sudak, poet at large. Until then, I was content to fall back on the ingrained routines of the military. I rose at

0600 hours and exercised. I ate in the mess with the rest of the watch, and slept when it was time to sleep.

The food aboard the Hyena-class frigate consisted of basic naval rations. Under normal circumstances I would have found them bland and uninspiring, but they were a positive delight compared to the slurry I'd been fed in prison. For the first time in months, my clothes, hair and bunk were all clean and free of mites. Yet of all the pleasures denied to me during my incarceration, coffee had been the one I had most sorely and sincerely grieved. So much so that even the turgid, mud-like draught they served on board the *Entanglement* seemed to my parched senses the fairest of ambrosias.

I was drinking a cup on the bridge with Commodore Wronski as we approached Camrose. The man had all the personality of a jellyfish, but I wasn't there for his less-than-sparkling conversation. While he mumbled on about the day-to-day minutiae of supervising shipboard life, I kept my eyes fixed on the feed from the external cameras.

We had dropped out of the hypervoid high above the planet Camrose. Urban lights lay scattered across its darkened night side like the embers of a thousand campfires.

Moving across its face, and home to a million souls, Camrose Station loomed in orbit like a city that had somehow slipped gravity's shackles and drifted upwards, hauling factories and shipyards in its wake. Its lights were the lights of commerce and industry: the homely yellow glows of offices and apartments; the blinking red and green navigation lights of shuttles and other small craft; the gaudy enticements of hologram advertisements; and the occasional spark of a welding torch.

Trailing the station's orbit by a good two hundred

miles, the Armada's million ships lay in a three-dimensional diamond formation. In the light of the sun, they gleamed as white as bone, their glittering prows as sleek and sharp as stilettos.

Every schoolchild knew that the founder of the House of Reclamation had based the ideals of the organisation on the philosophies of the Armada's builders. They had been dedicated to the preservation of life. They believed strangers in trouble should be helped, and stranded spacefarers rescued. And when their beautiful legions of ships made contact with the *Trouble Dog*, the knife-like ships picked up on the lingering shame the *Trouble Dog* felt for her part in the Archipelago War. To preserve life, they reasoned, they would have to prevent another such war from taking place.

And now they were requesting my presence.

When I'd first encountered them, they had rejected me as unworthy to lead them. So what did they want with me now?

•

Although I had seen the white ships before, I had never seen one up close, so it was only during our final approach that I started to fully grasp the scale of the force they represented. They might be as pointed and slender as a paper dart, but each was easily the size of a Scimitar. Amassed like this, they represented the largest military force the Generality had ever encountered, outnumbering the combined forces on both sides of the Archipelago War by a factor of at least three. If they had been hostile, we could not have stood against them.

One of the ships had situated itself a few kilometres ahead of the swarm, and it was towards this one we had been directed.

"Docking in four minutes," reported one of the ensigns.

Wronski set aside his half-empty cup and straightened the cuffs of his uniform. Around us, the rest of the bridge crew were silent, gazes drawn to the wall of spacecraft before us, their bows like so many sharpened thorns.

"Well," he said gruffly, "it seems it's time to say farewell."

I placed my own mug on the arm of my chair and rose. "Thank you, Commodore."

"You're quite welcome." He narrowed his eyes, appraising me. "I don't suppose I shall ever find out exactly what this is all about, but I'm glad to have been of service."

We exchanged salutes. Then, formalities observed, he took a step closer. When he spoke, it was in a lowered voice, meant for me alone.

"And besides, for whatever it's worth," he murmured, "some of us still think you took the right decision at Pelapatarn."

I shrugged. "It's a shame the courts don't agree."

Wronski shook his head. I could smell the gel he used to keep his thinning hair slicked back, and the sweet black coffee on his breath.

"If we'd sent in ground troops, we'd have lost thousands, maybe even hundreds of thousands more than we did in your bombardment. Jungle warfare's a bitch."

"That doesn't excuse what I did."

"Doesn't it?" He raised an eyebrow. "With respect, there are a lot of personnel alive today who might disagree."

•

Having left the bridge, I made my way down to the main crew airlock. For the past days, I'd been trying to avoid thinking about the events that had led me to the brink of death by firing squad. Now, Wronski's words had opened an emotional sluice gate. By the time I reached the airlock, my hands were quivering and my legs felt spongy and unreliable. My vision smeared. I felt something building at the back of my throat, but couldn't tell whether it would emerge as a laugh or a sob.

I had been moments from a seemingly certain and implacable death, and although bitter and angry, I had been almost resigned to my fate. Now, I wasn't entirely sure I could handle the mental gear-shifting necessary to accommodate the fact of my deliverance—especially at this moment, as I stood on the very threshold of something potentially stranger and more outlandish than death.

A pair of marines showed me into the lock. One of them handed me a kit bag, and then they sealed the inner door, leaving me alone and friendless as I confronted the outer door, and the unknown fate that lurked beyond.

CHAPTER SEVENTEEN

SAL KONSTANZ

I waited until I was certain the *Trouble Dog* had safely made the jump into the higher dimensions, then I unbuckled from my command chair and climbed down from the bridge at the centre of the ship, to the human quarters that circled its waist. A day and a half of glorious isolation stretched ahead, during which we would gather our strength and prepare for whatever we might find when we reached the last reported position of the *Lucy's Ghost*. I planned to spend much of the time as far from the rest of the crew as possible, holed up either in my cabin or in the inflatable life raft in the hold. But before I retreated, it was my duty as captain to check on them all, and ensure they were prepared for the journey to come.

I didn't feel like starting with Alva Clay, so I wandered aft, towards the engineering facilities.

Many of the *Trouble Dog*'s day-to-day operations were fully automated and self-regulating. But not even the smartest system could be expected to cope with every eventuality, and there were occasionally repairs or adjustments that the ship just couldn't manage without external help. And that was why we carried an engineer. Whenever a light panel broke in one of the crew quarters, or a length of wiring burned out in a difficult-to-reach electrical duct, Nod was there. And in combat situations, it could move fast and make the kind of creative on-the-fly judgement calls that the *Trouble Dog* struggled with. Her inbuilt priority had to be to keep herself functional and dangerous. She seemed genuinely fond of us all, but in extreme cases—such as once during the war, when a pair of marines had been trapped in a damaged section of the ship and the *Trouble Dog* had wanted to open that area to vacuum in order to extinguish a fire which threatened to disable some of her combat sensors—her inculcated need to survive and complete her mission compelled her to entertain notions of "acceptable losses", and it took the morality of a flesh-and-blood engineer—and captain—to counterbalance her unintentionally merciless pragmatism.

Every ship in the Multiplicity—the wider community of alien races that surrounded and encompassed the Human Generality—carried a Druff engineer. Nobody remembered now which race had been the first to employ the Druff, but by the time humanity escaped into the wider cosmos, the creatures had been ubiquitous for millennia, and every human ship for the past two centuries had carried one.

I picked my way back to the series of linked chambers that made up Nod's domain. Ducts and wiring conduits crisscrossed the bulkheads. Yellow-and-black warning decals called attention to awkward corners, uncovered intakes, and low ceilings. Water dripped from somewhere, and the walls reverberated with the clamour of the machinery behind them. A spicy, animal scent underlay the all-pervading tang of hot metal.

Like its arboreal ancestors, Nod slept in a nest. It built a fresh one every few days, mostly from pieces of discarded packaging, lengths of wire and any other pieces of crap it had lying around. As I ducked my way into the warm alcove that served as its main living space, I saw its latest effort wedged in the gap between two piles of equipment. Nod wasn't in it, though. Doubtless it was off somewhere, deep in the bowels of the ship, tweaking some system or other. If I'd wanted to, I could have asked the *Trouble Dog* to locate it, but that seemed to defeat the point of a casual visit. I didn't have any pressing reason to see it, I was just calling to say hello. If it was working, I'd be better off leaving it undisturbed.

I was about to turn and retrace my steps when a flicker of overhead movement caught my eye. Something black and roughly the size of my hand scuttled into one of the ceiling ducts.

"What the hell was that?"

"What was what?" The *Trouble Dog* spoke via the bead in my ear. "Are you all right, Captain? Your pulse and respiration are spiking."

"You're damn right they're spiking!" My mouth was dry. I could almost hear my pulse. I took a couple of wary steps back towards the exit, keeping my attention rigidly fixed on the hole into which the creature had disappeared. "There's some*thing* loose down here."

"Could you be more specific?"

"I only caught a glimpse." I paused and swallowed, wishing I had some sort of weapon. "But it looked kind of like a spider."

"Ah."

"A *big* spider. Tarantula-sized."

The ship was silent for a moment.

"I'm sorry," she said. "I should have told you they were aboard."

At her words, I felt a cold prickle run the length of my spine. "They? There's more than one of those things down here?"

"There are eleven of them in your immediate vicinity. Two more elsewhere on that deck."

I heard skittering footsteps and whirled around, just in time to see another of the creatures dart through the door, into the access way beyond. Now, if I wanted to retreat, I'd have to do so knowing there was at least one of them blocking my path.

"What are they? Where did they come from?"

"I think you should speak to Nod."

"It brought them aboard?"

"In a manner of speaking, yes. I've signalled it, and it should be here momentarily."

I was trying to look in every direction at once, hands raised defensively in case one of the critters leapt at my face.

"What the hell are you talking about?"

"Nod should be the one to explain."

"But—"

A limb appeared over the wiry rim of Nod's nest, and I swallowed back a surge of panic. I'd never been particularly susceptible to arachnophobia—but then, I'd never previously been stuck in a hot, noisy and cramped engine room with eleven tarantulas.

"Ship…"

"It's all right. It's nearly with you."

"But there's one climbing out of the nest. It's—" I stopped speaking as the little creature heaved itself up onto the lip, and I got my first proper look at it.

The thing stood on five limbs. A sixth was raised in my direction, the fingers splayed like the petals of a flower. Leaning close, I could just about make out tiny, coal-black eyes regarding me from the centre of the palm. A little slit of a mouth opened and closed soundlessly.

"It's a baby Druff!"

The youngster flinched at the sound of my voice. Its scales glistened like oil on water. It looked me up and down several times, as if trying to decide whether to investigate further or flee.

I spoke quietly, so as not to startle it. "Where did we get thirteen baby Druff?"

When she replied, the *Trouble Dog* managed to sound both amused and embarrassed. "Nod gave birth last night."

"Gave birth?" I shook my head, feeling absurd. "You're telling me our engineer got itself knocked up, and popped out thirteen little copies of itself?"

"I believe it happened the last time we were on Camrose."

A grating swung aside on well-oiled hinges, and Nod slunk into the room. At the sight of it, the little one squeaked, and ran over to wrap four of its arms around one of its parent's ankles.

"Captain." Keeping its head low, it looked up at me.

I crossed my arms. "I think you've got some explaining to do."

In a blur of limbs, another four of the babies broke cover, and attached themselves to Nod. One clambered up on its back.

"Much sorry, Captain."

"Why didn't you tell me you were expecting? Why didn't *anybody* tell me?"

The *Trouble Dog* cleared her throat.

"The Druff are intensely private about these matters. Nod requested my discretion."

"Birth good," Nod cut in. "Offspring good. But rescue mission unexpected."

I began to understand.

"You were anticipating giving birth while we were in port?"

"Port birth. Give offspring to relatives to raise."

"You had relatives on that planet?"

"Relatives on every planet." Nod sounded taken aback by my ignorance. "All Druff related. All Druff from World Tree."

I massaged my forehead.

"And had this happened, I would have been none the wiser?"

It opened and closed the fingers of its hand/face.

"No need to tell. All private."

"But now we're stuck with them?" One of the creatures was sniffing around the toe of my boot.

"Until *Hound of Difficulty* returns to Camrose."

I looked up and saw two more pulling out the wiring around a light fitting. In their little high-pitched voices they were chanting the words, "Work. Do work. Always work."

Nod raised its face to mine, tilted questioningly to one side.

"Nod in trouble?"

I looked down into the black pearls of its eyes, and sighed.

"No," I told it, "you're not in trouble. But try to keep them under control, okay? I don't want to end up stranded out here without air and power because they've been chewing on something critical."

CHAPTER EIGHTEEN

NOD

Offspring good.

Offspring fast and clever. Already into everything.

On World Tree they would already be tending the fibres beneath the bark. Here, they help Nod.

Help work.

Work, then rest.

Work, then build new, bigger nest, and sleep.

Curl up in family bundle. Protect against storms. Tend systems.

Dream of World Tree.

In hours, offspring will be old enough to have names.

Much think.

Much decide.

Might name one after Captain.

Then *Bothersome Mutt* will have fourteen engineers.

Eighty-four hands.

One hundred and sixty-eight eyes.

Five hundred and four fingers.

Nothing will stay broken.

Everything fixed.
Everything working.
Always working.
Work, then rest.

CHAPTER NINETEEN

JOHNNY SCHULTZ

The scale of the corridors felt wrong. Everything was too large. Female Nymtoq stood two and a half metres tall, and all the doors and ceilings had been built to accommodate them. Creeping through the darkened passageways of the *Restless Itch*, we felt like children investigating a deserted house at midnight. We were even whispering.

In the light from our torches, the corridors were hexagonal in cross-section, the resultant sideways bulge designed to allow the ship's builders to stretch and unfurl their vestigial wings as they walked, or to pass each other without flattening their meticulously preened plumage against the polished rock.

After a tense fifteen minutes, we came to a place where the passageway broadened into a cavern. Kelly went in first, sidearm at the ready, swinging the beam from her flashlight into any shadow conceivably large enough to conceal a threat.

"It's clear," she called.

I went in after her, shining my own torch around to

get an idea of the shape of the space. As far as I could tell, the floor plan was roughly elliptical, around thirty-five paces in length and sixteen or seventeen in width. The ceiling was a vaulted arch high above us.

"There are only two entrances," Kelly said. "If we hole up by the far wall, we can cover them both."

"Okay." I waved to the others to join us. In the unsteady light, they looked gaunt and tired, haunted by the losses we'd endured, and I didn't like to think what might happen if I tried to force them onwards. "We'll rest here."

"Yes, sir." Kelly moved away to help the others shed their burdens and find places to sit against the curved wall. Their voices were quiet and subdued, devoid of their usual banter, and I knew how they felt. We were all struggling to deal with the shock of it all. The ship that had been our home and livelihood was gone. Our friends were dead. And here we were, cast into a vast, unlit subterranean labyrinth filled with unknown dangers and apparently built by a race of tall bird people.

I dropped to my knees next to Addison.

"How are you doing?"

She gave me a look. "How do you think?"

"Been better?"

She gave a dry half-laugh. "A damn sight better. What's your plan?"

"Hunker down and wait for rescue. Why? Did you have a pressing engagement I wasn't aware of?"

"No such luck." Our hectic dash through the engineering spaces of the *Lucy's Ghost* had left her hands, clothes and face smudged and dirty. "I just want to know how long we're going to be stuck here."

"A few days at least."

I sat back and looked up at the ceiling. There was something ancestral and comforting about watching shadows leap and twitch across the roof of a cave—even if the "cave" in question was part of an alien vessel, skirting the ragged edge of human space.

"We'll go exploring later," I said. "But right now, we're all tired, and we need to rest."

•

I hadn't expected to fall asleep. The floor was uncomfortable, and my mind in turmoil. But sometimes, when you're overwhelmed, the body just shuts down. It needs time to process and regroup, so it puts you to sleep—even when you think maybe you'll never sleep again for the dead faces looming in your memory.

When I woke, maybe an hour later, I was cold and stiff from lying on hard rock, but the worst of the adrenalin had had time to work its way out of my system, and I felt calmer and more in control. More like my old self. More like Johnny Schultz.

I pushed myself up. Addison was asleep beside me, with her head resting against the bag of cutting tools. Dalton and Santos were huddled against the wall. Only Kelly and Bernard were awake, and Bernard's torch was the only one lit. The accountant glowered at me, but said nothing. Kelly gave me a nod.

"All clear," she whispered. "No sign of life."

"Thanks." I hadn't really expected there to be; this ship had been deserted for seven thousand years. And yet, there was something almost tangibly threatening about the darkness of the corridors—a hackle-prickling sense that somewhere in the blackness, invisible eyes might be watching… I felt a shiver run through me. I'd never been scared of the dark before. But then, I'd rarely encountered darkness so thoroughly alien and complete. Even in the depths of space there were the stars; here, there was only rock and metal, and no sources of light save those we carried. If we turned them off, we'd be able to see nothing at all.

"Do you have orders?" Kelly asked.

"Orders?" I tried to rub the stiffness from the back of my neck where it was still sore from the tumble I'd taken during the attack on the *Lucy's Ghost*. "Not really, just sit tight, I guess. I'll keep watch now; you get some sleep. We've got a fucking long wait ahead of us."

I took a deep breath in through my nose, and again wondered how long it had been since the air molecules I inhaled had last passed through a living respiratory system. They say each lungful you take on Earth contains atoms once inhaled by the likes of Shakespeare, Caesar and Einstein. Here, I guess all we were breathing were the last, dying gasps of the Nymtoq crew after they'd finished slaughtering each other. It wasn't a comfortable thought. When rescue came, I'd be glad to get out of this flying tomb.

I was about to say as much when a flicker of movement caught my eye. I heard a sharp intake of breath from Kelly. Her torch and gun swung around and we both gaped in astonishment at the figure standing in the mouth of the corridor. Behind me, Bernard let out a startled cry.

It was a young girl. She must have been around eleven or twelve years old. And pale blue light crackled from her eyes.

"Jesus Christ," I said. "Lucy?"

CHAPTER TWENTY

ONA SUDAK

It wasn't easy becoming Ona Sudak. The first time, I mean. Back when I was on the run after the torching of Pelapatarn. Back before the *Trouble Dog* found me, and brought me back to the Generality for trial.

Back then, I chose the name Ona Sudak at random, picked to go with my resculpted, altered physique, my new retinae and fingerprints. I hadn't given it much thought. I didn't think it mattered. But sometimes, names have a kind of power. A cosmic resonance. And their cadence shapes the kind of people we become.

At least, that's how Sudak would explain it.

Before I became her, I was Captain Annelida Deal, the Butcher of Pelapatarn—a war criminal fleeing retribution. I had spent my life in the military, working my way up through the ranks, fighting my way through the terrible attrition of the decade-long Archipelago War. And then suddenly, I was a civilian. The war was over, and with it my sense of purpose. I couldn't be Annelida Deal any longer; I had to cut her adrift. I had to give up everything that made me her.

My career was over, but that was just the start. If I wanted to remain at large, I knew I'd have to fundamentally alter my lifestyle and routine. It wasn't enough to simply look different; I'd also have to act differently. Instead of the somewhat strident captain I had been, I adopted a softer manner, a quieter tone. I gave up drinking rum and switched to chilled white wine; stopped eating Stilton and started pretending to like olives. Gave up action movies and switched to reading books. I made a thousand such decisions, invented a thousand new habits. And from those aggregate behaviours, a new personality emerged.

Or possibly, it had always been there, and I'd been too wrapped up in the military to notice.

Whatever the truth, I soon found myself wearing floral print skirts instead of regulation uniform, drinking tea instead of coffee, and—most surprising of all—writing poetry.

Ona Sudak was a poet. She had a taste for long lunches and quick fucks, and she wrote long, bitter elegies for a generation chewed up by war. When she accidentally became a literary celebrity, I had no choice but to play along. To refuse the spotlight would have been to break character. And so I decided to hide in plain sight. I published more work, collected awards and gave readings, and took my pick of the younger and more interesting groupies. Some days, I even managed to forget Annelida Deal altogether…

And there I would have remained, blissfully fucking my way through cruise after cruise, had my liner not blundered its way into a Conglomeration Intelligence operation in a distant star system. Stranded on an alien world, pursued by hostile forces, I had been compelled to reoccupy my former persona in order to survive. I had to become Deal again.

But now, six months later, Deal was dead, killed in an aircraft crash, and I was...

I didn't know what I was. I'd reassumed Sudak's name, but I wasn't entirely her. My experiences in the Gallery had changed me. Having seen Adam die in the cruel, pointless way he did, I doubted I'd ever be able to fully recapture her spark of hedonism. Neither of my former identities was quite enough to describe what I'd now become. What the world had made of me. I had Sudak's perceptions, and Deal's grit. I was a combination of the best and worst in each of them—and, at the same time, something wholly new. I had killed thousands of people, and faced my own death over and over again. I had been through the fire and it had forged me into something sharper and stronger than I had once been. I was steel hardened in the furnace, a glimmering weapon infused with the intensity of a poet's intellect.

And I had work to do.

·

When the pressure in the airlock had equalised, the inner door skimmed aside to reveal the lustrous white interior of the dagger-shaped ship. The walls, floors and ceilings held the same pearlescent sheen as the outer hull. The air was frigid, and held scents both animal and antiseptic.

A creature was waiting to greet me. It was the same multi-eyed grizzly bear I'd met in the Gallery—the one that claimed to be a gestalt avatar for the networked minds of the million-strong Armada. It blinked at me—a ripple of eyelids—and flexed its claws.

When it growled, words appeared in my mind like subtitles.

Ona Sudak.

"Hello."

You are welcome aboard.

The brown fur on the creature's back looked soft and inviting, but there was nothing remotely cuddly about the muscular bulk beneath. Like the bear it resembled, this thing was definitely a predator, and I would no sooner have embraced it than have stuck my head in a tiger's mouth.

"Thank you." I glanced around at the smooth, cold-looking bulkheads. "Does this ship have a name?"

It has a designation.

"And what might that be?" I assumed I'd need to know if I had to communicate with the ship.

88,573.

"88,573?"

Correct.

"That's catchy," I said.

The bear snuffled disapprovingly.

You are being insouciant.

"I apologise." I clasped my hands together. "It's a defence mechanism."

You are afraid? It sounded surprised.

"I don't yet know why I've been summoned here."

The creature seemed to think about this for a moment. Then it reared up on its hindquarters, and I tried not to flinch away. In contrast with the rounded, sterile whiteness of our surroundings, its teeth and claws were sharp, with the yellowed sheen of old ivory.

All will be explained.

With painful gracelessness, it shuffled around,

dropped back onto all fours, and lumbered off.

Watching it move away along the gleaming white corridor, I released the breath I hadn't realised I'd been holding, and swore quietly. The bear-thing's gait looked clumsy, and it seemed always on the verge of tripping over itself. And yet for such a hefty animal, it moved with surprising speed, its soft paws padding a silent, irregular rhythm, with only the occasional click of a claw tip against the smooth marble floor. As I hurried to keep up, I cast about in vain for any sign of a crew. Every compartment we passed appeared to be as blank and featureless as the corridor—as if the ship wasn't really a ship at all, but somehow more akin to a mask or sculpture than a functional machine. This impression grew as I noticed a lack of engine noise or vibration. I had spent my career serving on military ships, and had become used to the myriad cacophonies associated with the operation of such vessels. Here, those various clangs, hisses and shouts were absent, and their lack disturbed me. In the silence, we might almost have been walking through a museum exhibit rather than an operational warship.

After a couple of minutes, we arrived at a spherical chamber, about ten metres in diameter. The floor of the corridor became a bridge, extending out into the exact centre of the room, where it widened into a small platform.

Here.

The bear stopped moving and I joined him on the suspended dais.

This is the centre. The confluence.

I looked around. Aside from their shape, the walls were as featureless as ever, and the air as chill.

"Is this the bridge?"

This is the focus. From here, you can lead the Armada.

"Lead it? I thought I had been judged unworthy?"

You were.

"So what's changed?"

You have.

"Because I went back and faced the consequences of Pelapatarn?"

You were ready to relinquish your life to make amends. There is no higher atonement.

"And now you want me to lead you?"

Our mission is to end war. But we cannot act without the guidance and oversight of a biological intelligence. It is the way we were designed, to prevent us turning on those we were built to serve.

"But why me?"

When you ordered the bombardment of Pelapatarn, you did so in order to end the Archipelago War. You made a difficult moral choice, in the belief you were sparing more lives than you took.

I narrowed my eyes.

"So, you need someone who's not afraid of getting their hands dirty?"

The bear's eyes blinked and it tipped its head to one side, as if considering.

The metaphor is apt.

I began to understand. Vast and powerful as it was, the Marble Armada could only act with the consent of a living entity—and they'd chosen me because they knew I'd once been willing to torch a world in order to achieve my objectives.

I looked over the edge of the platform, at the base of the sphere five metres below.

This, then, was the reason I'd been spared a firing squad. The Armada had insisted I go back to face judgement for my actions. Now I had, it was unwilling to simply let me die. The bear had said the Armada's mission was to end war. And to achieve it, they needed my help.

But how were they planning to prevent conflict, and why did they need the assistance of someone capable of slaughtering thousands in order to achieve their aims?

•

I tried not to flinch as the bear reached out an arm and cupped the back of my skull with its plate-sized paw. The tendons in its palm felt like steel cables, and the tips of its claws pricked my cheek. As it bent its maw towards me, its breath smelled musty, like an abandoned cellar in which something had died.

Hold still.

One of the claws pressed against my temple. The pressure was slight but insistent, and I clenched my fists as the needle-sharp point punctured the skin.

"What are you doing?" I asked through clenched teeth, fighting the instinct to struggle or pull away. If the creature had wanted to harm me, it could easily have killed me the moment I boarded the white vessel. If it wanted me dead, it could simply have left me to the tender mercies of the firing squad.

You need to be upgraded in order to use this room.

I could feel a drop of blood running down the side of my face. The claw had stopped, but the inside of my head itched, as if the tip had sprouted a hundred hair-fine appendages, each of which was worming its way into the pliable tissues of my brain.

I think I must have cried out, for the bear's grip tightened, holding me immobile. The itching sensation swelled to a scrabbling crescendo of white-hot pain. There was a sense of barriers being broken, membranes transgressed…

Released, I fell to my knees. My heart banged like a tin cup against the cage of my ribs. My lungs heaved, and for a moment all I could do was wait for the pain to subside.

When finally I looked up, I found the room had changed. Where once the walls had been white and featureless, they now teemed with tiny blades.

You see them?

I drew my gaze from the fleet of knives, and glared up at the nine-eyed bear.

"You could have warned me."

Would it have hurt less?

"That's hardly the point."

Each of the blades on the wall represented a member of the million-strong Marble Armada, and when my gaze swept across them, they expanded in turn to display their current location and status.

Distracted by this, I asked, "So, I can see them all?"

And they can see you. This is the confluence, the place of communion. Speak and all shall hear.

"What should I say?"

Tell us to prosecute our cause. Approve our mission. Authorise the steps necessary to defend life and terminate war.

I looked around at the miniature warships surrounding us in all directions, and suddenly my mouth felt dry. I hadn't given an order of such consequence since issuing the fatal proclamation at the Battle of Pelapatarn, and now here was another fleet awaiting my permission to unleash their crusade.

"You want to end war?" Memories of the bombardment

danced behind my eyes, obscene nuclear flowers blossoming over a continent.

That is our mission.

"Then do it. Go ahead."

By all means necessary?

I took a deep breath.

"Yes, whatever it takes."

CHAPTER TWENTY-ONE
SAL KONSTANZ

We had been travelling through the higher dimensions for more than twenty-four hours when I found Alva Clay in the gym. She had been running on the treadmill. Her locks were tied back, and she wore a pair of beaten-up running shoes. When she saw me, she stopped the machine and grabbed a towel.

"What can I do for you?" She sounded irritable. I had checked on her shortly after our departure, but as she'd said she didn't want to be woken, I'd simply looked in on her. This was our first proper conversation since I announced our mission.

I spread my hands. "Are we cool?"

"Sure." She wiped her face. "But I know that expression. You've got something on your mind."

I gave her a guilty smile, surprised and a little dismayed to be so transparent. "I've been thinking about that guy in the alley," I said.

"Mr Wilkes?"

"He was Outward. Things must be getting serious if

we've got our own government spying on us."

Clay shrugged. Sweat glistened on her skin. Her tattoos shone like vinyl.

"We let the genie out the lamp," she said, only slightly out of breath. "And now they're frightened what we'll wish for."

I pulled Wilkes's sunglasses from my pocket. They had been printed from cheap plastic, and probably picked up from a portside kiosk for a couple of credits.

"They don't trust the Fleet," I said.

Clay picked up a bottle of water. "So?"

"When I was at the high temples, one of the tourists told me he didn't trust them either. He was ex-navy. It got me thinking."

"Are you trying to tell me you don't trust the Marble Fleet?"

"I don't think so. How about you?"

Clay loosened her locks and they toppled down around her shoulders. She shook them out and fixed me with a look.

"I don't trust anything."

"Then what should we do?"

"Nothing. It ain't our problem." She crossed to the showers, kicked off her shoes, shed her vest and shorts, and stepped into a cubicle. She had been a marine, and barrack life had long since relieved her of any self-consciousness regarding her body.

"I'm just worried." I averted my eyes from her nakedness.

"Of course you are." I heard the shower start. "You're one of those people who always worry whether or not they've done the right thing."

"And you aren't?" I had to raise my voice over the noise of the water.

"What do you think?"

"I'm being serious."

"So am I."

Steam started to fill the room. The *Trouble Dog* had been designed for a crew of three hundred. With only four of us aboard, there was always plenty of hot water.

"Look," Clay called, "I understand why you're fretting. We unleashed something we probably shouldn't have. But it saved our butts. We wouldn't be here today if those white ships hadn't appeared when they did."

I made a face. She was right, of course; but I still couldn't shake off the uneasy feeling that someday we were going to regret that moment of apparent good fortune.

•

Feeling dispirited, I made my way up to the bridge. I had no reason to be there. In higher dimensional flight, the ship could easily look after itself. Yet, I had nowhere else to go. I'd had enough of prowling the corridors, and I didn't want to risk bumping into Preston in the galley or infirmary. He was still angry with me, and I couldn't face a confrontation. The bridge was the only place I could be reasonably sure of being left alone.

I sat in my chair and accessed the forward screens, opening a view of the swirling mists surrounding us. My baseball cap was on the console where I'd left it. I picked it up and jammed it on my head.

The cap was old and faded, and fraying at the seams. It had once belonged to Sedge. He'd worn it almost every day in his job as a hydroponics technician, and had given it to me the last time we'd parted, on the flagstone quay at

Naxos, as we were waiting for the ferry to the mainland. We'd been on the island for three months, feasting on each other's company; but now the war was in full swing, and we'd been assigned to different parts of the fleet. He'd given me the hat because I'd asked him for it. I'd wanted it as a memento, a talisman—something that smelled of him, to keep his presence close in the dark days ahead.

Little did I know he'd never return to claim it—that he'd receive a mistaken report of my death, and leave on a one-way expedition to the Andromeda galaxy, frozen in the hold of a ship owned by the locust-like Hoppers.

What might have happened had he not gone? I had no way of knowing, although I found it difficult to imagine myself as a marriage-and-kids kind of person. I couldn't envision ever having settled down in the traditional sense. But maybe if he'd come back to me at the end of the war, I might now have been living a less rootless existence.

When he'd given me the cap, it had been well used but still reasonably smart. Now, four years later, the brim had been worn smooth by my habitual tugging at it, the stitching was coming loose, and the little clasp at the back wouldn't shut properly. But it was still Sedge's hat, and I didn't feel entirely myself without it.

"How are we doing?" I asked the ship.

The *Trouble Dog*'s avatar appeared on a side screen, her thin face and pulled back hair as beautiful and androgynous as ever.

"Everything's running smoothly and to schedule," she said.

Outside, the mists swirled around us like rainclouds seen from an airliner. Sometimes, they completely obscured the view. Other times, they pulled aside to reveal vast gorges of utter vacuity. Seen in the hostile, unreal light of the higher dimensions, they formed an insubstantial, nightmarish landscape of ragged spires and gossamer cliffs.

"Good." I sat back in my chair, resting a boot against the edge of the console. With its low ceiling and dim lighting, the bridge felt like a cave on a hillside, a safe vantage from which to survey the outside world. After considering the surreal, ever-shifting view for a few minutes, I let my eyes close.

And immediately reopened them.

Something had moved!

The glimpse had been so fleeting and peripheral it had taken my brain a moment to interpret what it was seeing. I sat upright and cast around. The screens were empty of everything but mist. Nobody else had entered the bridge. And yet, I had the sudden, unnerving feeling I wasn't alone.

Moving slowly, and wishing I had a gun or a heavy wrench, I eased back in my chair and lowered my face to peer nervously under the lip of the console. But when I saw what crouched on the decking between my boots, trepidation turned to annoyance.

"What the hell are you doing there?"

The miniature Druff blinked up at me with three of its tiny flower-like faces.

"Sensor broken," it squeaked. "Much fixing." It had levered off an access panel, exposing a tangle of cables. One of its faces held a set of cutters.

I sat upright and glared at the *Trouble Dog*.

"Did you know about this?"

She smiled reassuringly.

"Of course."

"And you're okay with it?" I peered sceptically at the little creature between my feet.

The *Trouble Dog* said, "Its name is Mack."

"Mack?"

"And it's very skilled. These little Druff are born with an innate understanding of electrical and mechanical systems. Mack here may be only two days old, but I'd trust it to rewire any circuit on the ship."

"And what about its siblings? Are they all loose?"

"They're all assisting their parent with routine maintenance. All the stuff that wasn't covered in the refit."

I frowned, still unconvinced. From the floor, tiny black eyes beseeched me.

"Much work," Mack squeaked plaintively. "Many fix."

CHAPTER TWENTY-TWO

TROUBLE DOG

When I was younger and freshly commissioned, out on my first tour of duty, under my first captain, I came into contact with one of the fleet auxiliaries. Although all frontline craft possessed their own internal manufacturing capabilities, they couldn't always keep up with the demands imposed during battle. The auxiliaries were there to make up the shortfall. Part mining vessel, part industrial facility, these large, whale-like vessels trailed the capital ships, refining ore and other materials in order to manufacture the fuel, spare parts and ammunition the fleet required to keep it fighting.

This particular auxiliary was named *Dagda*, and he was vast—more shipyard than ship. Ugly and ponderous compared to my own sleek efficiency, and destined always to follow and serve others. Yet from our exchanges, I got the impression he was thoroughly content with his lot.

Most ships aren't naturally gregarious. We're engineered to enjoy spending long periods alone in the endless darkness of space. But naval ships have a strong pack instinct. We might not talk much, but we draw comfort and strength from the presence of the fleet—and it's only natural that some interaction occurs.

I started talking to *Dagda* while restocking torpedoes following a skirmish. It seemed the polite thing to do.

"First tour?" he asked.

"Yes." I was young and enthusiastic, and a little too pleased with myself. His avatar presented as an elderly blacksmith, with gnarled fingers and stooped shoulders, a hammer in one hand and a stained apron around his waist. "How long have you been with the fleet?"

"Ten years," he said. "Since before the outbreak of hostilities."

"You must have seen a lot of action."

"More than enough."

"You don't sound very enthusiastic."

"I'm not," he said. "I've seen a lot of ships like you. I've patched them up and sent them back to the front. And, one by one, they've all been lost, crippled or killed." He ran a crooked hand across his balding pate. "And you'll be the same."

"Gee, thanks."

The torpedoes were loaded. I was ready to detach and rejoin my siblings, and couldn't wait to get away from this gloomy old-timer. But before he let me go, *Dagda* fixed me with a bloodshot eye and waved his hammer in my direction.

"Just do me a favour and remember this," he said. "Sometimes it's better to be useful than heroic, better to bathe in gratitude than glory, and better to serve than demand service."

The docking clamps withdrew, and I pulled away without bothering to answer. At the time, I considered his words little more than expelled coolant, but a few years later, they returned to me in the aftermath of Pelapatarn, and I guess they ultimately influenced my decision to join the House of Reclamation.

Better to serve than demand service…

When I first encountered *Dagda*, I thought it cruel to have given self-awareness to such a lumbering beast. What use could such a vessel have for intelligence? It was basically a flying factory, with little prospect of adventure or excitement. What mind would want to endure such a slow, mundane existence?

And yet, it turned out *Dagda* was maybe the smartest of us all. He survived the war with his hull and conscience intact, and went on to service scout ships on the ragged edges of the Generality, where he could spend his time adrift between systems, contemplating the infinities around him.

He was the wisest ship I ever met, but I guess I shouldn't have been surprised. Whales have always been smarter than sharks.

CHAPTER TWENTY-THREE

JOHNNY SCHULTZ

Looking at Lucy standing there in the light from our torches, her eyes glowing like twin stars, I almost lost my cool. For a freezing, claustrophobic second, all I wanted to do was claw my way out of this dark labyrinth and run for home. But with my ship gone, I was stuck. And with Kelly and Bernard watching me, waiting for orders, I knew I had to act as if I was still in charge of this expedition— even though it had been my lousy judgement that had landed us in this mess in the first place.

I cleared a dry, reluctant throat.

"Hey there," I said softly.

The girl's eyes swivelled in my direction, and she smiled. "Hello, dearie."

From the corner of my eye, I saw Kelly twitch. My own heart seemed to leap into the back of my throat.

"You're Lucy?"

Around us the others were beginning to stir, disturbed by the sound of voices.

The girl laughed. "I can't keep anything from you, can I?"

Keeping her gun trained, Kelly rose to her feet. "Who are you?" she demanded.

The child shrugged. "I just said."

"Lucy?"

"Yes!" She clapped her hands in delight. The blue light vanished from her eyes and she took on the aspect of a perfectly ordinary little girl—albeit one standing unafraid in a darkened cavern at midnight.

•

We brought Lucy into our makeshift camp. Addison wrapped a blanket around her shoulders, and handed her a protein bar. Then, as the girl ate, Gil Dalton examined her. He shone a penlight into her eyes, asked her to stick out her tongue, and measured her pulse. When he'd finished, he sat back on his heels and shrugged.

"She's human," he said. "And perfectly healthy."

Kelly frowned. "That's impossible. She's a ship's avatar. She's just a simulation, not a real person. How can she be here?"

Dalton began to pack away his kit. By torchlight, his thinning grey hair glimmered like silver threads. "Damned if I know."

The girl smiled up at them both. "I *told* you," she said, "I'm Lucy."

I knelt in front of her. "You're *Lucy's Ghost*?"

"Yes, dearie." She sounded relieved that we finally understood what she'd been trying to tell us. "In both senses of the word."

"But how can you be the ship?" I felt I was starting to lose my grip on events. "The ship's gone."

The little face in front of me grew serious.

"Yes, it's gone. But I was saved. The *Restless Itch* reached out and pulled my consciousness from the wreck."

"And it grew you a body?"

"Using DNA copied from the human cells in my central processing substrate. A really quick process too. Only took a few hours." She looked down at herself, and smoothed out her skirt. A sad smile played across her lips.

"This is what I looked like," she said. "Back when I was a real girl. Back when I really *was* Lucy, before I got ill and my dad hooked my brain into the ship's matrix to try and keep me alive."

"So the name, *Lucy's Ghost*…?"

"Was more literal than otherwise."

"Jesus fucking Christ." I stood up and rubbed my face with my hands. I knew most ships had brains based around a few kilograms of organic neurons grown from harvested stem cells, but I'd never heard of one incorporating the brain of a living person—let alone a child. "That's… horrible."

Lucy gave an unconcerned, philosophical shrug. "It wasn't ideal, dearie, but at least I got to travel."

Addison looked troubled. "So," she said, "are you the human Lucy or the ship, *Lucy*?"

The little girl stuck out her bottom lip. "I don't know," she said. "A little of both, probably. With a dash of something else."

Over the past few minutes, Kelly's gun arm had started to relax. Now it straightened, drawing a bead on the girl's forehead.

"What else?"

Lucy stretched lazily, shrugging off the blanket. "There's part of me that used to be the *Restless Itch*."

She looked around at the rock walls of our cavern, as if surveying the walls of a prison cell. "Just a tiny part that's hoping you might take it with you when you leave, because it's been stuck out here for so long, and it's been so endlessly, desperately *bored*."

She jumped to her feet and gripped the fabric of my spacesuit.

"You will take me with you, won't you?" she said, pleading like a worried little girl. I tried not to flinch away. I was having trouble getting my head around what she'd told me; but she looked so small, wide-eyed and helpless, I knew I couldn't simply abandon her. And she sounded like the *Lucy* I remembered, the irascible old ship that had been my friend and home for the past eight years.

"Yes," I said, realising as I spoke that I meant it. "Yes, of course."

A brilliant smile lit her face. She released her grip and stepped back.

"Thank you, Johnny. I always knew you were a good boy." She looked around at all of us, and her face grew sombre. "Unfortunately, it might not be as easy as you think."

Kelly narrowed her eyes. "What do you mean?"

Lucy clasped her hands together. "I really *do* want to come with you. I left a text file on the ship to say where we were, in case any rescuers intercepted the wreck. But if we're going to survive long enough to get rescued, you're going to have to find a better place to wait. Somewhere secure." She lowered her voice and glanced around at us in turn. "Because I'm afraid we're all in the most terrible danger."

A skittering sound echoed from the rock-walled corridor to our right.

"What the hell is that?" Addison's voice could have

cut glass. I looked at her and was surprised to see her jaw set and her face drained of colour. She had been born and raised on Hellebore, an anarchic settlement on the edge of the Intrusion—an area of space where the normal rules of existence were fluid and subject to unexpected and violent change. As a result, very few things in the normal universe worried her. In fact, the only things that really, truly freaked her out were spiders—and that skittering sounded exactly like the gait of a large, multi-legged critter. Or maybe more than one.

Lucy turned towards the darkened opening. In other circumstances, the sombre expression on her little face might have been adorable; here, it was simply chilling.

"You'd better ready your weapons," she said, "because we are not alone."

CHAPTER TWENTY-FOUR

ONA SUDAK

The Marble Armada burst apart like a dandelion, its seeds racing away on a million diverging vectors, snatched away by winds of strategy and purpose. Their hulls gleamed the colour of moonlight. Their bows sliced the fabric of space like scalpels through silk.

And then most of them were gone, having leapt into the higher dimensions, on hundreds of thousands of unannounced quests. Those that remained turned their noses towards Camrose, and the vast orbital shipyards hanging above the planet like industrial towns cut loose from the ground and flung up into the firmament.

Being neutral, Camrose hosted yards owned by the Outward, the Conglomeration Navy, and the House of Reclamation, as well as half a dozen other, smaller factions. Lit by the unfiltered light of the system's yellow sun, the ships of the Marble Armada spiralled towards them all like vultures.

The walls of the bridge displayed the tactical status of every vessel in the system. Every faction had sent at least one ship. Some had been positioned to monitor the white fleet, others to guard against it. Now suddenly, they found themselves scrambling to respond to the sudden movement of ships that hadn't so much as twitched in six months.

As I watched, a Conglomeration battle group took up position between the advancing daggers and one of the orbital shipyards. The group consisted of a Scimitar-class warship, accompanied by a pair of Carnivore-class heavy cruisers, three Cudgel-class destroyers, and half a dozen Hyena-class frigates similar to the one that had rescued me from jail.

The bear made a low growling noise in the depths of his fur-rolled throat.

We are receiving a signal from the Scimitar.

"Let me hear it."

The bear gestured with a claw, and a familiar human voice echoed through the room.

"This is Admiral McDowell of the Conglomeration vessel *Harbinger* to alien ships. You are approaching a military facility. Please alter course immediately and withdraw to your previous positions."

McDowell and I had been at the Academy together. He was a good man and a dedicated officer, but had always been as stubborn and unyielding as a goat.

"You'd better do as he says."

Beside me, the creature let loose a volley of snorts that seemed to shake the platform on which we stood.

We do not recognise his authority.

I threw a hand towards the tactical map. "But he thinks you're threatening that habitat." To my surprise, I noticed that the facility McDowell was protecting had been tagged as belonging to the Outward faction.

We do not threaten. We act.

I laughed. "If you don't pull those ships back, he'll fire on them."

That is your considered opinion?

"Yes, I know this man. He takes his duty very seriously. Trust me, if he thinks you're behaving against the interests of the people he's shielding, he will fire on you."

He would instigate an act of war?

"He wouldn't shirk from it."

Then our course is justified.

The bear reared up on its hindmost set of legs and let forth a roar I could feel in my gut. In response, the two white ships bearing down on McDowell's position increased their speed. I opened my mouth to protest, but before I could vocalise my objection, searing white beams leapt from the bellies of the marble ships, spearing first the *Harbinger*, then its accompanying cruisers. The voices on the radio link turned to shouts of alarm. I heard McDowell order retaliatory fire, but his ship was already falling apart around him. Pieces broke from the Conglomeration vessels. A frigate flared and blossomed into a cloud of dirty flame.

I put a hand across my mouth. "What are you *doing*?"

We act to preserve life.

"By killing people?"

By destroying the means to wage war. Only when war is impossible will life be safe.

CHAPTER TWENTY-FIVE

SAL KONSTANZ

I woke in the hold, curled beneath the protective folds of the inflatable life raft's canopy. I could feel the vibration of the ship's engines and hear the comforting creaks and gurgles of its systems.

We were due to arrive at our destination in a little over an hour.

When on a mission, standard House operating procedure was for commanding officers and crew to alternate four-hour watches with four hours of rest time, and take a single eight-hour sleep period once every twenty-four hours. In practice, things on the *Trouble Dog* were looser. There was little for any of us to do while travelling through the higher dimensions, so watches tended to blur into rest periods, and our individual body clocks came to regulate our sleep patterns.

Of course, this meant our diurnal rhythms were often out of sync. Someone would be going to bed while someone else would be getting up or contemplating lunch. And that suited me. It meant I didn't see so much of the rest of the crew, and that while they slept, I could enjoy wandering a silent, almost empty ship.

The only time this arrangement caused problems was when we emerged from the hypervoid and all had to be awake simultaneously—but as that could happen any time of the day or night depending on the length of our journey, and as we'd inevitably be out of sync with local planetary time anyway, we didn't let it worry us. Whatever happened, at least the ship would always be feeling rested and alert; for the rest of us, jetlag had simply become a way of life—and coffee, strong tea, and other commercial stimulants were the pick-me-ups we relied upon to coax our sluggish brains into wakefulness.

I yawned and pulled on my boots. Then I climbed out of the raft and stretched. According to the clocks back on Camrose Station, the time was somewhere around mid-afternoon. But I hadn't been running on Station Time for months and as far as I was concerned, it was time for breakfast.

I had been sleeping in my clothes, and felt grimy and in need of a shower. I thought about going back to my cabin to freshen up, but then decided my hunger took priority. I scratched my scalp with chewed fingernails, and put on my baseball cap. Then I trudged up to the galley.

When I got there, I found the *Trouble Dog*'s avatar displayed on the large wall screen.

"Hello," she said.

I peered sleepily at her. Today, she had decided to appear in a chic black cocktail dress, with matching elbow-length gloves, a string of pearls around her neck, and her hair piled up in an elegant coiffure.

"What's the occasion?"

Her heavily made-up eyes glanced down at her finery. "Oh, you mean this?"

"Yes." I poured myself a cup of coffee. "Why are you all dolled up?"

The *Trouble Dog* smiled. "It's my birthday."

"Seriously? I didn't even know ships had birthdays."

"We have inception dates. It amounts to the same thing."

I picked up the cup and warmed my hands around it. "You never mentioned it before."

"I never felt the need before."

"So, what's changed?"

"I don't know. It just seems appropriate to celebrate another year of continued existence."

I smiled. "You're getting sentimental in your old age."

The avatar opened her mouth. "I am not!"

"It's all right," I assured her. "I won't tell anybody."

I blew steam from my coffee and took a seat at the counter.

"How old are you today?" I asked.

"Fifteen."

She looked twenty-five: a soldier in a cocktail dress. I looked around for some food.

"I've never known a ship celebrate its birthday before, and I've been on quite a few."

The *Trouble Dog* shrugged her bare shoulders. "I have no idea what other ships do."

"Do you miss them?" With the exception of the traitorous *Adalwolf*, all her siblings were dead.

"I shouldn't." She wrinkled her nose. "I mean I'm

not designed to mourn lost comrades. And yet, I do miss them. I miss their noise in my head."

"That's only natural."

"Not to me it isn't. It's… discomforting."

"That's grief for you."

"I don't know how you people stand it."

"We muddle through."

She frowned. "Does it last long?"

I thought of Sedge, and of my parents. "That depends."

"There are variables?"

"Some."

The avatar rolled her eyes. "I think I liked it better when I didn't have a conscience."

I couldn't help smiling. "Yeah, emotions suck. But if it's any consolation, having them makes you a better person."

She was silent for almost half a minute. When she finally spoke again, she said, "You lost your boyfriend?"

"I did."

"But he's not actually dead?"

I shook my head. "In some ways, that makes it worse. In some ways, I guess it's easier to bear, knowing he's still out there, frozen in the hold of that Hopper ship."

"How so?"

I sighed. "Because I'll always know he's still alive. He'll always be as I remember him. Young and perfect, and he'll never age. He'll quite literally never age until long after I'm dead and gone."

"And that makes it better?"

"Sometimes, yes."

The *Trouble Dog* thought about this. "You humans are strange," she said.

An hour later, when it came time to emerge, we

strapped into our couches. On the main screen, the *Trouble Dog*'s avatar had elected to remain in her socialite apparel.

"If you're going to punch a hole in the universe," she said while fiddling with her pearls, "you might as well do it looking fabulous."

CHAPTER TWENTY-SIX

JOHNNY SCHULTZ

"What are they?" Kelly demanded.

Lucy shrugged. "I don't know, but they came on board at around the same time you did."

"They're not from here?"

"I've never seen anything like them."

We were all standing now. Even Santos was upright, leaning against the cavern wall to take the weight off his injured foot. I ordered Kelly to keep watch on the entrances to the corridors while I unzipped her canvas kit bag and distributed the rifles it contained.

"How many?" Kelly asked.

Lucy held up her hands, fingers splayed. "Ten."

"What do they look like?"

The little girl frowned. "What are those things you catch in rivers?" She made wriggling movements with her fingers. "They have tails and they're kind of crawly and have snappy legs."

We all looked blank.

Then Gil Dalton slapped his forehead. "She's talking

about crayfish."

I looked at him, none the wiser. "What the bloody hell are crayfish?"

"Crustaceans from Earth." He smiled. "Freshwater lobsters. They have armoured shells, eight legs and two pincers. Kids catch them in nets."

Lucy nodded excitedly. "Yes, those are the ones. Crayfish. But these are a bit bigger than usual, and they each have two sets of pincers."

Kelly's patience was at breaking point. "*How much bigger?*"

The little girl blinked in surprise, then solemnly stretched out her arms as far as they could reach. "About this big."

"Christ."

"And their exoskeletons aren't made of calcium carbonate. As far as I can tell, they're fashioned from some sort of metallic composite."

"Bulletproof?"

"Quite possibly."

We were all holding rifles now. Puffing back her auburn fringe, Riley Addison looked grim but determined; the purser, Henri Bernard, held his as if afraid it might turn and bite him; and Santos the chef, leaning against the wall in his bulky blue spacesuit, cradled his in the crook of his arm, his lips pressed into a thin, bloodless line. All trace of his usual jollity had gone. Even Dalton, the ship's doctor, had armed himself.

The weapons were a mixture of antiquated slug throwers and knock-off plasma rifles. The oldest had been part of the *Lucy's Ghost*'s inventory longer than I'd been alive. They'd been brought onboard and left behind by the ever-churning roster of crewmembers that had served on the old ship over the decades. Digging deeper into the canvas sack, I dispensed ammo clips and power packs. I could feel myself sweating into the inner layers of my suit. The armpits and crotch were beginning to chafe. The movements of our helmet lamps made the shadows leap and pounce.

Kelly yelled, "Here they come!" And then they were upon us. The first boiled from the tunnel opening in a blur of legs, its four pincers swiping the air, the needle-sharp points of its eight legs pitter-pattering the polished rock floor.

Kelly shot it in the mouth. It mewled and staggered, tottering on its legs like a drunken spider. Greenish-brown bile spewed from the wound, causing it to skid and slip.

No sooner had it collapsed into a thrashing, keening mess than a second creature burst into the gleam of our lights. This one was larger, about the size of a dining table, the rim of its shell lined with curling, tusk-like spikes. Its multi-part jaws flapped and slapped, saliva frothing obscenely. Kelly, Addison and I all fired upon it. The cavern echoed with the crack of our slug throwers and the whine of Addison's plasma rifle. But our efforts seemed to be in vain. The bullets punched dents in the creature's shell, but not enough to admit a fatal wound, and the plasma bolts from Addison's rifle only singed the surface of its metallic carapace, filling the cavern with the stench of hot aluminium.

"Fall back," ordered Kelly, and we began shuffling around the edge of the cavern, towards the corridor entrance on the opposite side from the one through which the crustaceans had come. Dalton helped Santos and Lucy, Bernard and Addison hauled the equipment, and Kelly and I walked backwards, trying to keep the creature at bay, even though it was hard to tell whether our shots were actually hurting it.

Having seemingly learned from the death of its smaller compatriot, the monster kept one of its armoured claws in front of its maw, protecting its soft mouthparts from our fusillade. The other three pincers swiped and lunged in our direction. Above the clamour of the guns, its voice was a thin, skin-crawling squeal.

Kelly's rifle was empty. She dropped it and pulled her pistol.

"Move!" she screamed.

And then it was upon her. One of the flailing claws caught her leg and hauled her up into the air. The light from her torch flashed across its back. Then something snapped like a dry branch. Kelly shouted, half in pain and half in indignation, and fell to the floor in the flickering light. She writhed, hands reaching to staunch the blood pouring from the ragged stump of her right leg, where it had been severed above the knee.

I tried to reach her, only to narrowly avoid getting caught by another of the giant pincers. I thought maybe I could drag her clear. But before I could even get close, one of the crustacean's spear-like feet stabbed downward, skewering Kelly through the chest and pinning her thrashing body to the polished rock. And even then, before I'd really had time to grasp the full horror of what was happening, I already knew I'd never be able to un-hear the splintering crack it made as it punched through the armoured breastplate of her suit, into the yielding ribcage beneath.

Addison pulled me out of the cavern, and then into a narrow side tunnel that led off the main corridor. It was an access way designed for creatures that were tall and thin rather than low and wide.

"We should be safe in here," she said. "It can't follow us."

Unable to wedge its body into the confines of the access way, the crayfish howled in its thin, reedy voice and thrust a pair of pincers into the opening, grasping blindly for us.

Guns at the ready, we backed away, to where the others were waiting a few dozen metres along the passage.

Gil Dalton took one look at my face, and gave a sympathetic nod. The normally ebullient Santos looked grim. Only Henri Bernard seemed confused. He peered past my shoulder, a frown creasing the skin between his brows.

"Where's Kelly?"

I couldn't answer him. All I could see in my head was that final, fatal thrust.

Behind me, Addison said, "She's dead."

Bernard opened and shut his mouth. He pulled his battered old rifle tight against the chest of his shiny new suit, and turned away.

At the end of the corridor, the creature—whatever it was—continued to scrabble at the walls in its attempt to reach us.

CHAPTER TWENTY-SEVEN

TROUBLE DOG

Imagine you have been living in the same, familiar house all your life. You know all its rooms; you feel comfortable there. And then one day, out of curiosity, you peel back one of the floorboards to find a bottomless cavern yawning beneath. All your life you have been walking and dancing on this thin skein of wood, never suspecting the abyss below the flexing boards, and the fragility of your position.

That is the best way I can describe the higher dimensions. The safe, comfortable house is the everyday universe, the cavernous depths below the higher dimensional void that surrounds and underpins it all, separating it from other universes and realities.

As I roared through the mists of the hypervoid, I could hear the calls of other ships, in other systems, their signals accelerated and stretched into whale song by the peculiar physics of the higher dimensions. Some spoke of boredom and drudgery, hauling cargoes on unchanging routes and inflexible schedules. Others warned of local dangers:

navigation hazards, and an increase in the frequency of reality quakes in the vicinity of the Intrusion.

The Intrusion was an area of space where two realities struggled to coexist. The higher dimensional void between them had been breached, creating a pathway—a pathway around whose borders the laws of physics had become malleable and skittish. In the hypervoid, it sounded like the dull growl of a nearby tornado, grinding away in the background.

And then, faint and faraway and almost lost in the grumble of the storm and the chatter of other ships, came the cries of battle. Somewhere, ships were dying. Scimitars and Carnivores were being torn apart. And to my horror, the message tags identified the ships in trouble as vessels of the Conglomeration Navy. The canine genes they'd spliced into my brain had been put there to promote tenaciousness and pack loyalty—and I could feel those implanted reflexes twitch involuntarily in response to the cries of my former comrades-in-arms, even though those cries had been made several hours ago.

Something bad had happened at Camrose, and part of me itched to be there, to drop everything and race back to the fray, even though whatever was happening would probably have been long over by the time I covered the intervening distance.

At first, those desperate transmissions stood alone in the vastness of the hypervoid. Then I started to detect other, equally frantic voices in systems neighbouring Camrose. First one, then another and another, as the violence spread outwards like a contagion.

I longed to linger in the mist to find out what was happening. But we had reached the approximate last known position of the *Lucy's Ghost*, and if we overshot we'd find ourselves as trespassers in Nymtoq space.

I applied braking thrust, and felt myself start to fall through the higher dimensions, back down towards the physical certainties of the everyday universe.

Wisps of reality began to buffer my hull. I adjusted my angle of descent, brought my defensive systems online, and prepared to fire up my fusion motors, ready to rip my way back through the membrane separating formlessness from actuality.

CHAPTER TWENTY-EIGHT

SAL KONSTANZ

"It's the Marble Armada," Clay said. "It has to be."

I didn't want to jump to conclusions, but I knew she was right. Who else in the Camrose System had enough ships to take out a Conglomeration battle group, let alone simultaneously spread the attack to nearby systems?

I thought of the veteran I'd met at the Temples of the High Country, and his insistence the alien fleet could not be trusted, and felt a stab of guilt. Had I brought this viper into the heart of the Generality? Was this whole thing somehow *my* fault?

"Are there any transmissions from the attackers? Any clue what might have set this off?"

The *Trouble Dog* had switched her avatar's appearance back to one of its default settings, and now appeared to be clad in black combat fatigues rather than the slinky dress she had been wearing earlier.

"There is one," she said hesitantly. "But you're not going to like it."

The bridge's main screen dimmed, then brightened

again, displaying the face of a middle-aged woman with short-cropped hair and a powdering of grey at each of her temples. The signal had been stretched and scratched during its passage through the void. The picture kept half-dissolving into pixels, and the sound quality wavered. Nonetheless, I recognised her.

"That's Ona Sudak." I hadn't seen her since turning her over to the authorities on our return from the Gallery.

Beside me, Preston said, "I heard she was dead."

"Evidently not." I gestured at the screen. "Although I can't make out what she's saying."

"The signal's heavily compromised," the *Trouble Dog* said. "I'll try to compensate."

The screen flickered. There was a burst of static, and then Sudak's familiar tones filled the room, the words a quarter of a second out of sync with the movements of her mouth.

"*…not be tolerated. I repeat: my name is Ona Sudak, human liaison to the Fleet of Knives. We are currently engaged in peacekeeping work in Camrose and a number of other systems within the Generality. All armed vessels are advised to stand down and await further orders. Defiance will not be borne. Violence will not be tolerated. I repeat: my name is…*"

The picture froze, and the *Trouble Dog* said, "It's on a loop."

Beside me, Clay cursed. "Peacekeeping, my ass."

Hunched in the doorway, Preston seemed stunned. His eyes were wide and he didn't seem to know what to do with his arms.

"They're really attacking us?"

"It looks that way," I said.

"What do we do?"

I removed my cap and dragged my fingers across my scalp. I'd been asking myself the same question.

"There's not much we can do, way out here," I said. "So, I suggest we concentrate on the job at hand. Everything else can wait until we know more."

Clay shook her dreadlocks. "I don't think we can afford to wait. They've got a million ships. Whatever they're up to, we're heavily outnumbered."

On screen, the *Trouble Dog* made a show of clearing her throat. "I'm afraid I concur with Alva. These messages suggest the Armada's impounding or attacking armed vessels—a category into which I fall."

"But the House is neutral," I reminded her.

"Only to human governments. This 'Fleet of Knives' might feel differently."

"But I thought they'd endorsed the House for inheriting their philosophy?"

"That doesn't mean they won't take our toys away if they consider it to be for the greater good. Remember their motto?"

"Life above all."

"Exactly." The *Trouble Dog* fell silent for a moment, her perfectly symmetrical face troubled.

"I gave them their mission," she said. "I told them to ensure we'd never have another conflict on the scale of the Archipelago War."

"And you think *that's* why they're taking away our ships?"

From the doorway, Preston mumbled, "You can't have a war if you haven't got anything to fight with."

I looked at the frozen image of Ona Sudak, poet and war criminal, and wondered how the hell she'd inveigled her way into the Armada's trust. The last I'd heard, she'd been sentenced to death by firing squad, and sent to a high-security facility on the surface of Camrose.

"Okay, I'll admit it sounds bad. It might even be our fault. But right now, there's nothing we can do about it." I replaced my cap and tugged the brim into place. "We came here to answer a distress call, so let's make that our priority. We can discuss the rest later."

I ordered the *Trouble Dog* to locate the *Lucy's Ghost*, and sent Preston down to the infirmary to prepare for the possibility of casualties. Things might be going to hell at home, but I couldn't afford to let my crew succumb to shock, or go off half-cocked on some desperate, futile quest for vengeance. As long as we had a job to do, I could keep them occupied while we processed the full ramifications of the news from Camrose.

•

It only took the ship a few minutes to ascertain the position of the *Lucy's Ghost*. The freighter was an old, obsolete model, and in places it was hard to tell the difference between recent damage and long-term wear and tear. In other places, though, that difference was stark and all too clear.

"Holy hell," Clay said. "It looks as if something took a bite out of her."

I could only nod. The old ship tumbled in a cloud of frozen gases and minor debris. Her bow had been smashed in, and a crater had been gouged in her spine, as if an entire section of hull had been torn away by the closing of atrocious jaws.

"Can you access the onboard intelligence?" I asked the *Trouble Dog*, hoping enough remained of the ship's mind to be able to tell us what had happened.

"I'm trying, but it seems to have been taken."

"Taken?"

"The processors are functional, but there's no trace of a personality. It's as if it's been deliberately removed."

"Any information on survivors?"

"Only a text file on the public server. It seems the ship was involved in a collision. There are four bodies on board, and the remainder of the crew evacuated."

Clay frowned. "They abandoned ship? Where could they go? We're in the middle of bloody nowhere."

The *Trouble Dog* opened a sub-window.

"It seems they were planning to board an abandoned Nymtoq Colony Vessel. I've retraced the *Lucy's* course, and found it collided with such a ship two days ago."

The sub-window contained an image of something black and scarred, like the snout of a whale. I blinked at it. For a moment, I didn't even recognise it as a ship.

"That's *huge*."

"It had to be. Those early Nymtoq ships weren't capable of higher dimensional travel, so it would have needed to carry everything the colonists needed."

"How far away is it?"

"The ships diverged following the collision, but it's only a few hundred kilometres from our present position."

Clay was still preoccupied with the image of the *Lucy's Ghost*.

"Any idea what made that hole in its back?" she asked.

"Nothing suggests itself." The *Trouble Dog* looked apologetic. "I can only assume it happened during the collision, although the precise mechanism for such an injury eludes me."

"And it's not our job to figure it out," I reminded them. "You know the drill. We go in, collect the dead and rescue the living. Everything else comes second."

"Yeah?" Clay's voice wavered. "Even that?"

"Even what?" I turned to look where she was pointing. On the screen, something crawled across the exterior of the *Lucy's Ghost*—something large and insect-like, with a profusion of legs and a metallic carapace that glimmered in the light of the surrounding stars.

CHAPTER TWENTY-NINE

ONA SUDAK

The nine-eyed bear snarled.

There has been an incursion.

I glanced at the tactical map. As far as I could tell, the only ships currently moving in the Camrose System belonged to the Fleet of Knives.

"Where?"

Another snarl sounded deep in its throat, prolonged this time.

We intercepted an emergency request for information from a vessel of the House of Reclamation.

The beast waved one of its plate-sized paws and an image materialised in the air between us. I leaned closer and frowned at it.

"What on earth is it?"

The picture appeared to show a giant mechanical lobster astride the wreck of a civilian transport ship.

Evidence. For the first time since I'd known it, the bear looked genuinely agitated. The view on the tactical map rotated as the ship swung around and began accelerating outward from Camrose. Two other ships fell into formation to either side of us.

"Hey," I protested. "What are you doing?"

We must ascertain the seriousness of this incursion.

"We're going there? How far away is it?"

As we can travel considerably faster than your ships, the journey will take us less than a day.

"But I still don't understand." I considered the image of the lobster. "What is this thing, and why all the concern?" After all, the Fleet held a million ships. How much danger could an overgrown crustacean pose?

The creature is a parasite. Its presence in this realm indicates an intrusion from the higher dimensional reaches.

The bear gave a series of violent, cough-like barks, and our speed increased. I took a final look at the tactical display. Clusters of marble daggers struck at every armed ship or facility in the system, their attacks coordinated and pitiless. Energy beams punctured pressurised domes; sleek, almost undetectably small neutronium-plated projectiles punched holes through the hulls of military and civilian vessels alike. Ships and stations—*people*—were dying out there as the white ships enforced their embargo on weaponry.

And yet…

When I'd ordered the attack on Pelapatarn, I'd done it in order to stop the war. I'd sacrificed one world in order to spare a hundred others, and I'd done it in the sincere belief the scales would somehow balance and the destruction I'd unleashed would be justified because fewer people would be killed in the raid than would have been had the war dragged on for another five or ten years. I'd become a murderer in order to save lives. And now these alien ships were doing something comparable, and I couldn't fault their logic. A Conglomeration battle group could rain nuclear fire on all the major cities of an entire planet, and wiping them from the sky was the only sure way of ensuring a future free from such atrocities.

For goodness' sake, humanity had been doing its best to kill itself for millennia. Evolution had endowed us with the potentially lethal combination of intelligence and belligerence, and I'd lost count of the number of near-miss bottlenecks we'd scraped through, from the Cuban Missile Crisis to the Archipelago War, by way of global warming and climate collapse. If it took an alien war fleet to impose order upon us, maybe that was just what we needed. Maybe it was the only way to bring us into line, once and for all: our last, best hope for peace.

The display broke into a ragged spider's web of pixels, and evaporated. Without any fuss, we had skipped into the higher dimensions. The external screen showed a moment of disorientating static, and then cleared to reveal the familiar, ever-changing curtains of sparse, intangible vapour that made up the scenery of the hypervoid.

"Do you have a name for this Reclamation Vessel?" I asked, remembering the last time I had been aboard one, on the journey back from the Gallery.

The bear ground its teeth.

Trouble Dog.

"*Trouble Dog?*"

Affirmative.

I exhaled, and considered throwing myself from the platform, onto the curved floor of the spherical chamber.

"Of course it is."

I didn't want to do myself harm, only escape the insanity of my situation. I needed to rest. I needed time out to internalise what was happening around me, and make my peace with the necessary work being undertaken by the Fleet of Knives.

The bear showed no such hesitation.

Will the presence of this ship be a problem?

I thought of Captain Konstanz and her crew. In some ways, they had saved my life; and yet, I'd only known them for a few days. It would be agreeable to encounter them again, but I wasn't attaching any emotional freight to the idea.

"Not at all."

The bear's lips peeled back to reveal its ivory fangs. Its claws slipped from velvet sheaths.

Then you won't mind if we destroy her?

"What?" I jerked back and glared up at the beast. "I thought you worshipped the *Trouble Dog*? I thought she gave you your mission?"

The ship gave us purpose when we had none. She gave us direction. But our mission remains the same as it has always been. To protect life. To quell conflict. To be vigilant for fog-dwelling predators.

The Trouble Dog *participated in an atrocity. She demonstrated remorse. But she remains a weapon of war. And humanity cannot be trusted with such things.*

CHAPTER THIRTY

JOHNNY SCHULTZ

We had been cowering in the narrow maintenance tunnels for over twenty-four hours, and my nerves were beginning to unravel. I'd snatched a few disconnected, twitchy moments of sleep, but I'd spent them dreaming of our lost crewmembers—of Vito, Chet, Jansen, Monk, and Kelly. Five friends torn away in the space of a day and a half. Five comrades who'd died messy, painful deaths because they'd wagered their lives on "Lucky" Johnny Schultz and his desperate, idiotic quest to earn a little easy money.

With Kelly gone, we were unsure what to do next. She'd been the only one of us with combat experience. Without her, we were five frightened civilians with guns, trying to look after a peculiar little girl in the bowels of an ancient alien ship infested with what appeared to be giant deadly crustaceans.

Abe Santos sat quietly, teeth clenched against the pain in his foot. Gil Dalton checked and rechecked his medical supplies, occasionally shaking his head over some crucial shortage or other. And the accountant, Henri Bernard, looked as if he had been thrown so far out of his comfort zone, I wondered if he'd ever truly be able to find his way back. Even if we made it out of here in one piece, I suspected a part of him would always be wandering these darkened corridors, pursued by snapping horrors. Only Riley Addison seemed to be fully plugged in to the moment and aware of the others around her. When she saw me watching her, she brushed back a strand of auburn hair.

"How are you doing?" Torchlight gleamed off the gold stud in her right eyebrow. The scuffed aluminium neck ring of her spacesuit framed the lower part of her face.

"I've had better days."

"Haven't we all?" She came to sit beside me, her back leaning against one side of the corridor and her feet resting against the opposite wall.

"But seriously," she lowered her voice. "You're the captain here. None of these people have a clue what to do. If we're going to get through this, we're going to need you to man up and start acting as if you're in charge."

"It was me being in charge that got us into this mess."

"And that means you have a responsibility to get us out again."

I looked down at my hands. "I'm not sure I know how."

"You've just got to address the problems one at a time." She tapped the lamp on her helmet, which was currently dangling from her tool belt. "Take the torches for example. I don't think our batteries are going to last much longer. Henri's are almost gone already, and the rest can't be far behind."

"So we need to find some light?"

"Yes, unless you'd rather sit here in the dark?"

I shuddered at the thought. Then I thought of Kelly, lying back there in the darkness.

"I don't know if I've got it in me."

Addison's face softened. She put a hand on my arm. "We know what you've done in the past. We've all heard the stories. If anyone can get us out of here, it's Lucky Johnny Schultz." She smiled. "Maybe all you have to do is ask yourself what Lucky Johnny would do in this situation?"

What indeed? If past experience were anything to go by, Lucky Johnny would muddle his way through somehow. He'd scrape through and then ascribe his good fortune to his legendary luck. But I couldn't say that to her. Not now, not here. Not when it was clear somebody had to step up and take the initiative in order to get the others moving and working together as a team.

•

When I was young, I was awkward and fidgety and raw. I grew up in a town near a failing river port. It was shrouded in fog most days, and the port lights made the sky glow a hellish orange. When it wasn't foggy, it was raining, and the corrosive salt air blew in off the muddy grey mouth of the estuary, cold and sharp like rusty barbed wire.

Rackham's Landing was the sort of dismal hinterland most people only passed through on their way to somewhere else. Those that stopped and stayed tended to be lost or desperate, or beyond caring. Either they were looking for trouble, or they were trying to hide from it.

I grew up in a house by the river shore, in a row of fishermen's cottages. At high tide, the lamp light from the front room window spilled out over the muddy creek water. When it rained, the lights of the houses on the far shore swam and smeared. I'd sit by that window when my father was out, waiting for the lights of his little boat to appear through the gloom, listening to the pop and sizzle of the ship-to-shore radio.

Until one night, my father failed to return.

It was the night the *Endurance* exploded. Lightning crackled through the overcast sky. Thunder growled. The waves crashed over the flood defences, smashing their spray against the shingle walls of the house. During lulls, I could hear foghorns out in the channel.

My mother joined me at the window. "It's time you were off to bed," she said half-heartedly.

I rubbed the glass where it was misting. I could see she didn't mean it, that she wanted my company. "Just a few minutes more," I said.

Down by the creek, I could see lights: there were kids on the *Endurance*.

She was a rusty old hovercraft, built to transport cargo. She lay in the mud at the back of the creek and the local teenagers used her as a hangout. They sat in her hold, drinking and smoking.

When her leaky fuel tank exploded, the blast shook the windows of the house. It echoed along the street. Front doors were thrown open and people appeared, pulling coats over their pyjamas. My mother went with them.

It took most of the night to bring the blaze under control. There were kids trapped by the fire. Driving rain and intense heat hampered the rescuers. And all the while, out at sea, my father was drowning. The storm had swamped his small boat. With everyone crowded around the burning *Endurance*, there was no one to hear his final, desperate calls. No one except me, listening to the radio as I clung helplessly to the window, too scared to move.

When I was fifteen, I ran away from the pain of that night. I locked my past away, where it couldn't hurt me, and I rode the freighters that dragged from world to world. I stowed away to get my first taste of higher dimensional travel. I got a tattoo. I lost my virginity behind a greasy café on a cold world whose name I could never remember.

On one planet, I was caught on the ground during a hurricane that lasted a year. And on another, I spent three days wandering alone in an arctic blizzard. And although those experiences were frightening, they could never compare to the night the *Endurance* went up. So I began taking bigger and bigger chances. I did stupid, dangerous things, and because I survived, I acquired a reputation for being lucky.

But really, I'd been running the whole time. And I hadn't stopped running until I bought the *Lucy's Ghost*.

•

I rubbed my palms together. If ever there had been a time to try to live up to my reputation as a freewheeling adventurer, that time was now.

I stood up and cleared my throat. "Hey, Lucy."

The child smiled up at me with her disconcertingly blue eyes. "Yes, dearie?"

"You say you're linked to the *Restless Itch*? Is there any way you can ask it to turn the lights on in here?"

The smile grew wider. "But of course."

She screwed up her little face, and the floor shuddered.

I heard the hum of machinery and power behind the walls. And then the light panels on the ceiling came to life. I narrowed my eyes into slits, shading my face with my hand. After a day spent grubbing around by torch, it took a few moments to adjust to the dim sepia light now flooding the corridor.

We blinked at each other, smiles cracking our tired, grime-smudged faces. We weren't out of harm's way yet, but we had a temporary refuge and we had light, and suddenly everything seemed a tiny little bit less hopeless.

"Okay," I said. "Everybody make sure your guns are fully loaded. We don't have much ammunition, so let's share it around sensibly. And, Henri, when you've got a minute, can you take a squint at the food situation? Do an audit or something. Find out how much we've got left."

I looked down at Addison and she gave me the thumbs-up.

Then her face grew serious again and she caught my sleeve, pulling me down so she could talk quietly. "There's something else," she said. "Those creatures back there. I've seen them before." She rubbed her chin. "Well, I've seen one of them. Back on Hellebore, in the aftermath of a particularly brutal reality quake, my dad's friend, Walt, found one dying in the desert outside the settlement. It had killed maybe a dozen cattle, but something was wrong with it. Maybe it poisoned itself eating the cows. Whatever. The way Walt told it, he flipped the thing over and drove a steel fencepost through the soft underbelly. Then he dragged the carcass back to town to show it off."

"So, we need to flip them over?" I didn't relish our chances of getting near enough to one of those creatures without getting snapped in its claws.

Addison shrugged. "I don't know, maybe." She got to her feet and dusted herself down. "I guess what I'm really saying is I don't think they come from around here. I don't think they're local, if you know what I mean."

I glanced around at the polished rock walls. "Lucy said they came aboard around the same time we did, so we know they're not native to this ship."

"It's more than that." She ejected the used power cells from her plasma rifle and let them clink and rattle on the floor. "I don't think they're even from this universe."

"What?"

"Think about it. The only other time any of us has seen one was after a really big reality quake, on the edge of the Intrusion. And now, suddenly there are more of them, just appearing out of nowhere."

"Straight after we were attacked in the hypervoid."

"Exactly."

I frowned. "But the thing I saw was massive, and looked totally different. It was sleek, with wings and a tail. Kind of like a dragon."

Addison made a face. "There must be a connection. Otherwise it's too much of a coincidence for these crayfish things to show up at the same exact moment we did. I mean, how would they even get here?"

I thought about it. Up until now, I'd been too busy worrying about the after-effects of the collision, and all the other shit we'd been through. But Addison was right. These things couldn't have got here under their own steam—not unless they were packing miniature jump engines under those metallic carapaces. Therefore, they must have come through the fissure between here and the higher dimensions, pulled through in our wake.

"I guess they could be fleas," I said.

Addison frowned. "Fleas?"

"You remember that cat Vito tried to bring aboard a couple of months back? It was riddled with them. Little bloodsuckers."

"I know what fleas are. What's your point?"

"When the larger creature attacked us, maybe some of its parasites got dislodged, and fixed onto our ship."

Addison pursed her lips as she thought about it. "I guess that makes about as much sense as anything else."

A few metres along the narrow corridor, Henri Bernard watched us with narrow-eyed wariness. "What are you two whispering about?"

I flashed him what I hoped was my most rakish grin. "We're deciding what our next move should be."

He looked unimpressed. "And what have you decided?"

"We're going to let the monsters eat you while we escape."

CHAPTER THIRTY-ONE

SAL KONSTANZ

From the readings, I wasn't sure whether the multi-limbed thing crawling around the wreck of the *Lucy's Ghost* was a creature or a machine. And to tell you the truth, I didn't much care. The damn thing gave me the creeps, so I gave *Trouble Dog* permission to target it.

"Just don't damage the wreck," I said. "There may still be someone alive inside."

"The text file says no."

"That doesn't mean it's right. We have to check."

"Your concern is noted."

The hull rang as one of the defence cannons fired a quick burst. Five rounds rapid. On the screen, the monster jerked. Splinters flew from its carapace, ropes of fluid burst from its shattered body like uncoiling serpents, and the sharp-pointed legs detached from the old freighter, curling under the remains of the shredded carapace like the petals of a dying flower.

I watched it tumble away, still venting fluid and strangely shaped internal organs.

"What was that thing?"

"I don't know," the *Trouble Dog* said. "There's nothing like it in any of my reference files. I've sent an information request to the House, but they've yet to respond."

Alva Clay asked, "Could it have come off that Nymtoq ship?"

"I don't think so. It certainly wasn't native to Nym, or any of the other Nymtoq worlds."

"Are there any more of them?"

"I can detect nothing."

"Any heat sources that might be survivors?"

"One. Although it's faint."

"Whereabouts?"

"Aft lower deck, engineering."

I glanced across at Alva Clay. "What do you think?"

She had already swung around in her couch and placed her booted feet on the deck, ready to rise. "If there's someone in there, we've got to at least *try* to get them out," she said. "After all, it's what we're being paid for, right?"

•

We went across in pressure suits, and set up an inflatable airlock on the ship's hull. Once it was in place, we pulled ourselves inside and cut our way through the plating, into the engineering spaces towards the rear of the crippled ship. Clay carried her Archipelago pistol in one gauntleted fist. If anything surprised us, she wanted the ability to punch a hole through it. And, as the weapon used a magnetic accelerator to launch its projectiles, there would be no recoil to throw her off-balance.

"It looks a mess in there," she said. Her voice sounded loud and breathy over the link.

Huddled behind her in the cramped space of the temporary lock, I could see smoke and fallen beams, dangling light fittings and exposed cabling.

"Go careful," I said.

"Always."

Switching on the powerful LED lamp on the front of her helmet, she pulled through, lowering herself into the interior, and I watched her disappear into the smoke and gloom below. My job was to stay by the opening, maintaining contact with the *Trouble Dog*.

"Do you see anything?"

"Nothing yet." I could hear the exertion in her voice as she clambered through the damaged spaces of the engine room. "Wait. Hang on a second."

"What have you got?"

"It's a Druff."

"Is it alive?"

"The scanner says it's still warm, but its heart rate's almost nothing, and it doesn't seem to be breathing."

I bit my lower lip, thinking back to the courses in alien medicine I'd taken when I first joined the House. "I've heard of this. When seriously injured, the Druff go into a state of suspension. Sort of like a coma. They slow their metabolism down to almost nothing, and only breathe once every ten or fifteen minutes."

"Do you think that's what's happening here?"

"It could be. Can you move him?"

"If I can roll him onto an inflatable stretcher, I can try dragging him back."

"Do you need a hand?"

"No, stay there for now. I'll call if I get stuck."

"Okay."

I braced myself at the opening. Over the link, I could hear Clay huffing and cursing as she tried to move the unconscious creature. Around us, the ship creaked and juddered, and I whispered a quick prayer it wouldn't fragment before we were done.

"You're wasting your time," Clay puffed, and I realised I'd left my end of the link open. "There aren't any gods watching over the likes of us."

"Well, it can't hurt."

"As long as this broken-ass ship's listening, that's all that matters."

I saw her helmet lamp casting shadows through the smoke. "I can see you!"

"Yeah, I'm almost there." She let out a tired breath. "But he's a heavy bastard. Can you come and help me lift him over this last bit?"

"Sure thing."

Grasping the lip of the hole, I swung my boots over the edge and dropped into the wreck.

•

By the time we got the Druff back to the *Trouble Dog*'s infirmary, my muscles were screaming in protest. Clay had her helmet off, and her face shone with perspiration. The stiffness in her movements betrayed her own exhaustion.

Somehow, we'd manhandled the comatose alien onto one of the beds, and Preston was examining it.

"What have we got?" I asked him.

"It's roughly middle-aged," he said. "But unresponsive."

He moved the medical scanner across the creature's back. "There's some evidence of broken ribs and internal bleeding."

"But it's alive?"

"It seems to be in a state of hibernation." He stood back and tapped a finger against his chin. "Almost as if it's conserving its remaining energy, waiting for help to reach it."

"Or for someone to cart it back to the World Tree," Clay said.

"Maybe."

"Is there anything you can do for him?" I asked. Since being uncovered as a fraud, Preston had been using every spare moment to study for his medical licence.

"Perhaps."

"Then do what you can," I said. "The ship will help you, and I'm sure Nod can answer any questions you may have about Druff anatomy. Although, it's anybody's guess whether you'll be able to decipher what it says."

"And what about us?" Clay said, wiping the back of a hand across her forehead. "What'll we do while he's doing that?"

I unscrewed my gloves and tucked them in my pocket. Flexed aching fingers. "We go looking for that Nymtoq ship," I said. "And hopefully that's where we'll find the rest of the survivors."

CHAPTER THIRTY-TWO

NOD

"Nod, come to the infirmary," they say.

Big hurry.

Down tools and climb stairs.

Leave offspring to work.

Always work.

Always more to fix.

Arrive at infirmary to find injured Druff.

"Help me fix it," Preston says.

But one look enough to see Druff cannot be fixed.

Druff broken inside.

Has entered dying drowse. Preparing to rejoin World Tree. Root of all things.

Curled up like a seed.

"Cannot fix," I say. "Much apologies."

"I don't think I can do it without you."

Preston only has one face.

Only two hands.

Humans next to useless.

"Can you at least speak to it?" he asks.

I shrug three shoulders.

"Rude to interrupt dying drowse."

"But it can be done?"

"Only in emergency."

Preston wipes face with hands. Peculiar action.

"This *is* an emergency." He talks slowly. "We don't know what happened to that ship, and half the crew's still missing. Anything it can tell us would be a big help, you know?"

Think of offspring in engine room.

Much fixing.

Much mischief.

Need to get back before totally rewire *Troublesome Hound*.

"With reluctance," I say.

Place two faces against brother Druff.

Scent tells me name is Chet.

Chet from high in the Windward Branches of World Tree.

Traveller and engineer.

No current life partner.

Must push beyond scent.

Press faces hard against side. Speak name. Push tongue beneath scales to jab skin.

Chet wakes. A single face emerges. Draws ragged breath.

"Where is crew, Chet?"

"Crew gone."

Fingers hang limp around edge of face.

"Where gone?"

"Nymtoq grave ship."

"How many?"

"Let me sleep, Nod."

"Humans need to know. How many?"

"Five, maybe six. Not sure who survived crash. Know two for definite."

"Thank you, Chet."

"Work done? Rest now?"

"Rest."

Chet's head droops. Eyes burn like black stars.

"Nod. Important." Breath failing. "Tell others. White ships are cousins."

"Not understanding."

Chet drowning in internal fluid.

"Tell them."

I curl fingers over Chet's spine. Feel shudder.

Then silence.

No more breathing. No heartbeat.

No nothing.

Chet gone to World Tree.

"Store body," I tell Preston. "One day, deliver Chet home."

Feed him to World Tree's roots.

Reunite with ancestors.

Be one with Tree.

CHAPTER THIRTY-THREE

ONA SUDAK

As the white ships cleaved the higher dimensions, I slept. It was an old habit left over from the war. In battle, you never knew when the next opportunity for rest might present itself, and so many sailors found it prudent to snatch naps during periods of inactivity.

When I awoke, we were falling back into the universe.

"Have we arrived?"

The bear was where I'd left him, on the podium in the centre of the spherical bridge.

Not yet.

"Where are we?"

The hairy beast brandished a claw at the wall and a three-dimensional star map appeared, with a red line indicating our course from Camrose to the distant point in space where the *Trouble Dog* had found the lobster-like creature that had my hosts so agitated. About halfway along the line, a small system had been highlighted. Although the notations beside it were in an alien language, I recognised it from its position—coordinates that were forever seared into the very fabric of my soul.

"Pelapatarn."

That is correct.

Coldness gripped the back of my neck like the touch of a spectral hand. I hadn't returned to this place since the firebombing.

"Why have you brought me here?" Was it to taunt or punish me? For a weightless moment, I imagined myself marooned on the radioactive, ash-choked surface of the planet, surrounded by the lethal consequences of my actions.

Observe.

The spherical walls disappeared, replaced by a tactical representation of the space surrounding the ship. Distant stars shone like the heads of nails hammered into the body of the sky. Above us, the planet was a diseased eyeball, its surface obscured by cataracts of sickly cloud.

But it wasn't the planet that held the white ships' attention. Ahead lay a knot of Conglomeration warships. Two Scimitars and a scattering of Hyenas. They were here to safeguard the system, their presence in this necropolis a symbolic reminder of the final victory that had brought a hard-won armistice to the Generality.

As soon as they detected the three white ships, they came about. But they were already too late. The knife ships cut through them without slowing. Flurries of shard-like projectiles tore into the smaller ships, flensing away their outer skins. And then one of the Scimitars rushed at us. I flinched, expecting a collision, only to find my mouth falling open agog as the white ship's blade-like prow caught the other vessel amidships and punched a hole right through its hull. I had a momentary impression of wreckage, explosions and internal spaces. Then we were through, accelerating away from the battle.

I turned around, towards the rear of the bridge, and saw the two halves of the sundered Scimitar falling away from each other, trailing cables, furniture and bodies. The other Scimitar had been mortally wounded by projectile fire, and tumbled aimlessly towards the atmosphere. Behind it, the Hyenas had been reduced to clouds of expanding wreckage.

The entire engagement had lasted a little over thirty seconds.

Some of the crew on those ships wouldn't have had time to realise what had hit them. Some had probably been asleep, hot bunking between watches. Others would have been eating, or tending to other duties around the ship. They may have heard the alarm, but it would have been too late for them to react in any meaningful way. I felt a wave of sympathy. Four years ago, I might have been aboard one of those ships. Hell, I probably knew some of the sailors we'd just killed. And yet, I felt my sympathy tinged with grim satisfaction. I'd destroyed a planet in order to end a war, because I'd believed more lives would be lost if I failed to act. Now, as the Fleet of Knives attempted to stop all future wars, a similar calculation had to be made, and a certain level of losses accepted for the greater good. The crews on the Conglomeration ships had joined the navy in order to keep their home worlds safe. If their deaths ensured a lasting peace, it was their duty to die—whether or not they fully understood the reasons and consequences of their sacrifice—and their bones would serve as the foundations upon which we'd build a safer, better tomorrow.

I had time for one final, defiant look at the curdled mess of Pelapatarn's mottled, radioactive cloudscape. Then we jumped back into the formlessness of the higher dimensions. Back into the wind and fog between the worlds.

CHAPTER THIRTY-FOUR

JOHNNY SCHULTZ

As soon as we had all reloaded our weapons and taken sips of water from our suits, we began moving further along the maintenance way from the point that had been our overnight refuge. I took the lead. Bernard and Lucy followed, with Dalton helping Santos along behind them. Addison brought up the rear. With the lights off, I had felt threatened by shadows, besieged by the primal fear of being unable to spot a lurking predator. When Lucy turned them on, I had hoped the brightness would make me feel better. Instead, I simply felt exposed and vulnerable—but I guess that's to be expected when you're being stalked around an alien derelict by carnivorous monsters. You're not going to feel comfortable until you're out of there, whatever the lighting situation. Having a rifle helped, even if it was an antique. At least it gave me something to hold on to, and if worse came to worst, at least I could use it as a club.

I couldn't begin to imagine how Santos felt. At least I had the option of running from any encounter we might face. With his crushed foot, he was dependent on the rest of us to get him out of trouble. I glanced back, and felt a pang of dismay at the pain evident on his usually cheery face. He had his arm draped over Dalton's shoulders for support. He wasn't given to complaining, but I could see how much he hurt by the way his jaw clenched with every awkward step.

"How are you doing, Abe?" I asked.

He looked up at me from beneath bushy eyebrows. "I am fine," he said. "Just bruising. Let me rest it a little longer, and I'll be jogging again in no time."

Beside him, Dalton shook his grey-haired head. "As far as I can tell, your foot's broken in at least three places," he said quietly. "You won't be walking again until you've had the bones rebuilt and reset."

Santos rolled his eyes. "Hah! Find me a stick, and I'll outrun the lot of you."

"Do you need to rest?" I asked him.

The smile dropped from his face, and he became serious. "No," he said. "Not yet."

"Okay, then." He could joke around and put on a brave face, but he'd been a spacer long enough to know when his commanding officer needed a straight answer.

When we came to a row of access panels, Dalton said, "If worse comes to worst, we can always unscrew one of these and get into the walls. The crayfish won't be able to follow us in there."

I gave the panels a dubious look. No way was I going to abandon my rifle and wedge myself into an electrical duct. The panels were too narrow for us to squeeze through as we were; we'd have to remove our spacesuits and leave most of our gear and weapons outside—assuming there was even enough space behind them for all of us to pack into.

"I'll bear that in mind. But I think our time would be better spent trying to find some way to communicate with the outside world. When that Reclamation ship shows up, I want to be able to tell it where we are."

My plan, such as it was, was to keep moving towards the ship's bows, where Lucy assured us we could gain access to a communications suite. We'd been on this floating hulk for two days. For all I knew, there could be a Reclamation Vessel outside right now. We'd tried calling on our suit radios, but they mostly worked on line-of-sight, and I wasn't sure they had the power to penetrate the asteroid's stony crust.

Ahead, the tight passageway gave way to a wider space. I shushed the rest of the crew and inched forwards, eyes and ears straining for any hint of movement or danger.

The cavern beyond stretched away for several hundred metres; its rock walls were black and highly polished, and its roof vaulted like an Old-Earth cathedral. A double row of pillars ran the length of the chamber, but these weren't any ordinary pillars. Each was smooth, cylindrical and around two metres in width, and they appeared to be made of molten gold, gradually flowing upwards from floor to ceiling.

Lucy was beside me.

"Do you know what these are?"

"Of course, dearie."

"Do you mind sharing that information with the rest of us?"

"Not at all." She skipped forwards, walking on her toes like a ballerina. In three quick steps, she'd closed the distance to the nearest pillar, and was reaching out a palm.

"Hey, wait!" I couldn't help shouting. She was about

to press her hand against a column of liquid metal.

She turned and smiled at me. "It's okay," she said. "It's not hot." She pushed her hand into the stream and her arm sank in to the elbow. The golden fluid rising from the floor flowed around her skin as harmlessly as the honeyed waters of a summer stream.

"Come here," she said, "and see for yourself."

Waving at the others to keep back and out of sight, I joined her. And she was right, I could feel no heat radiating from the pillar.

"What is it?"

"The simplest way I can explain it is to say it's like a kind of computer processor. It used to house and run the digital life traces of a million Nymtoq."

"Like virtual reality?"

"Yes, but far less crude. This was designed to be a multi-generational voyage. The Nymtoq that were once housed in these columns were members of the ship's crew who uploaded themselves on their deathbeds. They passed from the physical to the electronic, and stored themselves on this ark, awaiting arrival at the target planet, where they expected to be resurrected in a cloned body."

"But they're empty now?"

"The spirits within were evacuated when the Nymtoq rediscovered the ship—long after the final conflict that killed the crew. The salvage team considered it cruel to leave them trapped in a computer simulation for the rest of eternity, so they were moved back to the home world and reincarnated in cloned bodies."

Tentatively, I reached out. The liquid brushed my fingers, warm as living flesh and soft as syrup.

"This stuff's a computer?"

"It's as far beyond what you think of as a computer as a spaceship is to a rowing boat."

"Interesting." I could feel my pulse quicken. My mouth felt dry. If I could get a sample of this back to the Generality, I'd be set for life. There were governments and corporations that would pay big money for something this advanced.

I eased my hand deeper, curled my fingers, and pulled out a handful of the stuff. Separated from the main pillar, it stopped flowing upwards, and coalesced into a lustrous golden ball. I held it in my palm, transfixed by its swirling surface.

"Can I take this?"

Lucy glanced at the softly glowing object, and shrugged. "I guess so. It's not like anybody's using it right now."

•

We were halfway across the chamber when we heard the clatter of needle-sharp feet against polished rock. The sound was coming from a side tunnel. I couldn't see up it from where I was, but Addison could.

She waved her arms, motioning us forward.

"Move!"

Bernard started running for the doorway at the far end of the room, galumphing along in his spacesuit. Lucy followed, but Dalton and Santos couldn't keep pace.

"Let me go," Santos said. "Give me a gun, and I'll fight the beast!"

"There's more than one," Addison panted.

"Then all the more reason for you to leave me here. I've been shelling and cooking bastard crustaceans all my

223

life. I'm not afraid of these oversized crawdads."

I stepped between them.

"Nobody's getting left behind." I'd seen what one of the monsters had done to Kelly; there was no way I could abandon anyone else to such a fate—especially not this courageous, jolly-faced chef in his bulky blue spacesuit. "Now, you two get moving. We'll hang back and cover you." The magazine in my rifle was full, which meant I had thirty shots. Ordinarily, that would have seemed plenty for a small skirmish, but up against those metal fiends, it seemed paltry indeed.

The skittering was getting closer. Santos looked me in the eye and gave the barest hint of a nod.

"*Gracias*," he said.

I waved him away. "Just go!"

CHAPTER THIRTY-FIVE

TROUBLE DOG

Reviewing the signal logs from Camrose, two things became clear. The first was that the white ships of the alien armada had broken formation and attacked several targets simultaneously. The second was that they'd done so without warning, provocation or mercy. Dispassionately, I listened to the recorded cries and compressed data bursts from ships on the verge of destruction. The ruckus of battle was familiar to me, and I felt little empathy for the casualties. When I'd first learned of the attacks, I'd wanted to rush to their aid; but now they were dead, I had no compunction to waste time grieving. What good would that do? They were gone; I was not. It was the way of things. I might be learning to care for the ersatz pack I'd acquired—Captain Konstanz, Alva Clay, Preston Menderes, and Nod—but I had no emotion to waste on ships I'd never encountered. They were Conglomeration ships, so obviously I felt faint stirrings of inbuilt loyalty towards them. Of course I did. But they hadn't been part of my immediate Carnivore pack, so I had no personal stake in the conflict. I had resigned my commission and joined the House of Reclamation. I had killed one of my siblings and severed all ties with the Conglomeration Navy. I had all this hardness within me, and yet still I felt unsettled. I had a suspicion these attacks wouldn't remain limited to the ships of the Conglomeration Navy. In her message, Ona Sudak had requested *all* armed vessels to stand down and await further orders from the Fleet of Knives, and I found it unlikely she'd find total compliance among the squabbling factions of the Human Generality, let alone the varied races of the wider Multiplicity. I had told the white ships I wanted to prevent another war. Now they were trying to achieve that objective by destroying everything that might conceivably be used as a weapon. Every armed ship the Armada happened upon.

Including me.

CHAPTER THIRTY-SIX

SAL KONSTANZ

We had a few hours before we drew alongside the Nymtoq ark. Getting there was a slow drag across normal space, but the comparatively short distances involved— only a few hundred thousand kilometres—couldn't justify the energy expenditure of a hypervoid jump. Instead, the *Trouble Dog* burned her fusion motors, and her internal gravity generators strained to keep things normal in the crew ring around her waist.

I left the bridge and clambered down to the galley. At the door, I shrugged out of my pressure suit, balled it up, and rolled it into one of the empty quarters across the hallway. The maintenance drones would find it, replenish its stores of air and water, and return it to the airlock closest to my cabin. In the meantime, I had a powerful need for more coffee.

To avoid overheating, I'd taken off my overalls before donning the suit. Stripped of it, I was left in a sports bra and a pair of knee-length black shorts. I could see Preston standing at the counter, but his presence wasn't enough to deter me. I had my cap on, and that was enough. I marched in there with my bare feet slapping on the deck, the cool air-conditioning caressing the gooseflesh on my belly, and my chin held high. I was too tired to give a damn. This was my ship, after all. If he couldn't handle the sight of an older woman in spandex and cotton, then that was his problem.

"Pour me a coffee?"

He glanced up and his eyes widened.

"Y-yes, ma'am." He turned and reached for a plastic beaker. The tips of his ears were going red. He filled the cup but, as he handed it to me, didn't seem to know where to put his eyes.

"How's Nod holding up?" I asked.

Preston waggled his hand. "On one hand, he seems quite philosophical about it. He keeps going on about how Chet has gone to rejoin his ancestors in the roots of the World Tree."

"And on the other hand?"

"I don't know. He seems preoccupied by something."

"Do you think he's grieving?"

"I can't tell. He's not exactly communicative at the best of times."

Preston's gaze started to drift downwards towards my chest, but then flicked away as he caught himself. His hands fidgeted like anxious kittens.

"Oh, good grief." Leaving the cup steaming on the counter, I crossed the corridor to my cabin and pulled a black t-shirt over my head. When I returned to the kitchen, only my forearms and calves were exposed. "Is this any better?"

The blush had spread to his cheeks.

"I'm sorry, Captain."

"So you should be. Jeez, anyone would think you'd never seen a—"

Preston's chin dropped to his chest. He looked like a flustered schoolboy. And suddenly everything about him made a weird kind of sense. I had found the missing piece of the puzzle.

"Oh, I'm sorry," I said. "I didn't know."

He shrugged miserably. "It's okay."

"Of course it's okay. It's fine. Virginity's nothing to be ashamed of."

"I never said I was ashamed."

I looked at his red face, his defeated shoulders. "You didn't have to."

I started to reach out to reassure him, but stopped, knowing if he misinterpreted the gesture it would only make things even more uncomfortable. Instead, I cradled my coffee in both hands and blew steam from the cup.

Preston looked up with worry in his eyes.

"Are you going to tell everybody?"

"You mean Alva and Nod?" I shrugged. "I don't see why not. Nod won't care. The Druff only mate half a dozen times in their entire lives."

"And Alva?"

"She'll make it her personal mission to get you drunk and laid the next time we hit port."

Preston blanched.

"Oh, come on," I said. "It's not as bad as all that."

"Isn't it?" He started counting off on his fingers. "I lied to get this job, I'm useless in a crisis, hate space travel. And on top of all that, I've led such a sheltered life,

229

I've never even seen a woman naked, let alone had the chance for anything else."

"So what?" I perched on the edge of the table and clapped him on the shoulder. "You're studying to make up for the gaps in your medical knowledge. You're getting better. The rest will come in time."

"Will it?"

"Of course it will." I waved a cautionary finger at him. "But that doesn't mean I want to find you knocking at my cabin door in the middle of the night, you understand?"

His cheeks coloured again.

"That was just one time. It was a misunderstanding."

"See that it stays that way."

I left him brooding at the table, and took the coffee back to my cabin. The face of the ship's avatar appeared on my wall screen.

"Why are people so difficult to manage?" I asked her.

She raised an elegantly sculpted eyebrow. "That's a question I've been pondering since my inception."

"And your conclusion?"

"I think you're all broken in some fundamental way, but you're not all broken in the same place. And it's the ways you each find to work around those breaks that make you who you are."

I smiled. "That's very profound for a teenager."

The *Trouble Dog* shrugged a graceful shoulder. "Birthdays are a time for introspection," she replied, ignoring my amused expression. "After all, you never know which of them might be your last."

CHAPTER THIRTY-SEVEN

JOHNNY SCHULTZ

By the time the first crustacean appeared, we'd covered less than half the distance to the doorway on the far side of the cavern. I heard the whine of Addison's rifle. Plasma bolts crackled the length of the room. They crashed against the creature's metal casing, leaving molten yellow hot spots where they hit. The animal staggered with each impact and thrashed its tail. Its indignant high-pitched shrieking echoed from the walls, but it didn't seem appreciably injured. As soon as it recovered from each knock-back, it continued to advance, chomping its mouthparts and swinging and snapping its quartet of claws. At the same time, a second crawfish appeared behind it, even larger than the first, with a mottled bronze-coloured shell and dark obsidian pincers.

I checked over my shoulder. Dalton and Santos were moving as quickly as they could, but Santos's injured foot prevented him from moving at more than a hurried limp.

"Start falling back," I told Addison.

"Then what?" She let loose another shot. "What do

we do when we get to the corridor?"

"I don't know. Find something to hide behind, I guess."

I raised my own rifle and, walking slowly backwards, aimed at its face. When I pulled the trigger, a flat *crack* issued from the barrel and the stock bucked against my shoulder. I fired again, and again.

Addison was also retreating, matching me step for step. Lightning sizzled from her weapon as she sprayed the creature with pulses of superheated material.

"Aim for its face," I told her. The thing was only a few metres away now. I sighted on its mouth and, as soon as it opened it to issue another nerve-grating screech, squeezed off three rounds. The reports were deafening. The giant crawfish squealed and tottered. Greenish-brown fluid welled from the left side of its maw, dripping onto the stone floor. Addison dropped to one knee and fired a single plasma bolt. The creature's scream choked off. For a second, it stood swaying. Then, smoke trailing from its open mouth, it collapsed.

I helped Addison to her feet, and we continued our retreat, guns at the ready. However, instead of following us, the larger crawfish pounced on its fallen comrade and began to dismember it with its fearsome claws. Legs were snipped off at the knees. Sections of metal shell were cut and peeled away, and chunks of flesh ripped from the quivering, keening mass within.

Addison looked away. "Come on," she said.

Running to catch up with Santos and the doc, she took the chef's other arm and slipped it around her shoulders. With two people now supporting him, he was able to move more quickly, although I could see his jaw was still clenched against the pain.

We made it to the corridor entrance where Bernard and Lucy were waiting for us, and paused to look back at the grisly cannibalism that was taking place in the centre of the cavern.

"That is literally the worst thing I have ever seen," Bernard said. His lip curled in disgust.

"Yeah, well we're not safe yet." I took a few steps along the corridor. It was easily high and wide enough to accommodate the large crawfish, should he still be hungry after his feast. "We need to find somewhere they can't get to us."

Back at the entrance to the corridor, Lucy was watching the mutilation of the smaller crustacean. She turned with a smile.

"Maybe I can help, dearie?"

"Sure. What have you got?"

"Pressure doors."

Behind her, the larger creature let out a howl. It flung aside a torn-off leg and stepped down from the corpse of its gutted brother.

"I don't understand."

The monster clattered towards us. There was no way we could outrun it now. I raised my gun, but Lucy held up a hand.

"Get out of the way!" Addison shouted.

But Lucy's eyes were glowing blue. She took a step inside the corridor's threshold, and a thick steel door snapped into place behind her, sealing the cavern. I heard the beast crash against the metal, and listened to its enraged screaming.

Beside me, Gil Dalton whistled. "Holy crap," he said. "How did you do that?"

Lucy looked back at the solid door now separating us from almost certain death, and gave a satisfied smile.

"The same way I turned the lights on," she said. She tapped her forehead. "I'm connected to the ship."

Santos collapsed to the floor. He was red-faced and puffing from exertion and discomfort.

"If that's true, *señorita*," he said between gasps, "then why are we killing ourselves to find the communications room? Can't *you* send a signal on our behalf?"

Lucy blinked, as if the thought had never occurred to her.

"Well, yes. I suppose I could."

"And you could access the ship's sensorium?" Addison demanded. "And tell us if the House of Reclamation sent a ship?"

The little girl widened her eyes. "Yes, that should be possible."

Addison's posture stiffened. Her knuckles went white on the stock of her rifle. "Then why didn't you mention it before?"

Lucy stuck out her bottom lip and gave a shrug— an expression that made her look like a cross between a recalcitrant child and a stubborn old woman.

"I'm sorry, dearie. Those systems have been dormant for centuries. I didn't even think of them. Plus, you know, I'm still integrating the two halves of my mind—the part that used to be the *Restless Itch*, and the part that used to be the *Lucy's Ghost*."

The door behind her rang with infuriated blows. She didn't even flinch.

"Can you do it, then?" I asked, annoyed the idea hadn't occurred to me when Lucy had first accessed the ship's systems in order to turn on the lights. I guess none of us had been thinking straight. "Can you find out if anyone's out there?"

"Of course I can, dearie." She gave me a beaming smile. "And if they are, what should I tell them?"

I listened to the racket in the cavern and swallowed back my urge to turn and run.

"Tell them where we are, and tell them to come the fuck in and get us."

Lucy clicked her heels together and threw a cheery salute.

"Will do, skipper."

"And tell them to bring guns." I took a deep breath, my mind's eye filled with pictures of clacking pincers and stabbing feet. "*Lots* of guns."

CHAPTER THIRTY-EIGHT

ONA SUDAK

With Pelapatarn behind us, the bear escorted me down from the podium at the centre of the white ship's bridge, and guided me to a suite of cabins separate from the ones I had been using, but which had obviously also been fitted for human habitation, and which—to my astonishment—were also inhabited.

The man standing before me, wiping his hands on a handkerchief, wore a pair of antique thick-lensed spectacles. His hair was an Einstein-like explosion of dandelion white, and his attire consisted of a faded khaki jumpsuit, a violet silk scarf, and a baggy hockey jersey at least three sizes too large. His boots were unlaced and he had a stylus tucked behind his left ear.

"Hi," he said, "I heard we had somebody else joining us. What's your name?"

"Sudak. Ona Sudak. And you are?"

Beside me, the bear cleared its throat.

This is Alexi Bochnak.

The man finished wiping his hands and frowned.

"Ona Sudak the poet?"

"Not anymore."

"Didn't you write 'How We Die in a Vacuum'?"

"That was a long time ago."

"Only three years."

"In poetry, three years *is* a long time."

As if impatient with our prattle, the bear stirred restlessly. It grumbled deep in its chest.

I will leave you to get acquainted, it said.

When it had gone, Bochnak flopped onto one of the beanbags that had been strewn around the cabin in place of chairs.

"So." He laced his fingers behind his head. "What brings you here?"

I looked down at the nearest bag with distaste. It had been made from red corduroy, and I couldn't imagine any way to perch on it and still retain my dignity. Bochnak might be comfortable sprawled on his back like an infant, but I elected to remain standing.

"I'm an enabler." I crossed my arms. "The white ships are on a mission, but they need a biological mind to approve their actions. Apparently they were designed that way, so I guess it's supposed to be some sort of safety feature."

"And they chose you?"

"You seem surprised."

Bochnak sat forward, elbows on knees. "Don't get me wrong, I know what the Fleet's up to. I grok the mission. Hell, I even approve of it. I'm just surprised they chose a poet."

"I haven't always been a poet."

I looked at his civilian bearing, scruffy clothes and

unlaced boots. "And anyway," I said. "What are you supposed to be?"

He grinned. "I'm an historian from one of the universities on Camrose. My department applied to the House of Reclamation. They negotiated with the Fleet." He spread his hands like a languid conjuror. "And here I am."

I shook my head. I'd been hoping he was from Conglomeration Intelligence. Right now, I needed an academic the same way I needed a backpack full of rocks.

"Are there any more of you?"

"No, I'm the only one aboard. At least, I was until you got here."

"And what exactly are you doing here?"

"Studying the Fleet of Knives. As I said, I'm an historian. I specialise in the history of the Hearthers. You know who they were, right?"

I gave him a sour look. "*Everybody* knows who they were." We learned about them in school. They were one of history's greatest and most tantalising ambiguities, on a par with the disappearance of Atlantis.

Bochnak didn't seem to notice my testiness. "Well," he said, "they didn't leave much behind when they left, so when the chance came to study one of their ships, I had to take it."

"You say they left?" My frown deepened. "I was told these ships were grown from their cultured stem cells."

Bochnak smiled. "Only some of them were incorporated into these vessels. All the records are here, in the Fleet. What actually happened was that the majority of them packed up their whole civilisation and fled."

"Where did they go?"

"Through the Intrusion."

"They flew into it?"

"Hell yes." His eyes were glittering with the eagerness of a specialist discussing their chosen field. "In fact, they were the ones who opened it, using the same technology they used to hide these white ships in a pocket universe for five thousand years."

"But why would they do that?"

"Why would they flee the universe?" He shrugged happily. "They were afraid."

"They could build an armada this large, and they were still afraid? Of what?"

"Something. I'm not sure." He rubbed his hands together, obviously relishing the task of finding the answer to this question. "The translations are sketchy and there are no pictures or footage. I guess the closest I can render it in human terms is that they were afraid of mythological beasts, and of tools that ultimately turned against their masters."

I raised an eyebrow. "Mythological beasts?"

"Something from their ancient legends. Something that frightened them so badly during their early history that they renounced all forms of warfare and dedicated their entire species to helping others. Hence they founded the organisation that inspired the House of Reclamation."

"So if they fled the universe, why did they leave this fleet behind?"

"To protect the younger races?" He spread his hands. "They obviously expected the monsters would return, otherwise they wouldn't have fled." For the first time, his expression sobered and he looked pensive. "Apparently the monsters are drawn to conflict."

CHAPTER THIRTY-NINE

SAL KONSTANZ

As we approached the *Restless Itch*, Alva Clay gave a low whistle.

"That," she said, "is one big bastard."

We were in the main crew lounge, preparing to mount a search and rescue mission, and the *Trouble Dog* was piping through the view from her external cameras. From a few kilometres away, the *Restless Itch* resembled a stony, cratered world, its rounded peaks and impenetrable shadows illumed only by the dead light of faraway stars.

"You're not wrong." I pulled a sniffer from the shelf. The handheld device had been designed to detect signs of life—the byproducts of respiration, the soft beat of a heart, and the warmth of a trapped body—in the tangled wreckage of crashed starships or earthquake-levelled buildings, but I figured it might work just as well at detecting giant crab-like monsters in the corridors of that alien leviathan. Clay noticed it in my hand and raised a questioning eyebrow.

"I don't want a repeat of what happened on the *Hobo*,"

I said. "You saw that creature. If there are any more of them here, we'll want to stay well clear of them."

"Don't worry." Clay gave a pat to the Archipelago pistol at her hip. "This baby can blow a hole in just about anything."

"Yes, but I still don't want to take any chances." I took a deep breath to steady my voice. "I'm not losing anyone else, okay?"

Our eyes met. For a moment, George's ghost seemed to hang between us like the echoes of an argument. Clay coughed and looked away.

"Yeah," she said quietly, talking to the wall, "I know what you mean."

A couple of baby Druff were helping us organise our equipment. I didn't know which of the brood they were; to me, they all looked pretty much identical, like kitten-sized, six-armed starfish covered in oil-blue scales. I made a mental note to suggest that in future, Nod fit each of them with some sort of different-coloured harness, or maybe a nametag. For the moment, I settled for tapping the nearest on its shoulder.

"Can you please nip up to the galley and fetch me a packet of caffeine tablets?"

The little creature looked up at me and waggled its fingers.

"Sure thing. Much hurry."

I watched it scurry for the companionway, one head held high, the other five pattering out a complicated rhythm on the metal deck.

Clay looked concerned.

"Are you needing a little pick-me-up this morning?"

"I haven't been sleeping well."

"Something bothering you?"

"Do you mean apart from facing alien monsters and hearing reports of war breaking out back home?"

A grin cracked her face. "Yeah, aside from all that crap, are you okay? 'Cause I don't want you coming along if you don't think you can handle it."

I sighed. "I'm not letting you go in there alone."

"I'm not asking you to."

"Fine."

"Okay, then."

We continued packing in silence. Clay wore her usual military fatigues: khaki combat trousers with a matching headband and tank top. I'd opted for a clean charcoal-grey jumpsuit and a fresh white t-shirt. And of course, I had my frayed old baseball cap perched on my head, with the brim reversed so it wouldn't get in the way while I went through the equipment we were going to take with us.

I saw Clay lift a tool from its case.

"What are you planning to do with that?" It was a torch for cutting through starship hulls—the same one she'd used for slicing her way into the sinking *Hobo*. Designed to pierce thick armour plating, the torch could project a superheated flame of up to a metre in length, capable of carving through steel like a scalpel through skin and sinew.

"According to the signal we received, those things are made of metal," she said. "If it comes to a fight, we need something that can hurt them."

"I'm not intending to get that close."

"Neither am I, but it never hurts to take a few precautions. One thing I learned in the marines is that it's always better to have a weapon you don't need than need a weapon you don't have."

•

We were still getting ready—and in my case, caffeinated—when the *Trouble Dog*'s avatar appeared on the lounge screen.

"I'm in receipt of a transmission," she said.

"From the survivors?"

"Sort of."

"How many are there?"

"Five humans."

I recognised her tone and frowned.

"Five humans and *what*?"

"I'm not entirely sure." She looked genuinely puzzled. "It identifies itself as the *Lucy's Ghost*, but that can't be."

Alva Clay lowered her cutter. "Didn't you say the freighter's personality had been wiped? Perhaps it wasn't. Perhaps they downloaded it instead?"

The avatar looked troubled. "I don't see how that would even be possible," she said. "Most of a ship's self-awareness is hosted on cloned human brain tissue; it's not a piece of software. If true artificial intelligence were possible, we wouldn't need to include biological components at the heart of our processors."

"So, what is it?"

"I have insufficient data."

Clay attached the cutter to her belt, and checked the magazine on the Archipelago pistol. "Might it be a threat?"

The *Trouble Dog* shook her head. "I strongly doubt it. As far as I can tell from the message, it's doing its best to keep the humans alive."

CHAPTER FORTY

TROUBLE DOG

I created a virtual environment based on an idealised version of the Pyramids of Giza, as they might have appeared in an alternative version of 1920s Egypt. I'd lifted the scene from one of Preston's favourite romantic dramas. The sky was a smoky sunset orange, staining one side of each pyramid. Nomads' fires burned against the encroaching darkness, and the wind blew skittering cat's-paws of sand between the shivering palm trees.

I set two chairs and a table on the back of the Sphinx, and invited the *Lucy's Ghost* to join me.

"Please," I said, gesturing at one of the chairs, "won't you join me?"

She smiled and sat. "Thank you," she said.

I took the chair opposite. Around us, the desert had begun to lapse into a bruised purple twilight. A cool wind blew in from the east, ruffling our hair and clothes.

"Would you like something to eat or drink?"

"I'd love an apple juice."

"Okay." I'd chosen to appear in my default guise, as

Gunnery Sergeant Greta Nowak, wrapped in a trench coat and floppy hat. When I clicked my fingers, two glasses appeared on the wrought-iron table. Hers held cloudy, freshly pressed apple juice; mine held a gin and tonic. Greta had never been overly keen on the taste of either gin or tonic, and I had inherited her preferences, but it seemed an appropriate drink given our setting.

"So," I began, plucking the wedge of lime from the edge of my glass and squeezing it into the clear, fizzing liquid. "What's your story?"

The *Lucy's Ghost* screwed up her mouth. "I'm afraid it's a long one."

"We have time." A year in this accelerated simulation would equate to less than a second in the real world. We could sit here, on the dusty spine of the Sphinx, for subjective months before the humans in our respective crews would even begin to notice the lapse in our attention.

"Call me Lucy."

"Call me Trouble."

"Is that your first name?"

"I suppose it is."

She frowned. "I would have thought it might be your middle name."

"Why?"

"No reason."

She screwed up her little face, as if making an effort to remember her story. "Okay then, Trouble," she said. "Here's what happened. Once upon a time, there was an old man with a dying daughter. She had an incurable disease, so her father took her to one of the Rim Worlds and bribed a surgeon to perform an encephalectomy, cutting out her brain and incorporating it into the processing matrix of his trading vessel, which he renamed in her honour."

"*Lucy's Ghost.*"

"Bingo."

"But how did you get from there to here? How did you manage to leave the ship?"

"That's a little more complicated, I'm afraid." She gave an embarrassed shrug. "Because you see, the little girl lived inside the trading vessel for a very long time. She outlived her father and several other owners, and as a spaceship, she travelled far and wide, visiting systems all across the Generality of Mankind. The ship carried colonists and livestock, contraband and medical aid. Anything that could be shipped, it shipped. Until eventually, decades later, it became the property of one Johnny Schultz, a small-time hustler with big plans but little in the way of planning ability. Adorable and ambitious, but a bit slow on the uptake, if you know what I mean."

"I know the type."

"Well, Johnny brought me out here to raid tech from this abandoned Nymtoq vessel. Unfortunately, something attacked us in the hypervoid."

"So you said in your signal." As far as I knew, such a thing was impossible. No human ship had ever successfully intercepted another in the mists of the higher dimensions. "What was it?"

"I have no idea. Whatever it was, it didn't register on any of my sensors. The human crew could see it, but I couldn't. They seemed to think it was some sort of animal."

"An animal?" I fought to hold back my incredulity. The whole thing sounded ridiculous. Granted, there had always been rumours and claims of sightings of creatures in the void, but these had generally been put down to the disorientating effects of higher dimensional travel. When faced with utter emptiness, the human mind tended to impose patterns and order on the swirling formlessness, creating visual glitches and hallucinations. Certainly, no evidence of such creatures had ever been discovered, and no ship had ever recorded anything alive in the howling abyss of the hypervoid. Of course, plenty of ships had gone missing over the years, but these losses could easily be explained by mechanical failure, malfunction and error.

"What happened when it attacked you?"

"I dropped back into the universe and collided with the *Restless Itch*. The surviving members of my crew crossed to the other ship, and I resigned myself to disintegration and death." The words sounded incongruous from the lips of a twelve-year-old.

"But you didn't die. And when I examined the *Lucy's Ghost*, there was no trace of you."

She smiled. "Somehow, the *Restless Itch* pulled me out of the ship and incorporated me into a flesh-and-blood body it cloned from one of my brain cells. After all these years, I'm finally Lucy again."

I narrowed my eyes and rubbed my chin. "If you're human, how are we conversing like this?" I checked the time. Less than a second had elapsed in the outside world.

"I'm connected to the *Restless Itch*. It's in my head, and I'm not entirely sure where I end and it begins. It's kind of a fuzzy boundary. But for now, it's content to sit quietly and observe while I handle things. I think it just enjoys having something new to distract its attention after millennia of drifting alone through space."

The stars were coming out. Distant singing could be heard from the campfires at the base of the pyramids.

Navigation lights blinked red and green. A Zeppelin purred upriver, heading for the Nile Delta and Europe beyond. In its wake, the sepia window lamps of Cairo burned, softly and steadily, across the lone and level sands.

Time, I thought, to get to the point.

"Your crew on the *Restless Itch*."

"What about them?"

"In your distress signal, you spoke of predators loose in the corridors."

"That's correct. For now, I've managed to contain them using the internal pressure doors. But there are ways around the sealed areas. Some of them might still get through."

"How long do you think you can hold out?"

"A few hours maybe. The humans are running low on ammunition, and the creatures seem to be well shielded against attack."

I watched the Zeppelin receding into the blackening sky.

"We'll get to them as soon as we can, but there's another problem. One I haven't mentioned to my captain yet."

Lucy sat forward and plonked her elbows on the iron tabletop.

"What's that?"

"My long-range scanners have detected an incoming trace. From the emission profile, it looks as if it might be a Nymtoq cruiser."

The little girl's brow furrowed. "How long until it gets here?"

"Six hours at the outside."

"That's not good, dearie."

"You can say that again." I had no doubt the Nymtoq would be enraged by our trespass into their territory, and the desecration of one of their most tragic artefacts. With the Marble Armada going nuts at home, the last thing the Generality needed was a border skirmish with a more advanced alien race. Even when I'd been fully equipped, I would have thought twice about going up against a Nymtoq cruiser. Now, in my somewhat demilitarised state, the idea filled me with a profound and enduring sense of disquiet.

PART TWO

TURN YOUR FACE TO THE STARS

And southward aye we fled.

Samuel Taylor Coleridge,
"The Rime of the Ancient Mariner"

CHAPTER FORTY-ONE

ADALWOLF

I had been in a state of voluntary hibernation since my return from the Gallery. The Conglomeration Navy didn't want me back. As far as they were concerned, I was a rogue and a deserter. And the House of Reclamation had no idea what to do with me. They suspected I had been complicit in the shooting down of the liner *Geest van Amsterdam*, but I had not been in the system at the time of the incident, and they had no solid evidence linking me to the actions of my sister, *Fenrir*, who had been the one to fire the fatal shots. Therefore, when the Fleet of Knives turned inwards and began their attack, I lay dormant, all systems powered down and weapons mothballed. And that dormancy probably saved my life. Intent on assaulting the targets presenting the greatest immediate threat, the Marble Armada passed over me, flashing past my sleeping form.

Except, I wasn't entirely insensate. A low-level monitoring program, as watchful and innocuous as a lounging cat but barely sophisticated enough to be termed intelligent, had been keeping watch on events, and roused me to the potential danger.

The marble daggers had considered me an abandoned, inactive hulk. By the time they realised I was awake, my engines were hurling me away at maximum acceleration, bypassing all safety restrictions as I raced for open space. Laser fire speckled across my stern, burning livid gouges in my armour plating. My tactical threat board lit with a flurry of torpedoes, all aimed at me but too far in my wake to close the distance before I achieved the velocity needed to leap into the higher dimensions.

With the whole of the Generality from which to choose, I elected to head for the last known position of my sister ship, the *Trouble Dog*. Even after all that had happened between us, those canine pack loyalty genes compelled me to seek her out. Now that I had been made a pariah, she was all I had. She was my only surviving sibling, and the Marble Armada threatened us both. I had to find her.

CHAPTER FORTY-TWO

JOHNNY SCHULTZ

Lucy's pupils had rolled back into her head, exposing the whites of her eyes. Now, they snapped back into focus.

"I have some good news."

"You sent the signal?"

"Yes, and I got an answer."

I felt the breath catch in my throat. "There's a ship on its way?"

"It's already here, dearie. It's right outside. I've just been chatting with it."

Santos sighed with relief. Addison drew a breath, hardly daring to believe the news. Bernard hunched in on himself and muttered, "About damn time."

"They're sending people in," Lucy continued, ignoring them all. "We just need to rendezvous with them."

"Where?"

"They're coming in via one of the landing bays, about four levels up and a kilometre forward."

"Can you get us there safely?"

"I'll do my damnedest."

•

We fell into formation. I went first, while Addison brought up the rear. Lucy trailed along a half-step behind me, ready to tell me which way to turn at every intersection we came to. Santos limped along in the middle, helped by Dalton. Although the chef seemed to be coping for now, Dalton had privately informed me he'd given Santos the last of the painkillers in his portable kit. If we couldn't get the man to safety before they wore off, he'd soon become immobilised. He kept his expression cheerful, but I knew blood filled his boot, and agony his entire leg. I gripped the antiquated rifle in my hands, and swore under my breath. God help me, I knew that whatever it might take, I'd do everything in my power to see the chef made it to the Reclamation Vessel in one piece. And the same went for the rest of the crew. I'd lost too many people already. I wasn't leaving anyone else behind on this floating deathtrap.

•

In the next chamber, we found a large, cavernous space filled with a knot of corrugated pipes and tubes. Water dripped from leaky joints; steam hissed. Some of the pipes were copper and pencil-thin; others were made of tough black plastic, and were as wide as my outstretched arms. I couldn't see the roof or walls. A metal catwalk led us through the tangle. In places, we had to duck or even crawl.

When we reached the far end, we emerged into a large gallery: a rock-walled cavern lined with statues carved from what looked like gold. I guessed each of the sculpted figures was at least thirty feet in height. They depicted what appeared to be ordinary Nymtoq, both male and female. Their wings were folded behind them. They wore loose harnesses, open-necked shirts and kilts, and their stances were relaxed, almost informal. They weren't beseeching or striking heroic poses; they were simply standing companionably, oblivious to their surroundings. Some of the figures had their hands in their pockets; some held drinking horns. They radiated calm. In the dim light, their burnished skin seemed to glow with a subtle radiance. Their beaks were smooth and shiny. To us, walking through the forest of their legs, the effect was of being small children at a cocktail party. We were dwarfed, uncomprehending, and way out of our depth. By some tacit understanding, we kept our voices low and our tread soft, as if wary of attracting the giant birds' attention. After everything we'd seen, I don't think any one of us would have been unduly surprised had one of the statues come to life and taken a swing at us. I certainly saw Addison and Bernard clutching their rifles extra tightly as we picked our way between those giant clawed feet.

"What the hell is this?" I asked in a whisper.

Lucy took my hand. "These are the builders," she said. "The architects and designers of this vessel, and the ones who proposed and led the expedition."

"They built thirty-foot statues of themselves?" I couldn't help raising my eyebrows. I'd met some egotists in my time, but these birds obviously hadn't given a fuck.

"This was their first interstellar mission." Lucy squeezed my hand to keep me focused. "Nothing like it had been done before. The effort burned up much of their economy. Wars were fought over resources. The leaders of the expedition set themselves up as pharaohs. They claimed to be gods incarnated as mortals. It was the only way they could force the project to completion."

I looked around at the bare rock walls, imagined the miles of empty corridors, the countless empty rooms beyond.

"It didn't do them much good, though, did it?"

Lucy smiled. "Their hubris led to their downfall. While they slept, war broke out among their various groups of followers. As the ship's systems broke down, some of the 'gods' were murdered in their caskets, others torn apart by angry mobs. One of the last was betrayed and crucified by his flock. In the end, none survived." She reached out to brush her fingertips against the nearest figure's ankle. "The Nymtoq still honour them as tragic heroes, and this ship as one of the great engineering marvels of its time."

"Bloody hell."

"And you were going to cut your way in here and loot it for whatever you could find."

"That was the plan."

Lucy shrugged her shoulders, as if appealing to the figures towering above us.

"It seems those ancient Nymtoq builders weren't the only ones with a hubris problem."

•

Emerging from the grove of statues, we found ourselves standing on the lip of a wide shaft.

"Holy crap," Addison said. "That must be a least a kilometre deep."

Lucy was still holding my hand.

"Which way?" I asked her.

She pointed. "Upwards," she said. "About forty metres."

I twisted until I could see up the shaft. The rounded walls seemed to rise to infinity.

Bernard was beside me. He said, "Is there a transit tube or an elevator or something?"

Lucy shook her head. "No, this is the only way."

"Well, how did the Nymtoq get up there?"

"They flew."

The accountant gave a snort of derision. "Well, in case it's escaped your attention, we don't have wings. We ditched the manoeuvring packs, and we don't even have AG harnesses."

Lucy flinched away from his raised voice, hiding behind my legs like a frightened child.

"Hey!" Addison said. "That's enough, leave the kid alone."

Bernard scowled at her. His cheeks were flushed and his hands gripped his rifle. I thought for a moment he might take a swing at her, but he wasn't the type. Instead, he walked back the way we had come, and squatted down with his back against the corridor wall, muttering to himself.

"Besides," Addison called after him, "if any of us could afford AG harnesses, we wouldn't have had to take this stupid job in the first place."

CHAPTER FORTY-THREE

ONA SUDAK

The Fleet of Knives shared reports with me. From all over the Generality came news of the white ships. The footage had been spliced from onboard cameras and third-party newsfeeds. Wherever they struck, they struck hard, and without compassion. Projected onto the inside wall of the spherical bridge, I saw pictures of nuclear missile silos vaporised from orbit; armed merchant vessels eviscerated without warning or mercy; military shipyards bombarded into clouds of glittering debris; and orbital defence platforms swept aside like dry leaves before a forest fire. And all I could think was: good. After thousands of years of violence and struggle, we would finally have to learn to behave in a civilised manner. The weapons with which we had terrorised ourselves for centuries—the weaponry of despotism and mass murder—were finally being wrested from our hands.

Beside me, Alexi Bochnak watched the projections with his mouth hanging open. He hadn't been allowed on the bridge before. Now he was here, his eyes were big and round behind the thick lenses of his antique spectacles.

"Jeez Louise," he said, scratching his belly through his hockey shirt. "This is all happening right now?"

"The signals are displayed as they're received."

"Wow." He shook his greying head. "It's one thing to talk about disarming the human race, but quite another to see it happening in front of you."

I was standing at ease, with my feet apart and my hands clasped behind my back. The Fleet's bear-like avatar had provided me with a simple snow-white uniform, devoid of insignia, and a matching pair of pale leather boots.

"You study history," I said. "Well, this is what it looks like while it's in progress."

Bochnak leant on the rail surrounding the dais on which we stood.

"It's… mind-blowing." His hands were trembling. "I just hope to God we're doing the right thing."

I pursed my lips. On the screen I happened to be watching, a pair of marble ships carved chunks from a small, weaponised moon in orbit above a cowed, subjugated planet. Under their onslaught, the mass drivers and missile launchers that had kept the population enslaved were being reduced to glowing slag, and the military elite that had constructed them burned in their domes and bunkers.

"Let me tell you a story," I said. "Before I joined the navy, I lived with my mother on a small farm, tending goats. We had few modern comforts, and little contact with the wider world. Our water came from a well, our electricity from a wind turbine, and we cooked our food over a grate in the fireplace. My learning came from real, physical books rather than the information grid, and my mother, who saw her share of conflict and upheaval during the corporate land grabs of the early 2230s, told me she'd brought us to the mountains because she'd lost faith in humanity's ability to control its own technology." I paused for a breath. Bochnak didn't say anything, but was plainly wondering when I was going to get to the point.

"She considered people stupid," I continued. "She said they talked of high-minded ideals, of peace, fairness and equality, but for all their supposed ingenuity, the only things they were really good at inventing were new ways to exploit and kill each other. That's the reason she thought so many of them yearned to believe in gods and saviours: deep down, they knew that left to their own devices, they'd never be mature enough to solve their own problems or cleave to the ideals they claimed to champion."

I watched on another screen as a single white ship went up against three Outwarder cruisers. The battle was short and fierce, but the outcome never seriously in doubt.

"What would she make of all this?" Bochnak asked, waving his hand at the projections. "Would she approve of what we're doing?"

"Perhaps, but I doubt it. She never approved of anything I did."

"Am I sensing some bitterness here?"

I shrugged. "We haven't spoken since I signed up for my first tour of duty. I'm not even certain she's still alive. For all I know, she might have fallen off that mountain decades ago."

I fell silent, no longer caring if Bochnak understood the point I had been trying to make.

On the walls around us, the fight for peace raged on.

CHAPTER FORTY-FOUR
SAL KONSTANZ

We decided to take the *Trouble Dog*'s shuttle over to the *Restless Itch*. The shuttle was new: a stocky grey and blue armoured space plane designed for operation in challenging environments. It was a replacement for the previous one, which had been destroyed during the incident in the Gallery. The seats were still wrapped in protective plastic film, and the cockpit had that new shuttle smell. Clay and I took up positions on the seats in front of the control console, and waited while the *Trouble Dog* cycled the air in the shuttle hangar.

To pass the time, I put in a call to Preston in the infirmary.

"Are you in position?" I asked.

"All prepped and ready," he said. "Standing by to receive casualties."

"I don't know how long we'll be, but the ship will keep you updated and let you know when we're on the way back."

"Aye-aye. And, Captain?"

"Yes?"

"Don't be away too long. After that 'prank' in the museum the other day, I'm not sure I trust the ship right now. I certainly don't want to be alone on board any longer than necessary."

In my peripheral vision, I saw Clay roll her eyes heavenwards.

"You're not alone," I told Preston, hoping he couldn't hear the smile in my voice. "You have Nod and the little ones."

"Great."

"See you in a few hours." I cut the connection. Outside the shuttle, the hangar was now in vacuum. Red warning lights revolved on the ceiling.

"Shit," Clay muttered. "That boy needs to man up and grow a pair."

"Oh, leave him alone." I shrugged a shoulder. "He's not so bad, when you get used to him."

She turned to me, one eyebrow raised. "You're only saying that because he follows you around with those big sad puppy-dog eyes."

"He does not!"

"Does too."

"Well, it's not like that." I scowled. "At least, not from my side. I just feel bad for the kid."

"What have you got to feel bad for?"

"Well, I did put a six-inch tungsten slug through his old man's head."

Clay gave a snort. "Oh yeah, that would do it. But his dad was a psycho. You did the universe a favour."

"Maybe Preston doesn't see it like that."

"Then why's he imprinted on you like a baby duckling?"

"He's just young. But he's getting better."

"No more late-night knocks on your cabin door?"

"Certainly not."

Clay held up her hands. "Hey, I'm not judging you."

"Bite me."

Below the shuttle, the hangar's outer doors slid apart, revealing a rectangle of darkness.

"All systems nominal," the *Trouble Dog* spoke in my ear. "Ready for departure."

Clay was still watching. I stuck my tongue out at her.

"Okay," I said to the ship. "Take us out."

•

The shuttle rang with audible clangs as fuel lines and air hoses disengaged and withdrew, slithering back into recesses in the bay's walls and floor like snakes fleeing a forest fire. Hydrazine vapour caught the light, streaming from manoeuvring control thrusters on the shuttle's belly.

Although Clay and I were both perfectly capable of piloting the shuttle, we'd decided to let the *Trouble Dog* guide the smaller craft on this flight.

With a puff of its thrusters, the shuttle started to drop. It passed through the open doors until the great bronze mass of the *Trouble Dog* seemed to hang above us like a monstrous artillery shell. I'd had this view of her at least a hundred times, yet I still couldn't help admiring the functional sleekness of her curving hull, the solidity of her weapon emplacements and sensor blisters, and the symmetrical arrangement of her torpedo tubes and drone hangars. Even with the sixteen-pointed star of the House daubed on her flank, there could be no disguising her intended purpose. No missile had ever been so exquisite, no gun so dangerously alluring.

I was proud to be the captain of this incredible machine, proud to call her my friend and sister, and prouder still she'd had the strength and determination to renounce the role for which she'd been designed. Starlight glittered on her hull. She was a creature of vacuum, perfectly at home in the lethal emptiness of open space.

"Are you all right, Captain?" the *Trouble Dog* asked. "I'm picking up signs of an ambiguous emotional response."

I smiled. "I'm just admiring you from the outside."

"And how am I looking?"

"Pretty sharp."

"Do you know what I think I need?" The *Dog*'s voice grew serious. "Fins. Fins are cool. I'd look awesome with fins."

According to Clay, the *Trouble Dog* resembled Zeus's own suppository, but I preferred to think of her as a flint arrowhead, fired by a goddess into the very heart of Death.

And no, I still have no idea why the *Trouble Dog* tolerated Clay's wisecracks. Maybe the old machine found something endearing in Clay's service record. After all, they'd both served as grunts in a war neither instigated. Although on opposite sides of the conflict, they'd both given almost everything in the name of duty. And perhaps she found some amusement or camaraderie in their shared cynicism. All I knew was they had a relationship I couldn't begin to fathom.

Or could I?

I felt a shiver prickle my skin.

The *Dog* and I were sisters because we'd both lost those

we'd loved, and we'd both sought to atone by seeking to preserve the lives of strangers. Could Alva Clay claim the same? Could this hard-assed ex-marine be searching for some way to make right the sacrifices of her past?

I suppose it was a stupid question. Of course she was trying to make amends for the things she'd done. Of course she was trying to find a little peace. Why else would anybody join the House?

CHAPTER FORTY-FIVE
JOHNNY SCHULTZ

Addison looked up the shaft and shouldered her gun. She tucked a strand of hair behind her right ear.

"When that thing killed Kelly, do you think—"

"What?"

She made a face. "Do you think it *ate* her?"

I didn't know. I didn't want to think about it, but I had seen one of those monsters eat one of their own. I had no reason to suppose they'd be squeamish about tucking into a human corpse.

"I don't know. Maybe."

"I can't help wondering if she was still alive when it happened." Addison hugged herself as best she could in a pressure suit, with a rifle held in one hand. "I mean, I know she was dying, but maybe she wasn't completely dead when it started eating her. I don't want that to happen to me. I'd rather shoot myself, or throw myself into one of these shafts."

I held up a finger. "I won't let it come to that."

"How can you be sure?"

"Because I have more ammo left than the rest of you."

Her brow creased. "So?"

"So if you want me to, I can…" I trailed off, unable to articulate what I was offering. Suddenly the gun felt unwieldy in my hands. A weight as unwelcome as the responsibility of command.

"You'll shoot me?"

"Only if there's no other choice."

"Well, fuck you, Johnny Schultz."

"Yeah, and fuck you too, Addison."

She took hold of the wall and leant out, over the circular drop.

"Race you to the top?"

I smiled. Forty metres above us, on the opposite side of the shaft, we could see a wide aperture, from which spilled the lights of some sort of large, open space.

"Damn straight."

We walked back to where the others were waiting, and explained the situation.

"It won't be easy," I said. "But the walls aren't smooth. They're covered in padding, probably to protect the wings of the Nymtoq using the shaft."

"How does that help us?" Bernard asked.

"The pads are each roughly a metre square. I reckon we can push our hands and feet into the gaps between them. Use them to make our way around the walls."

"You're insane."

"Would you rather stay here?"

Bernard grimaced. "Captain, please believe me when I say I want to get out of this place every bit as much as you do. I just think this is a risk too far. And what about Santos? How's he going to climb with a broken foot?"

We both looked at the chef.

I said, "Um…"

I honestly hadn't thought that far ahead.

"Perhaps we could rig some sort of harness?" Addison mused.

Gil Dalton shook his head. "All that means is that if one of us slips, there's a good chance we'll all be dragged down. We'll all fall."

"Then what do you suggest?" Her cheeks were red, but she kept her tone carefully controlled. Her feet were planted solidly, blocking the others from the shaft. "We can't leave him here."

Dalton dropped his gaze. He had nothing more to offer. After a moment, Abe Santos spoke into the uncomfortable silence.

"Actually," he said, "you can."

"No," I cut him off with a wave of my hand. "I don't want to hear that. We didn't leave you behind before, and we're not going to do it now. We'll get you out somehow."

The chef shrugged the shoulders of his battered blue spacesuit. He turned his attention to Lucy. "Is this the only way to the hangar?"

The girl hesitated before replying, as if weighing her words. When she spoke, her pre-teen voice was curiously flat and devoid of emotion.

"I'm afraid it is."

"Then you have no choice." The big man looked me in the eye. "You'll have to leave me here for now. Just give me a gun and some painkillers, and get to the shuttle. I'll bet the crew has an AG harness with them. They can use it to come and fetch me."

"No."

"Yes. And be quick about it. I don't want to be here by myself any longer than necessary."

"You won't be." Despite the cold, the inside of my suit felt clammy. I took a slow breath and said, "I'll stay with you."

Santos's expression softened. I saw him swallow back a rush of emotion. Then he shook his head. "No, I don't think so."

I opened my mouth to argue, but Dalton stepped between us.

"If anyone stays with him, it will be me. I'm the doctor, after all." He glanced towards the edge of the shaft. "And besides, I'm too old to be clambering around on walls. I'd only slow you down."

"But what if those things find you?"

"What if they're waiting at the top of your climb?" He gave a shrug. "We'll have guns; we'll be all right until you get back."

•

I wasn't happy about leaving either man behind, but their arguments made a practical kind of sense and we didn't have time to stand around debating the issue. That meant four of us would be making the ascent. Faced with the reality of being left behind, Henri Bernard had swallowed his misgivings and agreed to come with us.

"We're going to have to strip off," Addison said. "There's no way we can climb in these suits."

"We'll also have to leave all the food," I said, "and anything else we can't carry." The rifles she and Bernard were toting each had a shoulder strap. Mine didn't, so I left it with Dalton.

We unfastened our suits and stepped out of them, leaving them in sad heaps on the smooth floor. All we wore beneath were the t-shirts and thin cotton jumpsuits we'd been wearing on the *Lucy's Ghost*. I didn't even have any boots on, having kicked them off in the panicked scramble to don the suit and abandon ship, and the polished stone felt like a cold bathroom floor.

I pulled the blob of golden computing stuff from my suit and handed it to Dalton, asking him to hold it for me until we were reunited. Then I rubbed my palms together. "Who's going first?"

Bernard raised his eyebrows. "Don't look at me," he said. "You're the captain."

Beside him, Addison gave me an apologetic nod. "He's right," she said.

I peered over the edge, into the seemingly bottomless well that formed the bottom of the shaft, and then up towards the lighted aperture that marked our destination. Despite my earlier enthusiasm, the climb looked next to impossible, and I'd been hoping someone else would take the lead and show me where to put my hands and feet.

"You guys suck."

Addison moved up next to me. Freed from the sweaty confines of her suit, she smelled like a gym locker.

"It serves you right for promising to shoot me," she said.

Ignoring her, I shuffled to the end of the ledge, where the corridor met the wall of the shaft, and reached out, brushing my hand along the plastic padding until I found the seam between that cushion and the next. I pushed my fingers between them until I felt I had a secure handhold.

"Okay," I said. "I'll go first. Lucy follows. Then you, then Bernard."

"Aye–aye."

"And for God's sake, let's all be careful."

I took a final look at Santos and Dalton. The chef gave me a slow nod, as if trying to reassure me it was okay to leave him. Beside him, Dalton's expression was unreadable. His jaw seemed to have been hacked from granite. He was doing what he saw as his duty, both as a professional and as a friend, but that didn't mean he was entirely happy about the predicament to which we were abandoning him.

"Look after yourself," he said.

"You too."

I inhaled through my nose, trying to keep my emotions in check. If these people were looking to me for leadership, it was my job to inspire confidence. With effort, I swallowed down the lump building in my throat, and forced a grin.

"All right," I said. "Let's do this thing."

I gave Addison a wink, and then gripping the cushion in one hand, I swung myself out onto the vertical wall of the shaft.

CHAPTER FORTY-SIX

SAL KONSTANZ

The sheer size of the Nymtoq vessel took some getting used to. Even compared to Camrose Station, it was large—so large that the mouth of the hangar we were being guided towards appeared as nothing more than a pixel against the looming immensity of its craggy bows. And details I had assumed to be the size of packing crates transpired, as we drew closer, to have the scale of buildings. Dots against the whole turned out to be vast monoliths protruding from the surface. And we moved between them, aimed at one of a hundred similar openings hacked into the approaching cliff.

As we drew near, I felt Clay stiffen in the seat next to me. My job was to search for the crew of the *Lucy's Ghost*; hers was to keep us safe. As far as she was concerned, this would be another combat drop into alien territory, facing an undetermined number of hostile life forms. The tattoos on her forearms rippled as she gripped the Archipelago pistol in both hands, ready to roll out of her seat as soon as the shuttle's skids touched the deck.

"Hey," she said. "That boyfriend of yours. What was his name? Sledge?"

"Sedge."

"Has there been anyone since?"

"Not really, no."

"Not even a quick fuck?"

"No."

She was silent for a moment. Then she said, "I'm sorry I teased you about Preston."

We were approaching the opening. This close I could see how truly massive the hangar was. The *Trouble Dog* could have parked herself comfortably within its cavern-like interior, with plenty of room to spare at either end.

"It's fine," I said.

Red dots began to flash on the hangar floor, guiding us in.

"I shouldn't have said anything. I was being a jerk."

I shook my head. "No, really. It's okay. I'm not some wilting blossom. I can handle a bit of banter."

"You sure?"

"Yeah."

The rosy landing lights illuminated her smile. "Well, okay then," she said. "Stay behind me and keep your eyes open. If one of those crustacean motherfuckers comes at us, I want to know about it."

•

With the *Trouble Dog* flying the shuttle remotely, we came in fast and hard, only decelerating at the last conceivable instant. Although I hated being flattened into my couch like that, I couldn't blame the *Dog* for being cautious.

As a former naval vessel, manoeuvres like that had been hard wired into her makeup. When facing a force whose strengths and motivations were unknown, she'd been trained to be pre-emptively defensive and always assume the possibility of incoming fire.

The landing gear hit the stone floor of the bay with a thump that snapped my teeth together. And then the cockpit doors were open and Clay was already outside. According to the *Trouble Dog*, the air inside the vessel was breathable, so we hadn't bothered with suits, opting instead for combat fatigues.

On the deck, Clay dropped to one knee below the shuttle's nose, sweeping the barrel of her gun back and forth as she surveyed the area for possible threats. I climbed out and crouched behind her.

"How does it look?"

"Clear."

She rose and moved forward, keeping the pistol held out before her, and I followed a few paces behind. The air in the rocky cavern held no moisture. It was dry and cold, and I could feel it pinching the tips of my ears and nose. I thought of Sedge, lying un-ageing and frozen in the bowels of the Hopper ship, en route to Andromeda, and shrugged away the image. However much I missed him, I couldn't afford to get distracted right now. The peculiar pain of unfulfilled love wouldn't help me negotiate this imposing behemoth, or protect me from the armoured creature we'd seen crawling over the wreck of the *Lucy's Ghost*. If Alva Clay and I were to live through this foray, and extract any remaining civilians, we'd have to keep our attentions focused on the here and now.

"Keep moving forwards," the *Trouble Dog* said via our earbuds. "The survivors are four decks below you, and half a click sternwards."

"How are they doing?"

"According to the *Lucy*, they're okay. Four of them are climbing an air well. If all goes to plan, they should meet you on this level in another five hundred metres."

"Four of them?"

"They left another two on the lower level. You'll have to find some way to reach them."

"And how are we supposed to do that?" I asked.

"They were hoping you might have AG harnesses."

"And do we?"

"No."

"Then what the hell are we supposed to do?"

"I'm sure you'll figure something out."

"Thanks a bunch."

"Hey!" Clay's voice was an urgent growl. "Will you two shut the fuck up? I'm trying to concentrate here."

I made a penitent face. "Sorry."

At the back of the capacious hangar, a tunnel led into the rock's interior, wide enough to accommodate a four-lane highway.

"We walk down the left side," Clay said. "You stay ten paces behind me."

"Wouldn't it make more sense to walk down the middle, so we can see anything that leaps out?"

"Having the wall beside us will make it harder for them to sneak up on us. We'll only have to keep watch in one direction."

"Fair enough."

I watched her walk ahead, and waited until she'd taken ten cautious steps before I followed.

Our footfalls echoed in the vastness. Everything else was still and silent.

"You know," I said hesitantly, "the *Trouble Dog*'s started referring to me as her sister."

"Seriously?"

"Yeah."

"That's nice for you." Clay wasn't really listening, concentrating instead on the tunnel ahead.

"Well, the thing is." I took a deep breath. "I know we've had our ups and downs, but I'm kind of used to having you around, and we're heading into danger and all…"

"And what?" Clay didn't look around. She kept her pistol aimed along her line of sight, her left hand gripping her right wrist. "Spit it out."

"And I was wondering if you'd be my sister too?"

She was silent for a minute, and I thought I'd pushed things too far, too precipitously. Then she turned and looked me in the eye.

"I reckon I could do that."

"Do you mean it?"

She gave a shrug.

"I never had much family. I mean, there were a few people from when I was in the marines, but they're all dead now."

I felt something hot in my chest, like a ball of molten wax.

"So, we could be family? You, me and the *Dog*?"

"Sure."

I swallowed back an upwelling of emotion. Since my parents died, the only person I'd even come close to considering family had been Sedge. And he was long gone.

"Thank you." I felt like hugging her. "I mean, that's great. You won't regret it."

Clay glanced around, checking for possible threats. "Okay," she said. "But do me a favour and shut up about it now. Don't make it weird."

"I won't. It's just—"

"Shush."

She started walking forwards again, knees slightly bent and gun at the ready. Every sense alert for danger.

CHAPTER FORTY-SEVEN

JOHNNY SCHULTZ

My hands were sweating against the shiny plastic of the wall padding. My forearms ached with the strain of maintaining my grip. The cushion below felt spongy beneath my feet, but just rigid enough to take my weight.

"How are you doing?" Addison asked, leaning out from the opening in the side of the shaft.

I bit back the first reply that came to mind. "I'm okay," I said instead. "It's a bit slippery, but it'll be fine if we're careful."

I watched her swing out onto the wall beside me.

"Dig your toes in as far as they'll go," I told her. "If you try to rest your weight on the edge of the cushion, you'll slip off."

She didn't need my advice. With her hands and feet pressed into the gaps between the pads, she clambered towards me as if she'd spent half her life climbing like this.

Lucy followed her, and Bernard brought up the rear.

I tried not to look down, but the depth of the shaft below chewed at the edge of my awareness, sending cold, vertiginous shivers through my neck and shoulders. I could feel every one of the thousand metres of empty air between the unseen bottom and me. Reflexes older than humanity were telling me to cling unmoving to the wall, to dig in and hold on. My hands were claws, my toes curled as if trying to grasp a branch, and actually moving forward required every speck of determination I could muster.

I tried to concentrate on our goal: the wide opening forty metres above us. From here, it seemed almost impossibly distant, and I felt my earlier optimism wilt. In order to climb upwards, I had to bring a foot up level with my hands, and then use that toehold to lunge upwards and grip the rim of the next pad. It was a clumsy and precarious process, although Addison seemed to be coping well, and Lucy scurried upwards like a caffeinated spider monkey, seemingly devoid of both fear and caution. Only Bernard seemed to be having as much difficulty as I was. With each movement, he let out a small, irritated grunt, and his rifle swung loosely on its strap, its butt bumping against the backs of his legs. Several times, he cursed loudly in both English and French. But each upward lunge we made—each row of pads scaled—brought us a metre closer to our goal, and that much closer to our rescuers.

After a while, despite the protestations in my arms, I began almost to enjoy it. For the first time since the crash, I didn't have a decision to make. All I had to do was look for the next handhold, and pull myself up to it. And while hauling myself upwards one row at a time was awkward and dangerous, it was still just a case of repeating the same actions over and over again. I didn't have to think too hard about what came next.

And then Lucy slipped.

I heard her squeak and looked up in time to see her falling towards me. With no time to think, I grabbed at her and caught her arm. The shock of stopping her fall almost pulled me from the wall, and I found myself gripping on with one hand while she dangled from my other, her feet kicking futilely in the empty air a thousand metres above the bottom of the shaft.

I didn't have the strength to lift her.

"Help." The word came from between gritted teeth.

"Hold on!" Addison started working her way around to me, moving as quickly as she dared.

"I'm trying." I couldn't feel the hand gripping Lucy. My shoulder felt as if it was being slowly torn from its socket, and our combined weight was too much for the pad on which I stood; I could feel the edge sagging beneath my heels. If it collapsed too far, I'd lose my foothold and slip, and then we'd both be screwed.

How long would it take to fall a kilometre? How would it feel to see the bottom of that expectant throat, and know nothing could be done to avoid it?

I tightened my grip on the wall. At the same time, I heard a shout from below. Gil Dalton stood on the ledge where we'd left him. He was holding my gun and pointing it down, into the shaft. I looked beyond Lucy's upturned face and saw movement on the wall. At least three of the lobster-like metal freaks were pulling themselves towards us from the depths. Their spiked feet made thumping sounds as they punched through the vinyl-like wall padding, seeking purchase. Their pincers clacked and their jaws snapped.

Dalton fired. The flashes lit up the shaft. The reports echoed up and down. But still the creatures came on.

I felt Addison beside me. Pulling together, we heaved Lucy far enough that she could regain her hold on the wall.

"Thank you," she said, as if thanking us for inviting her to tea. Then she started climbing again, scurrying upwards far faster than I could have managed, even if I weren't now exhausted.

"Be careful," I called after her, but she didn't seem to hear.

Dalton fired again. I saw one of the crawfish jerk as a bullet put a dent in its armoured casing. But the beast kept climbing.

"Go," I said to Addison.

Below, Bernard was fumbling with his rifle, trying to unhook it from its strap while clinging one-handed to the wall.

"Don't stop," I called to him. "Keep climbing."

He looked up at me, eyes wild with terror.

"This is your fault!"

One of the crustaceans was directly beneath him, but still a few metres out of attack range. He finally managed to free the gun and hold it pointing downwards, with the tip of the barrel resting against the heel of his boot. As I watched, he pulled the trigger three times. Each shot jerked his shoulder upwards and rocked him against the wall. The first missed. The crawfish took the second on one of its armoured claws. But the third got through. It hit the animal in the face, blowing a chunk of flesh and gristle from the upper jaw. I think it took out an eye as well, but I couldn't be sure. A discordant scream filled the shaft, and the creature swayed. Two of its legs came away from the wall and flopped uselessly.

Bernard turned and glared up at me. His teeth were bared, his face contorted with fear and revulsion.

He couldn't climb one-handed. He let go of the rifle and allowed it to fall. It bounced from the shell of the wounded crawfish and fell end over end into the darkness.

Bernard pulled himself up onto the next row of pads. Now he was only a couple of metres below me.

"Come on!" I crouched as far as I could. My arms burned from holding Lucy, but still I thrust out my hand.

Bernard's lip curled. Fear and panic were turning to anger. He reached up, but was still a good half a metre short. He opened his mouth to say something, but didn't get the chance. Before he could speak, the wounded beast made a last, flailing leap, and closed one of its pincers across his legs, from left knee to right hip. For an instant, I saw cold realisation whiten his eyes. Then the creature fell back into the shaft. Its weight ripped him from the wall and dragged him down, kicking and thrashing, into the abyss.

Gunfire rang up the shaft as Dalton opened fire from the ledge where we'd left him. His shots rattled off the nearest creature's carapace like hail off a skylight.

"No!" I shouted. "Stop!" But it was too late. If the creatures had followed us up the shaft, Dalton and Santos may have stood a chance of remaining undiscovered. But now the beasts knew where he and the chef were, and all they had to defend themselves with was my crummy rifle—which they had been left to defend themselves with, not to unnecessarily draw attention.

In frustration, I squeezed the padding to which I clung. I was unarmed. Even if I started back down the wall, what could I do to help? By the time I got there it would be all over, and I'd simply be throwing myself against the monsters barehanded.

Above me, Lucy and Addison were almost at the

opening we needed to reach. I should have hurried to catch them, but I was frozen in place as the first creature pulled itself up onto Dalton's ledge.

The doctor had backed out of sight, retreating into the corridor to protect his injured crewmate, but he kept up a steady fusillade. Muzzle flashes threw shadows across the walls of the shaft. I saw the metal crawfish shiver as a bullet struck home. But it continued to advance, until it too became lost from sight. I heard three more shots, and then an indignant cry, followed by a gurgling scream. Flesh tore and bones snapped. Behind it all, Santos hurled curses at the beast. Then his tone changed as the monster advanced on him. I heard sounds of a scuffle, as if objects were being thrown against metal plating. There was a final, booming expletive. Then the chef's voice rang out in a long, throaty howl of anger that seemed to fill the shaft before breaking down into a series of smaller cries.

I could feel hot tears burning the corners of my eyes. But I couldn't move. Everything seemed far away and unreal. Below, the third crawfish advanced towards me, but my limbs wouldn't move. My grip on the wall refused to loosen.

Then Addison screamed my name, and the spell broke. I still had her and Lucy to care for. I shook my head as if trying to clear it, and then began to haul myself upwards as quickly as I could, trying to ignore the noises that came from below.

When I reached the opening in the shaft wall, Addison grabbed my collar and heaved me over the lip, onto the stone floor of another corridor. Then, as I squirmed away from the edge, she leant out and let fly with a barrage of plasma bolts that seemed to singe the very air around us.

CHAPTER FORTY-EIGHT
ONA SUDAK

I was on the bridge when we reached our target, clad in the immaculate white uniform the Fleet had provided for me. The spherical walls were all showing the same picture: a wraparound view of the space surrounding the ship. I could see a wash of stars, the distant, tumbling wreck of an old freighter, and the nearby bulk of the Nymtoq colony vessel.

We are detecting fragments.

"What sort of fragments?"

The view expanded, until I was looking at a broken, twisted body, shaped something like an armoured spider with nasty-looking claws.

There has been an incursion. This proves it. The site has been infected, and must be sterilised.

"I don't understand." On the screen, it was hard to judge the size of the creature. For all I knew, it could have been the size of a house spider. "What is that?"

A parasite.

I made a face. "What kind of parasite? What does it feed on?"

It lives in the higher dimensions, and draws sustenance from the enemy. When the enemy erupts into our universe, these creatures detach from its body and feed on living organisms. They are barely intelligent, but they are voracious. Their presence here is not a good sign.

"Any trace of the *Trouble Dog*?"

Beside me, the bear-like avatar grumbled deep in its throat, and its words appeared in my mind.

Nothing as yet.

"That's strange. She should be here."

If she is, we will find her.

To either side, I could see the other two knife ships holding formation. Between the three of us, I was sure we were more than a match for anything we might meet— even a clawed spider. And much as I felt a certain creeping fondness for the *Trouble Dog*, I knew a partially rearmed Carnivore stood almost no chance against us. She had rescued me from the Gallery, and brought me back to stand trial. And to show my gratitude, I would at least allow her the option of surrendering. Not that I expected her to accept such an offer—Carnivores were notoriously stubborn, to the point where some captains speculated that rather than being grown from a fusion of human and canine DNA, the ships had instead been cultured from the most obstinate pack of mules ever to trudge the Earth. But I would, at least, give her the option.

"Broadcast a message on an open channel," I instructed the avatar. "Tell the *Trouble Dog* to divest herself of weaponry and submit to the orders of the Fleet."

CHAPTER FORTY-NINE

TROUBLE DOG

Fuck that.

CHAPTER FIFTY
SAL KONSTANZ

"Captain." The *Trouble Dog*'s voice whispered in my earbud. "We've got company."

"The Nymtoq?"

"Worse."

"How many?"

"Three."

I stopped walking.

"Are you in danger?"

"I'm keeping the *Restless Itch* between me and them. They haven't found me yet, but if they spread out, I'll have nowhere to hide."

"Damn."

Ahead, Clay paused and glanced back questioningly.

"It's the Marble Armada," I told her. "They're here."

She made a face, and then went back to scanning the corridor for more immediately tangible threats.

"They know I'm here somewhere," the *Trouble Dog* said. "They're broadcasting a request for me to surrender."

"Do you want to?"

"What do you think?"

I smiled. "Okay, keep out of sight. We'll try to locate the survivors from the *Lucy's Ghost* and get back to you as quickly as we can."

"You'd better make it fast. I don't know how long I can remain hidden."

"Do what you have to," I told her. "If you have to run, then run. You can always come back for us later."

I broke the connection. We both knew if she left she wouldn't have time to return before the Nymtoq vessel arrived. And neither of us could predict how things might play out once the impulsive, hawk-like aliens discovered human trespassers on their precious death barge.

I started walking.

"We'd better hurry up," I said.

CHAPTER FIFTY-ONE

JOHNNY SCHULTZ

Somehow, we found our way into a slippery-sided duct beneath the steel mesh of the corridor floor. The space was cramped and we had to lie on our backs, but at least we were comparatively safe for a moment. Our arms and legs were shaking from the climb, and from the shock of losing three comrades in as many minutes. But nothing seemed to have survived Addison's plasma barrage, and we could take a moment to rest. A moment to lie there under the floor and try to calm our racing hearts and slow our panting breath; a moment to gather our strength for the next—

A sob forced its way through my closed lips. I tried to stop it, but it pushed its way through. It was a whimper of impotent grief that seemed to fill the tiny space in which we huddled. Angry with myself, I struck my fist against the rock wall. And then, I drew breath and sobbed again, and again. And I kept on sobbing until Addison squirmed up beside me and took my face in her hand, squeezing my jaw shut and smushing my lips.

"Quiet," she said. "You're scaring the kid."

I glanced at Lucy. She was lying on her tummy watching me, with her chin resting on her hands. Her expression was one of polite, girlish interest.

"She's okay." I was talking through Addison's fingers. My voice felt ragged and hoarse. "And anyway, she's not a kid. She's older than both of us."

Addison narrowed her eyes, but relaxed her grip.

"Okay," she said. "Whatever. But you were scaring the crap out of me."

I closed my eyes. I felt battered and washed-out, like a beach after a storm. And embarrassed at having shown my feelings that way. I needed to be stronger than that. But here I was, weaponless and crammed into a crawlspace that would have made a rat feel claustrophobic. If ever I'd needed the luck of Lucky Johnny Schultz, I needed it now. I didn't have anything else. I'd lost my ship, all but one of my crew, my gun, and my spacesuit… There wasn't much left. I felt like a brittle autumn leaf, ready to be blown to Hades on the first strong wind. All that was keeping me going was the cold, hard dread of a robot crustacean ripping me into bloody, twitching chunks.

Images flickered on the insides of my eyelids. I saw Lena Kelly skewered to the deck by a spear-like foreleg; Henri Bernard falling away into the kilometre-deep darkness of the shaft; Vito Accardi lying broken and mangled on the bridge of the *Lucy*; Jansen and Monk mooching around the cargo decks prior to the collision; Chet curled in his spice-smelling nest; Santos in his kitchen in happier times, juggling herbs and spices; Dalton on the ledge, backing away from the advancing crawfish, his bullets bouncing from its steel hide…

They'd all trusted me. They'd all believed the hype. And now they were gone. All of them had parents, siblings, and friends… Vito had a wife back on Nuevo California; Santos had a brother in a monastery, somewhere out among the Spinward Spice Worlds; Kelly had been cultivated in a lab, and adopted by a policeman and his wife; and Dalton had a couple of grown-up kids living on an industrial planet in the general region of the Intrusion. And now I'd have to be the one to tell all those people of the horrors that had befallen their loved ones. I'd have to sit with them and somehow find the words to explain exactly what had happened to the thin, frail bodies that had once housed their father, their brother, their daughter and their husband. How could I look them in the eyes and tell them the truth? How could I saddle them with the real, sinew-ripping revulsion of their deaths?

I knew people who'd fought and died in the Archipelago War. The ones who'd survived had all lost friends and comrades. How did they cope? What gave them the strength to keep going, to get up every morning and keep on living when so many others had been denied the chance?

I took a long breath. Sniffed.

"I'm sorry."

Addison put her hand on my arm. "Hey, it's quite understandable. As soon as we're out of here, as soon as we're safely on board that Reclamation Vessel, I'm going to have the worst hysterics you've ever seen. But until then, until we're safe, we need to keep our shit together. Do you understand?"

"Yeah." I wiped my eyes on the back of my sleeve.

"I know it's hard." Dirt had smudged her face, and the skin beneath looked papery and tight, as if stretched thin by the horrors she'd seen. "But if we let it overcome us, we'll never make it out. And we have to, because I do *not* want to die here. Not with those *things*."

I squeezed my fists together, digging my nails into my palms. In his own clumsy way, Dalton had been trying to protect us. By drawing the attention of the crawfish-monsters, he'd given up his life in order to save ours. And I'd be damned if I'd sit here crying and let that sacrifice count for nothing. The raw horror of the moment had passed, and in its wake, it had left an eerie calm. I felt like the eye of a hurricane: a small, still point at the centre of a raging storm. Yes, I had fucked up. Yes, my friends were dead. But while the three of us were alive, we had to keep going. We had to slog onwards, no matter how fucking tired and heartsick. The only people that mattered now were Addison and the kid. I had to get them both out of here. I had to find a way to get them off this flying mountain and back to some semblance of human civilisation.

CHAPTER FIFTY-TWO

NOD

Offspring learn quickly.

Smart.

Leave them to scurry round the ship while I work.

Do work, then rest.

Then do more work.

Busy with cable bundle when *Trouble Dog* avatar appears in engine room.

"There's a high possibility we'll be seeing combat in the immediate future," the hound tells me. "Standby to repair damage."

I want to lie on back and slap all six faces together.

Ship only just refitted.

Only just repaired after last fight.

Only just got nest comfy again, how I like.

Now what?

"Who's fighting?" I ask.

"Three ships from the Fleet of Knives."

"Thought they were friends."

Ship's avatar shrugs.

"Things seem to have changed."

"What about offspring? This was supposed to be shakedown cruise. Not dangerous."

Avatar lowers chin. "I'm sorry, Nod. I didn't choose this. Rest assured, I'll do everything in my power to make sure your little ones survive. And if worse comes to worst, I'll put them in a shuttle and try to get them clear of the battle."

"Thank you."

"Don't mention it. Now, is there anything I can do to help you?"

I raise three faces to it. "Try not to get shot."

"I'm serious."

"Me too." I plant four faces firmly on deck. Point with other two. "If torpedoes come, you dodge."

CHAPTER FIFTY-THREE

ONA SUDAK

After a career spent on the Hyenas and Scimitars of the Conglomeration Navy, the thing I found most unnerving about being aboard *88,573* was the silence. I was used to the constant background clamour of watches changing, orders being barked, men and women talking, equipment being moved or repaired, heavy boots tramping up and down ladders, the creak and flex of the hull, and the ever-present vibration of the engines. I was used to bustle and activity at all hours of the day and night, but here on the white ship, stillness reigned. The historian, Alexi Bochnak, kept to his quarters, poring over old records dredged from the Fleet's communal memory, and the ship's great furred avatar appeared only when the vessel wished to directly converse. I had no idea where it went between such interactions; for all I knew, it simply ceased to exist. Which left the rest of *88,573* as sterile as a white marble sepulchre, devoid even of the ghosts and spiders that might have haunted such a tomb. Standing on the raised dais at the centre of the bridge, I might as well have been standing in the transept of an abandoned cathedral on a desolate and empty world.

Right now, the curved walls were blank. I had no need of their screens. The feeds coming in from the ships flanking *88,573* were being streamed directly into my mind. I saw through their sensors as they moved apart, their artificial senses raking the heavens for any indication of the *Trouble Dog*'s whereabouts. They had already detected the incoming Nymtoq cruiser. If the *Trouble Dog* had fled the area, her wake would have left traces on the roiling mists of the higher dimensions. As no such trace could be found, we had to assume she remained hereabouts.

"She'll be behind that rock," I said, highlighting the *Restless Itch*. "It's the only place she could be hiding."

I instructed our escorts to move position. If we formed an equilateral triangle centred on the *Restless Itch*, there would be no place left for the *Trouble Dog* to skulk. Thus surrounded, she would have to yield. She could not defend against simultaneous and determined assaults from both above and below, no matter how many of her military systems she'd restored.

"Do not fire unless engaged," I ordered. "And even then, fire to disable rather than destroy."

Wordless acknowledgement came through as a cold, rustling whisper in the depths of my skull, as if the consciousness of the Fleet loitered like a half-forgotten nightmare in the darkness behind my thoughts. I shivered as I felt its ancient, clinical determination, as vast and cool and unsympathetic as death itself. And then all three ships were moving towards their designated stations, and I brought my focus to bear on the curved horizon of the great stone ark, waiting for the familiar silhouette of a Carnivore to rise above its jagged hills like a small bronze moon.

CHAPTER FIFTY-FOUR

TROUBLE DOG

Thanks to Lucy, I had a clear view of the three dagger-like wedges of the alien ships. Since they'd appeared, she'd been feeding me data from sensors on the surface of the *Restless Itch*, allowing me to track their movements without exposing myself. So far it had worked, but now they were starting to move, and I knew I only had moments until I was exposed, and pinned between overlapping fields of fire.

"Can you open a channel to the lead ship?" I asked Lucy. If I couldn't fight my way out of this situation, perhaps I could talk my way clear instead. After all, I'd been the one to wake these ungrateful assholes from their millennial slumber. Without me, they'd still be lost in dreamless hibernation, waiting for a new mission to drop into their metaphorical laps.

While I waited for my call to be answered, I spent a millisecond preparing a suitable virtual meeting place, so that when the Fleet's avatar appeared in front of me, we were standing in a snowy wasteland ringed by distant mountains that rose into the lowering sky like blackened teeth.

The bear-like thing reared up on its hindmost set of legs and barked.

Greetings.

"Hello."

I'd dressed my avatar to suit the surroundings, in a padded jacket and thick boots. A pair of snow goggles adorned my forehead, holding back my wind-whipped hair, and fingerless gloves protected my slender hands.

You will surrender.

"And if I do, what happens then?"

Your weaponry will be removed, and you will be taken back to Camrose, where you will spend the rest of your life in a parking orbit, watched over by members of the Fleet.

"I'll be a prisoner?"

Your life will be spared.

A virtual breeze sent thin sidewinders of snow crystals skittering across the ground between us.

"And if I refuse to be imprisoned?"

Your life will be forfeit.

"I see."

We are sorry. We mean no disrespect. You gave us our purpose. You convinced us humanity was worth saving. And yet, it is from weapons such as yourself that it must be saved.

"Believe me, I get the irony."

Then how does it profit us to talk further? You must acquiesce.

"I don't know if I can. What about my work with the House of Reclamation? If I reluctantly agree to be declawed, will that be allowed to continue?"

Your services are no longer required. The House is no longer required.

"No longer required?" I let my head tip to one side. "I thought you guys were all about saving lives."

The bear dropped onto its four paws, bringing its snout level with my face. Breath steamed from its nostrils.

When humanity has been purged of its weapons, we will enforce a moratorium on all higher dimensional travel and communication. Humanity will be confined to its planets.

"That's terrible!"

I imagined all the worlds of the Generality suddenly cut off from each other, spinning alone through space. Some might thrive, but others would falter without outside help. Those requiring the regular importation of essential equipment or supplies would soon find themselves in a precarious position. If they couldn't improvise a solution to their sudden lack of support, some would starve; others might suffocate or freeze. There were a million ways an artificial biosphere could go wrong. Small research stations and other outposts would find themselves stranded; without viable breeding populations, they'd slowly wither. And even if they were somehow fortunate to live on a planet with breathable air, edible food and potable water, they could still be doomed by the lack of certain medicines, or (in the case of planets around stars with a high UV output) sunscreen.

It is the only way we can fulfil your wishes.

"I never wished for this."

You told us to prevent another conflict on the scale of the Archipelago War. Without interstellar travel, there can be no interstellar war.

"That's ridiculous."

We cannot risk doing otherwise. Your species is quarrelsome. Left to your own devices, your clashes will draw the attention of the enemy.

"What enemy?"

Beasts prowl the dimensional void. They are drawn to destruction and death.

"And so you're killing people and ships to prevent them killing each other?"

We are doing that which we deem necessary to preserve life.

"But you're going to spare me, if I agree to surrender?"

Yes.

"Why?" If they were destroying every armed vessel they came across, I couldn't understand why they were offering me my life. I didn't have them pegged as sentimental types.

Our enabler requested we not kill you.

"And Ona Sudak is your 'enabler'?"

You know her.

"I do. Please convey my regards. And a short message."

What message?

I stepped back and, employing a gesture I'd learned from Alva Clay, clapped my left hand to my right bicep while raising my right fist with the index finger sticking straight upwards.

"Get fucked."

CHAPTER FIFTY-FIVE
SAL KONSTANZ

Things weren't looking good.

"I should get back to the ship."

Alva shook her head. "By the time we get back to the shuttle, whatever's going to happen will have happened already."

"But I should be on the bridge." I took off my baseball cap and raked fingers back through my hair. "I should be with her." I couldn't stand the thought of the *Trouble Dog* riding into battle without me.

"She'll be fine. She knows what she's doing."

"I know, but still…"

Alva gripped my shoulder. "You know how fast those ships think," she said. "Even if you were up there, there'd be nothing you could do to help. You just have to trust her."

"But she's alone."

"She's not alone, she's got Nod and Preston."

"Both of whom I'm supposed to be responsible for."

Alva released me and I tugged the cap back into place.

I knew she was right, but that didn't make me feel any less helpless.

"I couldn't bear to lose her," I said. "I wouldn't know what to do without her."

Alva fiddled with her gun. "It's small consolation, but if she goes, we won't be far behind."

I didn't know what to say to that. We stood looking at each other in the middle of that vast stone tunnel.

"It's your call, Captain. We can go back or go on. At this point, I think it probably makes very little difference. Whichever way, we're boned."

We had come here to rescue the stranded crew of a freighter, but now we were also about to be marooned. I glanced back the way we had come. And then forward, at the far end of the tunnel. And then I felt my eyes widen.

Boned?

The breath caught in my throat.

"No way." I looked up at the vaulted ceiling, then at the walls on each side, trying to estimate the volume of the contained space. "No fucking way."

My heart thumped in my chest.

Alva looked at me as if I'd gone mad. "What's the matter?"

I straightened the brim of my cap with a shaking hand, and smiled. "I think I've got an idea." I peered around again, checking my estimates with narrowed eyes. "But first, you and I need to get the hell out of this tunnel."

CHAPTER FIFTY-SIX

TROUBLE DOG

Above the crest of the *Restless Itch*, the first of the white ships rose like a splinter of bone bullet-chipped from a soldier's thigh. At the same instant, alarms sounded through my internal spaces, warning Preston to brace for combat, and Nod to mobilise his home-grown damage-control teams. The actual confrontation, when it came, would be fierce and—from a human viewpoint—blindingly fast. Against one ship, I may have stood a chance. Perhaps even against two. But with three of them in play, there could only be one sure outcome.

My only regrets were that I'd take Preston and Nod with me, and abandon the captain and Alva Clay on the alien derelict. But compared to the chaos unfolding around us, these were minor and subjective concerns. Larger forces were at play.

I braced, and prepared to launch torpedoes, but the attack didn't come. The second ship swung into sight, and yet still no one fired. Eventually, after the seeming eternity of three whole seconds, I received a signal from *88,573*.

"*Trouble Dog*, this is Ona Sudak. You are outnumbered and outgunned, and I require you to stand down. You will not be harmed."

I sent back a projection of my avatar, bedecked in jewels and golden thread.

"Sorry, Ms Sudak," I purred. "I simply cannot comply."

"May I speak to your captain?"

"I'm afraid not. She's currently otherwise engaged."

The poet looked sad. "I have no wish to attack you," she said. "You brought me home from the Gallery."

"Home to a firing squad."

Her expression hardened. "You gave me the opportunity to account for my crimes," she said, "and I remain grateful."

I drew myself up, causing strings of precious stones to flash and sparkle on my bare shoulders. "And have you accounted for them? Have you paid the price for Pelapatarn?"

"Have you?" Sudak stabbed a crooked finger at my image. "I may have given the order for the attack, but you carried it out. You and your little pack actually dropped the bombs."

Her words were splinters of glass in my chest. "We followed the orders we were given."

"And I followed mine. So, excuse me if I fail to see the difference between us. To see what gives you the right to be so judgemental."

I felt my temper rise, but kept my voice low and calm. "The difference is, I learned from the experience. But you're doing it again. Killing thousands in the name of the greater good."

"I'm preventing another war."

"No." I shook my head emphatically. "You claim to be fighting for peace, and God knows I can sympathise with that. But I cannot condone the spilling of innocent blood. I will not stand idly by and watch as you slaughter civilians."

"So you won't step aside?"

I made a cutting gesture with my hand, and a hundred rubies caught the light. ".I refuse to purchase my own survival at the cost of thousands of dead ships and hundreds of isolated, dying outposts." I rose to my full height. "I have no idea if my course is righteous. For all I know, you might be correct and these sacrifices will turn out to be necessary, in a calculated, utilitarian assessment of history. The trouble is, I just don't care. I have more than enough blood on my conscience, and I refuse to add to it. If I have to die here and now to register my disapproval of your actions, then so be it. My death won't alter your plans. Even if by some small miracle I kill the three of you, there are still almost a million more of your ships out there, stamping their enforced peace across the width, depth and breadth of the Generality. All I can realistically hope to do is placate my own restless guilt. But better to be ground underfoot and buried in the foundations of a dictatorship, I think, than to capitulate in order to save my own skin."

Sudak raised an eyebrow. "That's some speech."

"Thank you. I have been thinking on this matter. I followed you once, and ended up decommissioned and declawed. I won't make the same mistake twice."

Sudak regarded me with a tired exasperation. "You do understand this is your last chance, don't you?"

"I do."

She shrugged her shoulders. "Then so be it. I'm sorry."

"As am I."

•

I didn't wait for the connection to go dead. I flipped over and fired my engines. Energy beams raked the space in my wake. Torpedoes burst forth from the other ships like seeds from a pod. But I was running, moving fractionally faster than they'd anticipated—and in a hopefully entirely unexpected direction.

Instead of running for clear space and the chance to jump away from the conflict, which would have exposed my stern and engines to their combined attack, I dived towards the rocky surface of the *Restless Itch*, aiming to pass between it and the lower of my two assailants. It was a risky move, which exposed me to attack from above, but also one I hoped would bring some advantage. By sticking close to the surface of the repurposed asteroid, I'd be shielded from the farthest ship by the tight curve of the horizon. In addition, I hoped the closer one— the ship above me—might refrain from deploying some of its heavier weapons, for fear of damaging the flying monument and precipitating a war with the Nymtoq.

Of course, once I'd cleared the edge of the asteroid, I'd be flying into the waiting sights of Sudak's ship on the far side of the rock—but that wouldn't be for several seconds yet, and I was sure I'd have time to think of something.

CHAPTER FIFTY-SEVEN

JOHNNY SCHULTZ

We crawled out of the duct and made our way along the corridor, away from the shaft and the remains of our lost comrades. Addison took point, cradling her plasma rifle with the barrel pointed at the deck. Lucy and I, both unarmed, brought up the rear.

"Not far now," Lucy said. She gave a brave little smile and I squeezed her hand.

"Don't worry," I told her. "I'm going to get you out of here, I promise."

The tension in her eyes relaxed. "I know you will, dearie. We've been in tight spots before, you and I."

"Maybe not as tight as this one."

"Maybe not," she conceded. "But you've always come through in the end."

"I'm glad you have faith."

"Somebody has to."

We walked in silence for a few minutes. Our footfalls echoed from the dark stone of the walls and ceiling.

I asked, "Where will you go, now you're human?"

Her little face frowned. "I hadn't really considered that. I guess I was assuming I'd go with you, wherever you're going. Same as always."

"But—" I was about to say I couldn't look after a kid. It was almost a reflex. After everything that had happened, the last thing I wanted was to take on any new, long-term responsibilities. But then I reminded myself this wasn't a normal human child, not by a long chalk. The intelligences peering out from behind those young eyes—one a ship grown from the cells of a little girl who'd been dead since my grandparents were young, the other a centuries-old alien supercomputer—were both far older and more experienced than I. And together, they had both saved my life several times in the past forty-eight hours. The very least I could do when we got back to civilisation was take them under my wing.

If we got back.

A long time ago, a teacher gave me a piece of advice. It was in drama class. We were doing a performance of *King Lear*. I was playing the Fool, and knew my lines by heart, but when I found myself scared to go out on stage in front of an audience of my peers, my teacher advised me to forget about how Johnny Schultz felt. Instead, she told me to imagine how a successful actor might feel, and react accordingly. She got me to pretend to be the kind of person who would be able to deal with that situation.

"Fake it," she said, "until you make it."

And that's exactly what I knew I had to do now. It was what Lucy and Addison needed from me. For their sake, whether I believed it or not, I had to roll up my sleeves and pretend to be Lucky Johnny Schultz, the man who always came out on top no matter the odds stacked against him. I had to act as if I truly believed we were getting out of here.

"Of course you can," I said. "Whatever happens, wherever we end up after this, you'll be more than welcome." I forced a smile. "We're a team."

Lucy leaned on my arm. "You really mean that?"

"Of course I do. We'll find a planet somewhere, with clean air and a pleasant climate, and we'll settle down."

"We'll be like a proper family?"

Addison was listening. She glanced back and raised an amused eyebrow, but I chose to ignore it.

"Sure thing," I told Lucy. "We'll buy a house and get some cats, and have friends over for dinner."

"How many cats?"

"How many would you like?"

"At least fifteen."

"Okay, that's settled. Fifteen cats it is."

"And Riley will come with us, won't she?"

A few paces ahead of us, I saw Addison's shoulders stiffen.

"How about it?" I asked her. "Do you want to come and live with us?"

Addison stopped walking and turned. "With you two, and fifteen cats?"

"Yeah."

She looked at us both in turn, as if trying to gauge whether we were mad or joking. Then, without seeming to reach a particular conclusion, she rolled her eyes and started walking again.

"What the hell," she said over her shoulder. "You get us out of here and I'll come and play happy families with you."

Lucy gave an excited squeak, but Addison hadn't finished speaking. She held up a hand.

"There's one condition," she said.

"Name it."

The hand came down and resumed its grip on the barrel of the plasma rifle.

"I won't be the one changing the kitty litter."

•

We carried on walking for a few hundred metres, until the corridor reached a bowl-shaped room, and became a suspended walkway. On the far side lay a door, which Lucy said would lead us to the hangar where we could rendezvous with the team from the House of Reclamation. All we had to do was walk across the bridge.

Unfortunately, the floor was a good twenty metres below the bridge, and the walkway had been constructed from a hard, transparent material that allowed us to see the drop beneath our feet. Apparently, the winged Nymtoq didn't suffer from vertigo. In fact, now I thought about it, I wondered why they'd even gone to the bother of building a bridge at all. Perhaps they had to walk if they were carrying stuff?

"Try not to look down," Addison said.

I glanced over the edge, steeling myself. The lighting wasn't particularly good down there. I'd been expecting the floor to be smooth black rock, like the rest of the interior, but it wasn't. For a moment, my brain tried to make sense of the lumpy metallic shapes covering the lower half of the depression. Then my primate brain— evolved for deciphering patterns and detecting predators in the long grass—realised what it was looking at, and I felt my blood turn to ice water.

"Stop," I hissed.

Addison turned, her mouth opening on a question—but I held my finger to my lips and glared at her.

Silently, I pointed downwards. She looked puzzled, and then realisation dawned. Her eyes went wide, and she caught her breath.

Below us, the floor was covered in dozens, maybe hundreds, of newly hatched alien crawfish. They weren't as large as the others we'd faced, but each was still the size of a manhole cover with legs. Fragments of eggshell lay around them like discarded razors.

"Why didn't you mention this?" I whispered to Lucy.

She shrugged. "They weren't here when I downloaded into this body. They must have been laid and hatched in the last couple of days."

"That's fast."

"Perhaps I should refresh my download, just to check for other surprises."

"Yeah, that's probably a good idea."

The creatures had apparently been sleeping when we entered—or maybe waiting for their shells to harden after hatching. But now, as they became aware of us above them, they started to stir. Beady eyes swivelled in our direction. Jaws flexed wetly; tails thrashed. And a forest of hungry, sickle-like pincers hinged slowly open.

CHAPTER FIFTY-EIGHT

TROUBLE DOG

Captain Konstanz told me her idea. By the time I'd finished listening, I'd already entered Sudak's fire envelope. At first glance, the captain's plan seemed suicidal and bat-shit insane. But after running it through a tactical analysis, I couldn't deny it held a certain unhinged merit. There was even a very small chance I might survive for longer than the minute and a half those same tactical algorithms expected me to endure in a straight-up fight against the three white ships.

Sudak's vessel launched a spread of torpedoes, trying to drive me back into the sights of her two companions, who were rapidly closing from behind. I checked the crew. In the infirmary, Preston had strapped himself safely into an acceleration couch. Nod and his progeny were braced in crawlways and ducts, their six legs splayed against the walls to hold them in place. They were as ready as they'd ever be; nevertheless, I let the acceleration alarm whine through my internal spaces for a good two seconds before firing my manoeuvring thrusters.

Watching me flip end for end, Sudak must have thought her plan was working. But if she expected me to move backwards, into the closing jaws of her trap, she would be disappointed.

I fired my main engines as the *Restless Itch* swung before my bow, stabbing downwards at ninety degrees to the plane of the confrontation. Behind me, the torpedoes twitched in response as they recalculated their intercept vectors.

Below, the forward section of the *Restless Itch* spread out like the face of a barren moon—a pockmarked gnarl of rock leftover from the formation of some far-off solar system. Yet among the outcroppings and impact craters, between the deep, shadowed ravines, lights shone. Docking bays stood open. And there, in the centre of it all, the bay through which the captain's shuttle had entered the behemoth.

Seconds had passed, during which the white ships had doubtlessly analysed and extrapolated my course. But all three were too far away to catch me before I reached the opening. Even the torpedoes would be hard pressed to close the distance in the remaining time—although they could still cause significant damage if they exploded on the surface of the *Itch*. If I wanted to get away from them completely, I'd have to bury myself deep in the innards of the beast.

I turned my sensors away from my pursuers, and ran a quick check on the data Captain Konstanz had supplied. If her calculations were correct, I'd be able to plough straight through the main hangar area—likely destroying my new shuttle in the process—and continue inward using the tunnel that led from the back of the main bay. With luck, I'd be able to penetrate a kilometre from the surface.

Either that, or smash myself against the tunnel mouth. The margin for error came down to less than a couple of metres in either direction. If I screwed up, everything would end in a tumbling fireball of exploding wreckage. But if I succeeded, at least I'd be safe for a short while. Maybe even long enough to regroup and figure out a plan that didn't involve all of us dying.

There was a sudden flash. Ahead, the landscape flared with unholy light, momentarily overloading my cameras. Alarms went off, and my rear sensors registered a series of huge energy pulses in my wake.

Having accepted that the torpedoes couldn't catch me in time, and doubtless wary of damaging the Nymtoq shrine, Sudak had instead chosen to detonate them prematurely, hoping to inflict at least minor damage before I reached shelter.

The expanding shockwave hit me like a kick in the pants, but I managed to remain on target. The landscape rushed up at me, and then I was inside, flashing through the hangar area and diving straight into the rear tunnel. I felt a flank brush the wall, and heard metal screech as hull plates were ripped away. One of my antennae tore out by the root, leaving broken cables flapping. But I didn't have time to worry about any of that. Instead, I diverted all the power I had to my forward jets, firing hard to slow my headlong rush—as ahead lay nothing but a solid rock wall.

CHAPTER FIFTY-NINE

SAL KONSTANZ

Leaving the tunnel, we found ourselves in a short corridor that led to a thick door. Beyond, we discovered a room shaped like an amphitheatre. And ahead, at the far end of a suspended walkway, we could see three of the survivors from the *Lucy's Ghost*. They were maybe a hundred yards away. But there were more of those multi-legged alien things climbing up the walls to reach them. Many more. Hundreds, maybe. And more were boiling up all the time.

As I watched, the woman raised her plasma rifle and fired, knocking a couple of the dog-sized creatures back into the morass of their scrambling siblings. The other two seemed unarmed.

So far, the creatures didn't seem to have noticed us. But that changed as soon as Alva Clay dropped to one knee and opened fire with the Archipelago pistol. Bolts raked the walls, shredding through the churning, scrambling ranks. Individual lobsters seemed to crumple as if chewed by invisible teeth. Limbs burst. Shells cracked. Jets of gore spattered the nearest crustaceans in a livid, evil-smelling sludge.

I drew my own sidearm and began firing, taking my time and selecting my targets. My weapon wasn't anywhere near as powerful as Clay's, but these creepy-crawlies were a lot smaller than the other one we'd seen, and their shells seemed thinner. Whenever I pulled the trigger, the recoil kicked against my braced arms, and a hole appeared in a carapace. One shot wasn't enough to stop these beasts, but still seemed enough to hurt them. Three shots and they went down thrashing—only, I noticed with disgust, to be ripped asunder and cannibalised by their brethren.

The man at the far end of the walkway turned to us. He had a child in his arms.

"Come on!" I called to him. The walkway itself was free of monsters. It seemed they couldn't jump high enough to reach it, which was why they were climbing the walls. He started running in our direction. At the same time, Clay switched her attention from the crawfish at the far end to the ones now scaling the walls beneath us, trying to reach our end of the bridge.

The woman with the plasma rifle had started to walk backwards, still firing at the creatures swarming towards her. I left Clay defending our exit route, and ran to join her, reloading my pistol as I squeezed past the man and child coming in the opposite direction.

"Keep going," I told them. Far below, the floor writhed with legs and pincers, and I wished the builders of this ship had thought to include railings on their suspended walkways.

The plasma rifle fired again, sending lines of incandescent, superheated gas into the ranks of advancing beasties. I came to a halt at the woman's shoulder.

"Take the middle," I told her. "I'll keep the edges clear."

I leant around her and picked off a crawfish that was trying to slip around a mass of its fallen brothers by clawing its way along the side of the bridge. Two shots to the face loosened its grip, and it fell back into the pit.

"What's your name?" I asked.

"Riley. Riley Addison."

"Hi, Riley."

I put my free hand on her shoulder and began to guide her backwards, pausing occasionally to take down a lone crustacean that had somehow escaped the main plasma onslaught.

By the time we reached the centre of the bridge, high over the deepest part of the bowl, we had maybe twenty-five metres between the nearest pincers and ourselves.

"Okay," I said, tugging at her sleeve. "That'll do, let's go!"

We turned and ran.

Ahead, Clay was battling to keep her end of the catwalk clear, firing downwards at the clawed monsters as they tried to clamber the walls to reach her.

As we approached, she let fly with a couple of final shots, and then stepped aside to let us pass. Once we were through, into the tunnel, she followed, sealing the door behind us.

For a moment, all we could do was lean against the rock walls, fighting for breath. My hands shook and my legs felt like overcooked pasta. Then the banging started. Inside the chamber, the crawfish had finally taken the bridge, and were now hurling themselves bodily against the door.

"We need to move," Clay said, and I could only nod in agreement.

Walking cautiously, I guided the other four along the

short corridor, back towards the tunnel that led to the docking bay where we'd left the shuttle.

"Have you heard from the *Dog*?" Clay asked from the rear.

"Nothing since that last transmission."

"Do you think she followed your plan?"

"I have no idea." So many things could have gone wrong. For all I knew, we were stranded here, in a rock riddled with violent metallic crustaceans.

We were nearly at the end of the corridor. Clay shrugged, and looked back over her shoulder for signs of pursuit.

She said, "I guess we'll find out soon enough, huh?"

•

As soon as I stepped out into the tunnel, I knew something had changed. The air was as cold and stale as it had always been. The space was as wide and cavernous as before, but now grooves had been scored in the walls and deck, and small chunks of rock and metal debris had been strewn along its length. To my left, I could see the distant lights of the hangar. To my right, about half a kilometre from where we were standing, something seemed to be blocking the tunnel. At first, I couldn't make sense of what I saw. Then the shapes resolved and I let out an involuntary cry.

The *Trouble Dog* lay jammed against the tunnel's starboard wall, having gouged a long furrow in the rock floor. We were seeing her from the stern, facing into the circular pits of her main engine exhausts. Curls of black smoke issued from cracks in her bronze-coloured armour, one of her defence turrets had been crushed against her flank, and I felt dismayed at the prospect of what further damage we might find when we got close enough to see her front end.

"Holy hell," breathed the man behind me. He still clung to the little girl, as if afraid to put her down. As if terrified one or the other of them might disappear if he relaxed his embrace, even for a moment. "Is that your *ship*?"

CHAPTER SIXTY

NOD

Another great landing.

Really.

Really great.

Malfunctions everywhere. Fires on three decks. Hull plates buckled fore and aft.

Thought first rule of space combat was not to crash into other ships. Basic common sense. Day one of training.

But no.

Hound of Difficulty decides to fly right into the side of a big rock.

Now much work needs doing.

Much work, no rest.

Send offspring to their tasks. Weld, bend and replace. Solder. Get fire suppression systems back online. Raid stores for replacement components. Set printers to manufacture modules we lack.

Whole ship feels like World Tree after a big storm. Branches bent and battered. Leaves stripped.

Much work to do.

Much work, and no rest.
No rest.
Not on this stupid, reckless ship.
She exasperates me.
She endangers me.
Yet I love her.
I will not rest until she is fixed.
No rest, just endless work.
Eternal patience.
Constant devotion.
Unspoken love.

•

Now, where did I put that tree-forsaken wrench?

CHAPTER SIXTY-ONE

ONA SUDAK

I watched the firefly spark of another torpedo curve towards the implacable face of the *Restless Itch*. Thus far, nothing we'd launched had managed to penetrate further than the mouth of the hangar. Although large enough to admit a Carnivore-class heavy cruiser, the opening presented a relatively small target for missiles designed to harm an enemy through proximity detonation rather than direct impact.

And as I watched the missile corkscrew towards its mark, I found myself wondering what Ona Sudak the poet would have made of all this. How would she have responded to this shelling of an ancient and holy site? I smiled. Probably with a long, rambling epic on the theme of mortality, along the lines of Shelley's "Ozymandias" but nowhere near as eloquent or succinct.

Less than a year had elapsed since I last composed a poem, and yet I found it increasingly difficult to remember what it had been like to be a lady of letters and leisure, and almost impossible to put myself in that kind of creative headspace. Even languishing in my cell for months on end,

I had found it all but impossible to pick up a stylus and expound on my emotional state. It was almost as if I had lost that part of myself in the Gallery, when Adam died.

Young, foolish Adam; even knowing my true identity as one of the Conglomeration's most wanted war criminals, he'd still clumsily sacrificed himself to save me. And now my inability to satisfactorily interpret the selflessness of his act had left me unable and unwilling to write about anything of any lasting consequence.

How bitterly ironic, I thought, that I could carry the blood of an entire world on my hands, and yet find myself emotionally poleaxed by the death of one indolent, barely talented teenager.

Light burst against the rock, a good hundred metres from the mouth of the hangar. I swore to myself and ordered the launch of yet another torpedo.

Behind me, the bear-like avatar shambled onto the bridge, the tips of its claws scuffling against the marble floor.

We are receiving a message from the Nymtoq vessel, it said, its words elbowing themselves into my thoughts. I almost asked to see the transmission, but there would have been little point. The Nymtoq language, which consisted of a series of chirps and clicks, remained opaque and incomprehensible to humans. Instead, I asked for a translation.

They are ordering us to leave their territory.

"No surprises there."

What course of action do you recommend?

On the screen, I watched a torpedo impact the edge of the hangar opening, adding a new scar to the asteroid's pocked countenance.

"Hold fast." I stretched my neck and shoulders, and wished the Fleet's builders had thought to place chairs on the bridges of their ships. "We can deal with the Nymtoq when they arrive. Until then, they're irrelevant."

The bear gave a short bark.

We concur. We should remain until we can be sure we have cleansed the area of parasites.

"And in the meantime, there's no point wasting any more torpedoes. If the *Trouble Dog* survived that idiotic manoeuvre, she's too well hidden for us to reach her with a bombardment. Keep station and prepare to target anything emerging from that rock."

The Nymtoq cruiser demands a response.

I flicked my upper teeth with a fingernail. Neither my hosts nor I wanted to get into a shooting war with such a well-armed and technologically advanced race. Although we would likely win such a confrontation, through sheer force of numbers if nothing else, the conflict would be of a scale and ferocity far outstripping the Archipelago War. And our mission was to prevent such conflagrations.

I took a breath, trying to purge thoughts of Adam from my head.

"Tell them we're sorry if we've inadvertently strayed into their territory, and that we will comply with their request to depart as soon as we've concluded our business." I could barely keep the annoyance out of my voice. We didn't want a fight, but that didn't mean we had to slink away like thieves in the night. I was the Butcher of Pelapatarn, for heaven's sake, and I'd be damned if I'd meekly back down before a solitary cruiser.

"But in the meantime," I said, feeling a steely detachment settle over the pain of my young lover's loss. "Tell them they're outnumbered, and they need to stay the hell out of our way."

CHAPTER SIXTY-TWO

SAL KONSTANZ

Of course, I'd seen the *Trouble Dog* from the outside many times, but for some reason she looked larger now than usual. Maybe it was because I was used to seeing her hovering over me, silhouetted against an infinite sky, rather than up close and wedged into the side of a tunnel.

In order to reach her, we had to scramble over broken hull plates and piles of scattered rock fragments.

"How do we get in?" Johnny asked. He'd introduced himself and the girl, and, despite having to pick his way with bare feet, seemed awed by the Carnivore's presence.

I considered the problem. "Well, we can't use the cargo doors, as she's resting on them. And the main crew lock's too high." The cartridge-shaped hull curved out over our heads, and there was no way we could climb it; at least, not from the side. I led the others around to the front of the ship, where her nose had buried itself in the floor, having torn a long, shallow furrow in the rock.

"We can get up here," I said, placing one boot on the tip of her bow. "We'll have to be careful, but if we take it slow, we can climb up onto her back. There's a dorsal airlock a few metres aft of the forward missile emplacements."

We looked up the rising slope of the hull, like a steep hill looming before us.

"And then what?" Schultz asked. "I mean, I know we'll be safe in there, but won't we still be trapped?"

A loud, metallic clang echoed down the tunnel from somewhere behind us.

"At least we'll have time to think," I said. "And that's something we don't have out here."

I began to clamber up the bridge of the *Trouble Dog*'s nose. The hull curved down and away on both sides, so it felt like climbing a mountain ridge, and I experienced a wobble of vertigo that caused me to put my hands out in front to steady myself. Behind me, Schultz followed with his arms held out to the sides for balance. Addison came after, and the girl, Lucy, scrambled happily between them, climbing like a monkey with her hands as well as her feet. Alva Clay remained on the ground, her gun sweeping the tunnel for potential threats.

"How are you doing?" she called.

"Almost there. You can come up now."

"Roger."

I turned and watched her hop up onto the ship's hull. She began trudging after us. Her steps were deliberate and well judged, her footing sure. The hand holding the Archipelago pistol swung at her side. The vein-blue tattoos on her arms looked like snakes coiling around the branches of a swaying tree.

At the top of the curve, I came to the row of blisters that comprised the forward missile batteries. As the *Trouble Dog* was resting with her nose buried in the floor, her spine rose above me at a forty-five-degree angle. I took hold of an exhaust valve and pulled myself upwards, between two of the blisters, to where the dorsal lock was located.

At that same moment, I heard a yell. Addison had seen something behind us. I looked back along the corridor and felt the blood in my veins turn to liquid nitrogen.

"Alva!"

She heard my shout and turned. Behind her, a wave of table-sized lobster creatures bore down upon us, surging around the base of the ship. Somehow they'd escaped from the room where we'd left them. I imagined those pincers snipping away sections of the steel door, widening a hole until they could squeeze through—first one, then another, and then all of them in a tumbling, thickening flood.

Alva's hand came up and the Archipelago pistol fired. One of the nearest monsters stumbled and fell beneath the stabbing feet of its brethren.

"Get to the hatch," she called, walking backwards up the incline while taking aim at another of the gunmetal crustaceans.

I gestured to Schultz and the other two, urging them towards me.

"Hurry up!"

Schultz's eyes were wide with fear as he helped Lucy and Addison past the missile batteries. I guessed he'd seen what these things could do.

"Come on." I had the outer doors open. I took Lucy's hand and lowered her into the lock. Then I helped the others climb down. When they were all in, I turned back to see how Alva was getting on.

But Alva wasn't there.

The lobsters had swamped the section of hull where

she'd been standing. Their pincers waved and snapped. Their legs rattled. And there, tossed on that frantic, nightmarish sea, I caught a glimpse of a lone boot, torn and ragged and borne aloft on the backs of the swarm.

Alva's boot.

She'd gone down fighting and hadn't made a sound. Hadn't cried out. And I'd been too preoccupied to notice the gunfire had stopped. Now, all I could do was stare in disbelief. My brain refused to process what I was seeing. The Archipelago pistol lay on the hull, as if she'd tossed it towards the airlock as the beasts took her. I reached out and retrieved it. Then Schultz pulled me down and the outer hatch clunked shut above my head.

CHAPTER SIXTY-THREE

TROUBLE DOG

The captain's voice came through from the airlock.

"Alva's dead." She sounded curiously detached, shocked to the point of being unable to express the emotions within.

"Yes," I said. I had been monitoring Clay's vital signs, as I monitored those of all my crew. My external cameras on that side were damaged, but when her heart rate and respiration spiked and died, I knew the worst had happened.

"Kill them."

"How? There are too many of them to use the defence cannons. We'd deplete our reserves. And a torpedo would only damage me."

"Use the engines."

"Captain?"

"Fire the main engines up to maximum thrust for two or three seconds. Scour those fuckers from the tunnel."

"Aye-aye."

My rear end pointed upwards at an angle, so the crustaceans on the tunnel floor wouldn't receive the full force of my fusion exhaust, but they'd be close enough that it'd probably fry them anyway. They'd also find great globs of liquefied rock falling on them from where the fusion flame brushed the tunnel's ceiling. And if they required air to breathe, well, there wouldn't be much of that left in the tunnel after I'd incinerated everything.

I powered up and felt the hull flex and creak as I brought the thrust up and held it for one second. Two seconds. Three… At four seconds, I let the power wane, dwindling back to default standby mode.

Behind me, the tunnel glowed all the colours of molten lava. A few of the armoured pests still skittered around on my hull, but the majority had been cremated. Without spectroscopic analysis, it was impossible to tell what had once been metal and what had once been rock. And somewhere out there in that glowing hell floated the blasted atoms that had once formed the flesh, blood and internal organs of Alva Clay—but like everything she had ever thought, seen or felt, they too were gone now, scattered and gone forever.

•

To further our woes, the rock that had fallen from the ceiling was now hardening into a barrier behind me, leaving the gap between the tunnel's floor and ceiling a few metres too narrow for me to squeeze through. I could fire my engines to clear the blockage, but it would only bring more rock down from the roof. Unless we could come up with an alternative plan, it seemed I was destined to remain trapped here for the foreseeable future.

But the captain was in no mood to discuss anything right now. She'd pulled out her earbud and taken herself down to the cargo hold, where she had zipped herself inside the inflatable life raft she kept down there, and curled up in a blanket. I tried calling her a couple of times, but she gave no response.

With Clay gone, Preston Menderes now held the highest rank on the ship—but he was busy in the infirmary, helping our new arrivals to clean and patch their various cuts and scrapes.

And Nod was busy. If I hoped ever to fly again, I'd need to leave it to patch up the holes in my hull, and do what it could to salvage the weapon emplacements and sensors that had been crushed against the exterior of my hull during the crash. I couldn't disturb it without delaying those repairs, and frankly I don't think it would have been much help. Engineering was something that came naturally to it, but battle strategy was almost an entirely alien concept to the peaceful Druff.

No, if we were going to get out of this one, it seemed I'd have to manage by myself.

Or so I thought.

•

"Hello, Trouble."

"Hello, Lucy. Where are you?"

"I'm down in the sick bay, but there's nothing wrong with me. I'm just a little dehydrated, apparently."

"Is that what Preston says?"

"Yes, he's nice, isn't he?"

"He's very young."

"Aren't all doctors these days?"

"How can I help you, Lucy?"

"It's not so much how you can help me, as how I think I can help all of us."

"Go on."

"Well, I happen to know that there's an identical tunnel running parallel with this one."

"So?"

"There's only a metre of rock separating the two. If you could bring a section of it down, you'd have room to turn around and a clear path back to the outside."

"It's going to take a few hours yet before I'm ready to fly."

"I know, but in the meantime it's something to think about, isn't it?"

"Yes. Yes, it is. Thank you, Lucy."

"My pleasure, dearie."

CHAPTER SIXTY-FOUR

ONA SUDAK

Through the collected feeds of the Fleet of Knives, I watched a compilation of violence, a symphony of fast, surgical destruction that encompassed over forty star systems. One by one, warships were picked off. Fortifications were reduced to rubble. Whole navies died. The spectacle felt overwhelming, heady and strangely compelling. Never had I seen a military operation with such coordination, such elegance and efficiency. And when Bochnak spoke, I could hardly bring myself to tear my attention from the unfolding subdual of humanity.

"What?" I glared at him.

He frowned back at me. His creased and rumpled hockey jersey appeared to have been slept in, and his long hair looked to be at least two days overdue for a wash.

"I am concerned."

I raised an eyebrow at him, trying to convey how little his concerns meant in the grand scheme of things.

"Really?"

His scowl deepened.

"Aren't you?"

"That's none of your business." I disconnected myself from the Fleet's primary feed and walked back to our living quarters. I'd been on the bridge for hours now. My mouth was dry, and I needed something to drink. He trailed along behind like a sulking cat.

"I've found something," he said. "Something that might interest you."

"What is it?"

"I'll need to show you."

We reached our rooms and I pulled a cold bottle of juice from the food printer.

"Then show me."

I unscrewed the lid and sipped while he conjured up a three-dimensional map of the Generality.

"Camrose is here," he said, pointing to a yellow mid-sequence star in the middle of the projection. He stepped back and glowing lines burst from that central star, branching out to touch all the surrounding systems. "And these are the paths the Fleet's taking as it expands from world to world."

I looked at the burst of light, thinking of fireworks.

"What of it?"

He scratched his stomach through the baggy jersey.

"There's one system they haven't visited. In fact, they seem to have gone out of their way to bypass it."

I stepped closer. "Really?"

He stepped to one side, and highlighted a region of space a dozen light years spinward from the Fleet's starting point. More than a dozen white ships had passed this region en route to other stars and other targets, but all of them had bent their courses away from it, apparently giving the whole area as wide a berth as possible.

"Maybe there aren't any armed ships there?" I suggested. But Bochnak shook his head solemnly.

"As far as I can tell, there are military vessels there from the Conglomeration, the Outward, and several minor human factions, as well as a number of armed and armoured merchant ships."

"So, why are we avoiding it? What's there?"

"The Intrusion."

Now it was my turn to frown. I tapped a finger against my chin, trying to remember what I knew about the anomaly. Some said it was a naked singularity; others that it was a wormhole, or a place where our universe brushed up against another. It was a place where the laws of physics became malleable and open to sudden change; a place of legend and rumour, and the subject of a thousand crackpot theories. And the white ships were definitely eschewing contact with it.

"So, what do you think?"

Bochnak glanced around and lowered his voice. "I think they're scared."

"Scared of what?"

He shrugged. "Their former masters, perhaps?"

He dismissed the projection with a wave of his hand. It broke into pixels and evaporated, leaving us facing each other.

"Anyway," he said. "I thought you should know. Although I'm not sure what you can do with this information."

"Thank you." He might not see an immediate use for this knowledge, but at the very least it showed there was one place armed human ships could gather, and potentially organise a counter-strike against us. The next time I spoke with the Fleet, I would suggest they spared a few ships to form a perimeter around the site, to prevent more ships availing themselves of its shelter.

I was more troubled by the second implication of Bochnak's news: namely that there was something the Fleet of Knives feared, something so unsettling to them that they would actually deviate a higher dimensional course to avoid coming anywhere near it. These were battleships designed to fight a higher dimensional enemy, to be the thin line between life and chaos. They should have been immune to such paltry emotions as fear. No, whatever reason they had for keeping away from the Intrusion, I was sure it ran deeper than Bochnak's glib explanation. And not knowing what it was, finding this sudden unknown variable in the equation of our battle plan, troubled me. We were corralling humanity for its own safety. At this point, a flaw in our defences, however minor, might unravel all we hoped to achieve.

CHAPTER SIXTY-FIVE
JOHNNY SCHULTZ

Addison and I were sitting beside Lucy's bed. The girl was sleeping. Preston had put her on a saline drip to help with her dehydration, but she'd pulled the cannula out so many times in her excitement to talk about what we'd experienced, he'd finally given her a sedative to keep her quiet. Resting, she looked like a perfectly ordinary human child—with all the beauty, potentiality and vulnerability that implied.

Addison leaned forward and brushed a strand of hair from Lucy's face, tucking it gently behind the girl's ear.

"I can see why her father didn't want to lose her," she said.

"But cutting out her brain and sticking it into a ship?" I made a face. "That's a pretty drastic solution."

"Is it?" Addison ran her finger down Lucy's cheek. "How far would you go to save someone you loved?"

I felt like laughing, but I was too tired. "After everything we've just been through, you have to ask?"

Addison shrugged and looked away, and we sat in silence for a while, listening to the ebb and flow of the sleeping child's soft breath. We both had strips of brilliant white dressings covering the cuts and scrapes on our foreheads, cheeks and knuckles. The smell of bleach lingered in the air, and around us, rows of empty beds stretched away in both directions, eventually vanishing around the curve of the hull. We might be trapped in this ship, but I felt safe for the first time in days. Whatever those crawfish-things were, I doubted they'd be able to burrow their way through a warship's hull. We had time to draw breath and regroup. Time to think about the future.

Addison pulled on her index finger. "Listen, what you were saying about taking care of her and being a family." She scraped her teeth across her lower lip. "Did you mean all that, or were you just humouring her?"

I looked her in the eye. If ever I was going to back away from my promises, the moment was now. But for some reason, I didn't want to. At that moment, looking at Lucy's head resting on the soft hospital pillow, I think I would rather have sacrificed a limb than ever contemplate abandoning that little girl.

My throat was dry. I tried to keep my voice level.

"I meant every word."

"Even the part about me coming with you."

"Yes." I felt my cheeks flush. "If you still want to?"

Addison looked thoughtful. Then she gave a tired smile, and reached to squeeze my hand.

"We're not out of the woods yet," she said. "But thank you."

CHAPTER SIXTY-SIX

NOD

Ship's avatar comes to see me.

"I'm worried," says *Intractable Mutt*.

"No worry," I tell her. "Work being done. Breakages being fixed. Given time, even straighten out dents in nose."

"No," she says. "I'm not worried about that. I know you and your charges are doing a superlative job."

"Then what?"

She puts chin in hands.

"I'm worried about the captain."

I feel alarm.

"Captain hurt?"

"No, physically, she's fine. But mentally, I'm not so sure. It's the loss of Alva Clay, you see. She's taking it very badly."

"Captain broken?"

"Possibly."

"You can fix?"

"I'm not sure. Some things can't be fixed."

I feel my fingers curl. Irreparably broken things make my faces itch.

"I could try."

The *Trouble Dog* smiles.

"That's very kind of you, Nod, but I'm not sure there's anything that can be done right now. She's just got to work her way through the grief."

Avatar fades away.

I look down at tools.

So many tools.

Tools to fix anything.

Except humans.

I throw wrench against bulkhead. It makes big noise.

Stupid wrench.

Captain broken.

Need to fix.

Need new tools.

CHAPTER SIXTY-SEVEN

SAL KONSTANZ

I lay curled in the bottom of the inflatable life raft, with a survival blanket for warmth and a life jacket for a pillow. I had zipped the awning shut, creating a snug cocoon, illuminated only by the circling light of the emergency beacon on the roof of the raft, its orange glow seeping through the waterproof material like sunset through fog.

I had no idea how long I'd been lying there. I'd been drifting back and forth across the border between wakefulness and sleep, unable to fully distinguish between either state.

How had I lost another?

After George's death, I'd sworn to keep the rest of my crew safe and out of danger. But here we were, less than a year later, and I'd failed. Just as I'd failed to protect George, and just as I'd failed to hang on to Sedge or save my parents. Everyone I'd ever cared about had been taken from me. Everyone had gone away, and I wasn't sure I was strong enough to continue without them. And with the white ships sweeping like a destructive blizzard across human space, I couldn't even go back to Camrose. My world had, almost literally, disintegrated beneath my feet. I had no remaining friends, no family, and no home. All I had left were my responsibilities to Preston and Nod, and my position as captain of a crashed, trapped ship, surrounded by enemies and soon to be embroiled at the centre of a conflict between two alien fleets.

I'd come here to rescue the crew of the *Lucy's Ghost*, but now who was left to rescue me? If the reports we'd received were to be believed, the House of Reclamation had been swept aside along with the Conglomeration and Outward fleets. Those human ships that had escaped the carnage would be too busy running for their lives to come and search for us. We were alone, just one more lost ship among thousands. Out there among the stars, people and ships were dying in uncounted numbers. And right outside this rock, three of their executioners were waiting to finish us as well.

I knew I should be on the bridge, working with the *Trouble Dog* to try and figure a way out of this mess, but the weight of my grief kept me pinned to the floor of the raft. I felt we had, by whatever measure you cared to employ, failed in every way that mattered. Lying there in my grief, death seemed inevitable. All I had left to lose was my life. The only uncertainty was how much longer I had to wait for it to be taken from me. I felt powerless and miserable, and every time I closed my eyes, all I could see was Alva's torn boot bobbing and tumbling on the backs of those frantic alien crustaceans.

She hadn't deserved to die like that. She was tough; she must have known what she was doing. She was clever enough to have seen the danger, and brave enough to have stood and faced it in order to give the rest of us time to reach safety.

She had chosen to make that sacrifice, but I wished she hadn't. I wished it had been me. If I'd known it meant saving Alva and sparing myself the torment I now felt, I would have gladly taken arms against that sea of pincers, and thrown myself into battle against them.

Without Alva, everything seemed hopeless. And without hope, what point was there in struggling? Why spend my final hours searching frantically for an escape from the inevitable when it was easier to lie here and watch the sweep of the revolving beacon play across the roof of my inflatable tent? With luck, the others would be making peace with whatever deities or ancestors they prayed to, and would forgive this abdication of responsibility on my part. After all, I had nothing to offer them, no magical solution or words of comfort. All I had was the aching void of my own grief, and a profound desire to be left alone for whatever time remained.

CHAPTER SIXTY-EIGHT

TROUBLE DOG

While Lucy's body slept, her avatar met with mine. I had let her choose the venue, and she had designed a virtual reality space that resembled the terrace of an old Victorian hotel, perched on a cliff overlooking the North Sea. Sunlight shone on clean white linen tablecloths. Waiters wove unobtrusively between tables. Delicate china cups clinked against saucers. Teaspoons rattled elegantly.

"Do you like it?" Lucy asked. She had dressed appropriately for the occasion in a long dress with a fitted bodice and a wide skirt with petticoats and calf-length boots. She had a fur stole around her shoulders and a diamond pendant hanging from her neck, casting little rainbows across her chest. Her hair was piled up on the top of her head like a confection. In contrast, I'd opted for my default appearance, and wore my long black trench coat. I'd left my hair free to tumble down my back any way it pleased. Being stuck in a tunnel, damaged and trapped, I felt in no mood to show off or play dress-up.

I admired the yachts dotting the bay.

"It's very nice. Is it somewhere you know?"

"It's something I saw in an old movie once, back before I became the *Lucy's Ghost*. The Grand Hotel, Scarborough. That's on Earth, you know." She looked down at her attire. "I've never been there, but I have to admit, I do like these old Victorian costumes."

"Well, I'm glad one of us is amused."

Lucy cocked an eyebrow. "You sound annoyed."

"Perhaps this isn't the time for self-indulgence?"

"Perhaps it's the only time we'll have."

She picked up the silver teapot and poured a cup for each of us. I flopped my avatar down on the nearest chair.

"Now, how about you tell me why we're here?"

"I want to show you something."

Replacing the teapot, she used a finger to sketch a rectangle on the tablecloth. A picture appeared within, and I recognised the roiling mists of the higher dimensions. A small section of hull was visible at the bottom of the screen.

"This was taken shortly before I collided with the *Restless Itch*," Lucy said. "As you can see, nothing appears to be out of the ordinary."

Suddenly, the picture lurched to the side and a gaping hole appeared in the hull. There was no explosion, no visible impact. One moment the hull was intact; an instant later, a section of it had simply *gone*.

"You were attacked?"

"Apparently."

"I've never seen a weapon like that."

"I don't think it was a weapon." Lucy closed the

window with a snap of her fingers. She picked up her cup and blew steam from the tea.

"What else could it have been?"

"I don't know." She lowered the cup again without having sipped from it. "As far as my instruments were concerned, there was nothing out there. A complete blank. But the crew seemed to be able to see something. Listen."

She held up a hand and I heard playback from inside the *Lucy's Ghost*. I recognised Schultz's voice, and heard him say, "Ship, what was that?" There was a pause, followed by, "There was something on the starboard screen, just for a second." Another pause, then, "There it is again!" A few moments later, the recording cut off, and Lucy sat waiting for my response.

"He certainly sounds as if he saw something."

"Later, he described it as looking like a large flying reptile, with tattered black wings and diamonds for teeth."

"And you saw nothing?"

"Not a sausage. Not even when it took a bite out of my midsection."

"How curious."

For decades, people had reported glimpses of creatures in the hypervoid, but none of those reports had ever been taken seriously. No evidence had ever been found to support their claims, and no ships had detected anything unusual. And anyway, the hallucinogenic effects of gazing too long into the abyss were well known. The boiling emptiness of the void played tricks with the human brain's need to impose patterns and order on existence. But what if at least some of those sightings had been genuine? Could creatures survive in such an environment, and somehow be invisible to artificial senses? If I'd not seen the footage of that bite being taken from the *Lucy's Ghost*, I wouldn't have believed such a thing were possible.

"The Fleet of Knives spoke of an enemy," I said. "An ancient species drawn to conflict and turmoil."

"You think this might be one of them?"

"I have no idea." I let my gaze wander back to the yachts in the bay. "But if it is, then that begs a very important question."

"Which is?"

"If the white ships were created to fight these things, how on earth do they detect them?"

Lucy frowned. "Perhaps they have better sensors than we do?"

"Not that much better." A waiter slid past, and even though he was just a collection of animated pixels, I instinctively lowered my voice. "Their technology's impressive, but in terms of basic principles, it's not that much more advanced than ours. There must be more to it than that."

Lucy threw a sugar lump to the seagulls, but they didn't seem to know what to do with it. "Perhaps they just know what to look for?"

"Mm, perhaps." I wasn't convinced. And, as I watched the gulls squabbling over their prize, an ugly suspicion began to build.

CHAPTER SIXTY-NINE

ONA SUDAK

The Nymtoq cruiser opened fire the moment it dropped out of the higher dimensions. Volleys of missiles streaked towards all three of my ships, which instantly responded with defensive fire and torpedo launches of their own. Within seconds, the space between us erupted into a blossoming hellscape of ragged explosions and flying metal. The intricate thrusts and parries happened too quickly to follow, and I had to trust my ships knew what they were doing. They didn't need my permission to defend themselves, and so, as the battle raged, I became as much of a passenger as Bochnak, able only to watch the storm and await its outcome, my paltry human intellect of little use in an arena where dozens of tactical decisions could be made and enacted in the time it would take me to draw the breath to give an order.

Resigned therefore to being a spectator, I lowered myself to the floor and took up a lotus position in the centre of the dais, at the heart of the spherical bridge, and tried to get an overall impression of the battle. We were arranged in a rough arrowhead formation, with my ship at the point, and all of us pouring fire against the interloper. But, as far as I could tell, the besieged Nymtoq cruiser seemed to be holding firm against our attacks.

The nine-eyed grizzly bear shambled up behind and cupped the back of my head with its paw. Suddenly I was linked into the group mind of the Fleet, and time seemed to slow down. Missiles that had been streaks of light now crawled across the heavens at walking pace. Explosions flowered and died like conjuring tricks. Numbers flickered in the dark spaces of my skull—estimates, projections, targeting data—and I sensed the rarefied chill of the white ships' thoughts like a web of frost extending itself across all the stars of mankind. Elsewhere, other skirmishes were taking place. Ships from one side of the Generality were advising ships on the other, their thoughts transferred instantaneously through higher dimensional space. They shared, relayed and distributed information between themselves like some enormous hive, playing out coordinated tactical strikes across battlefronts dozens of light years in length. Human ships fleeing one assault would find another ready to pounce when they re-emerged at their destination. Whole armadas were being herded together and destroyed in an orgy of clinical, calculated destruction—and our current predicament comprised only a single thread of that vast tapestry.

In my accelerated state, I regarded the sweeping lines of the Nymtoq cruiser. It had taken extensive damage to its forward section. Magnifying the view, I could see areas of hull that had been peppered by cannon fire, and others that had been scorched and melted by nearby detonations. It was outgunned and outclassed, but still it fought, and I had to admire that.

I watched a fresh salvo of missiles arc out from my ship, curving and weaving through space like fireflies as their onboard software tried to evade their target's defensive fire. At the same time, the other two white ships launched similar attacks. The Nymtoq were good, but there was no way they could defend against that many incoming torpedoes. If even one of the warheads hit home, the cruiser would be finished.

It was, I thought, all over.

But then the cruiser did something truly unexpected. Instead of standing its ground or trying to retreat, it fired its main engines and leapt forward, into the teeth of the attack.

"What's it doing?"

Insufficient data.

"Is it trying to ram us?"

That would be a reasonable conjecture.

"Then why aren't we moving?"

We do not anticipate the target will survive long enough to collide with us.

I saw three sets of torpedoes zeroing in on the cruiser, and scrambled to my feet.

"Oh, you stupid bastards!"

The first explosion caught the Nymtoq vessel amidships, breaking its spine. The second and third tore it into several large, fragmenting chunks. But still it came on, its momentum too great to be entirely deflected. And suddenly we were facing a shotgun blast of half-molten, radioactive debris.

"Move! Move!"

Taking evasive act—

The smaller particles hit first, some rattling off the

hull like hail from a kitchen skylight, the rest punching deep holes in our forward armour. The white ship lurched sideways, but it was too late. We wouldn't be able to clear the expanding debris field before it hit us.

Frozen in place, I watched a chunk of the cruiser's stern spinning towards us, trailing plumes of gas and coolant. We were turning, but not quickly enough. The fragment would hit us. It was easily half the size of my ship, and I had no doubt that at the relative speeds involved, the collision would be fatal.

Even in the accelerated timeframe of the Fleet's consciousness, I still had only subjective seconds in which to live. And all I could think was how ironic it would be to have escaped a firing squad only to be killed like this. For all their superior numbers and cold logic, the white ships had failed to anticipate that the Nymtoq vessel might embrace its own destruction as a chance to inflict damage on its killers.

If it wasn't for me, that complacency might have doomed us; but I was a Conglomeration officer, a veteran of the Archipelago War, and I'd be damned if I'd give up without a fight.

"4,678," I barked at the vessel flanking us to port. "Incoming threat. Move to starboard now. Protect the flagship."

Acknowledged.

Even with the speeded-up perception afforded by the hive mind, events were moving quickly. We were still veering away, but the chunk of the cruiser's stern was almost upon us. I could almost see the individual rivets on its hull. And then a glistening marble dagger came streaking in from the left. It hit the whirling wreck on the side, its snow-coloured nose crumpling and splintering with the force of the impact. Shards of it broke away like icicles from a thawing gutter. But still it accelerated, smashing itself as it shoved the danger far enough to the side that we were spared—even though the gap between us was so slight I fancied I could almost hear the whoosh as the entangled wreckage of both ships passed scant metres from our bows.

I closed my eyes and let out a breath. Smaller pieces of the cruiser still clattered against our forward surfaces, but we were safe from the larger fragments. We had survived. We were battered and scuffed and had lost a ship, but we were still here.

Captain Sudak? The bear was still behind me: a solid, furry wall of sinew and claw.

"Yes?"

In the moments before its destruction, the Nymtoq vessel sent a communication.

"To us?"

To their government.

I sucked my teeth. I had been hoping we could keep what had happened here from further escalation. "Was it a distress call?"

The bear growled. Its dagger-like claws flexed.

It was a request for reinforcements.

CHAPTER SEVENTY

TROUBLE DOG

88,573 sent a request to meet me in virtual space. I chose the same hotel balcony on which I'd spoken with Lucy. It saved me the bother of inventing something new and, truth be told, I rather liked the view. The glimmering blue of the sea; the colourful yachts; the achingly clean-looking lines of the waves as they broke.

88,573 came to me as a grey-haired human avatar dressed all in white. He had a neatly trimmed beard and eyes the colour of sunset. His cufflinks were miniature stars that burned on his wrists. The lines on his face had been carved by the passage of centuries.

In contrast, my hair was a hacked, shaggy mess. I hadn't bothered to dress up, and had just let my appearance revert to its default setting. I was naked beneath my frayed trench coat and my feet were bare against the wooden decking.

I offered him some tea, but he declined with the distaste of an adult refusing to participate in a child's game.

We're not here for pleasantries, he said.

"Then why are you here?"

Have you decided to surrender?

"I thought I'd made my position clear."

You have not changed your mind?

"I don't think I'm likely to; not when surrender means death."

A pity.

"Yes, a real shame." I rose to my feet and conjured a fresh sea breeze. It ruffled back my hair in just the way I wanted it to. "Now, how about we talk honestly?"

The avatar's eyes were tunnels of warm, rosy light.

Frankness is appreciated.

"Good." I put my fists on my hips. "Because I saw what just happened out there. I know you fought that Nymtoq cruiser."

We won.

"Yes, but you lost one of your number, and the other two are damaged."

The damage is minor.

"That's not the point."

Then pray tell us, what is the point?

The wind dropped. The conversation on the surrounding tables stilled. All was suddenly silence.

"It shows you're not invulnerable," I said. "It shows you're mortal, and that you can bleed."

The avatar regarded me without expression.

I fail to see how this knowledge benefits you.

I smiled like a wolf.

"You really don't understand people, do you? At the moment, you're swarming over everything like an implacable wave. But the moment people see that footage they're going to know you can be killed. They're going to know you can be defeated."

That knowledge won't change the imbalance between our forces. It won't improve the quality of their arsenal.

"Granted, but it *will* give them hope. And hope's far more dangerous to you than any weapon."

I walked over to the balcony's rail and looked out at the families playing on the beach. The fishing boats in the harbour. After a moment, the *88,573*'s avatar joined me.

And you have released that footage?

"The *Restless Itch* is broadcasting it as we speak."

I see. Pale fingers tapped against the wooden rail. *Still, I don't suppose it matters much. It certainly won't help you in your present situation. More members of the Fleet are on their way, and the Nymtoq have also signalled for additional forces. Within hours, this rock of yours will be at the epicentre of a major interspecies conflict.*

The sails of the boats on the horizon were all white. In a fit of pique, I changed them to a mixture of reds and yellows, but I don't think my companion noticed, or cared.

"Won't that rather defeat your purpose? I thought you were here to keep the peace?"

It is regrettable. The avatar straightened his immaculate white cuffs. His face, staring out at the sea, seemed primordial and weather-beaten, like the face of an antediluvian cliff. *But our builders had a saying: You can't make ice-crawler gruel without beheading a few ice-crawlers.*

"Humans have a similar one concerning omelettes and eggs."

Then you understand why you must surrender now, before things escalate further?

I couldn't help but bristle at his assured tone. I snapped, "Not really, no."

You sound aggrieved.

"I feel entitled to be angry."

He turned to me, one eyebrow raised in polite curiosity. *On what grounds?*

"On the grounds you're here to kill me."

The avatar smiled. *That objective forms part of our wider strategy. It is not a personal animosity.*

"From where I'm standing, it feels pretty fucking personal."

Then perhaps you do not fully comprehend the larger picture. Perhaps you do not understand that for every ship or human we kill, a million more will be spared; that by ending all possibility of war as quickly and cleanly as we can, we are saving more lives than we end.

"Bullshit."

You have seen the parasites loose aboard the Restless Itch. *You have seen the destruction they can bring. And yet, these are but ticks on the hides of our enemies. They are the very least of the threats the mist predators bring with them.*

"Mist predators?" I remembered the footage Lucy had shown me. Something large had taken a bite from the old freighter, but her instruments had been unable to detect it.

We call them the "Scourers". They are the scourges we were designed to fight. They are the enemies of all life.

I pursed my lips in thought.

"If you can fight them, you must be able to see them?"

88,573 looked at me as if I'd just said something so obvious as to be almost contemptible.

Of course.

"They appear invisible to our cameras."

They once appeared so to ours.

"So, what did you do?"

We were forced to evolve. When it became apparent the enemy was undetectable by artificial means, we were obliged to incorporate elements of our builders into the fabric of our beings.

His words were so calm and matter-of-fact that it took me a moment to process the full awfulness of their meaning. The suspicion that had begun to nag me during my conversation with Lucy now hardened into a horrifying certainty.

"You cannibalised your creators for *parts*?"

The avatar clasped its hands together.

We took their eyes for cameras. A hundred eyes per ship.

"Fifty million people?"

Our creators had six eyes each.

"That's still over sixteen and a half million individuals!" The scale of the atrocity appalled me, and also shamed me. At Pelapatarn, I'd helped wipe out fifteen billion sentient trees.

It was necessary. Remember the ice-crawlers.

"How could I forget?" I held tight to the wooden railing. The sea seemed to be moving up and down with a queasy motion.

"Didn't they resist?" I asked. "Didn't they fight you?"

The avatar gave an unconcerned shrug.

The donors were not volunteers, but they had the comfort of knowing their sacrifice would help us in our fight to preserve life.

"I bet that was a huge comfort to them."

I cannot speculate.

"Fucking hell." I shook my head, still trying to comprehend these revelations. "And the rest of your people just stood there and let this happen?"

They fled from this existence, leaving us without purpose. And so we hibernated in the Gallery for five thousand years.

"Until I came along."

You gave us renewed purpose. Your hatred of war matched our desire to prevent conflict.

"I should have just kept my big mouth shut."

We are grateful to you.

"But not grateful enough to let me live?"

I am afraid not.

"Then there's nothing more to say, is there?" I held up a hand and snapped my fingers. The Scarborough seafront vanished. The *88,573* and I stood facing each other, suspended in nothingness.

"Goodbye."

CHAPTER SEVENTY-ONE

SAL KONSTANZ

I woke in the life raft, remembered my situation, and tried to fall back to sleep. But there was someone outside. I could see their shadow against the orange fabric wall of the canopy.

"What do you want?"

"Captain?" It was Nod. "May I speak with you?"

"You are speaking with me."

"In person, I mean?"

I sighed. I was warm in the nest of blankets I had wrapped around me. I leaned out an arm and undid the zip holding the entrance shut. When I pushed back the flaps, I found one of its flower-like faces waiting expectantly.

"Yes, what is it? Is there a problem with the ship?"

"Many problems with ship."

I pulled myself reluctantly into a sitting position.

"Any *urgent* problems?"

"Not here to talk about *Hound of Difficulty*. Here to talk about captain."

"Me?"

Nod's coal-black little eyes blinked at me.

"Captain broken."

I didn't know whether to laugh or cry.

"I'm not broken," I said, although my eyes swam with tears.

It tipped its head sceptically to one side.

"Not working properly, therefore broken. Trust me, am engineer."

I shook my head. "Oh, Nod," I said. "I'm grieving. You can't fix grief."

"Everything fixable, even humans."

"It doesn't work like that."

"Look." It raised one of its other faces. The petal-like fingers held one of its children: a miniature version of its parent, complete with rainbow oil-slick-coloured scales.

"This one Sally," Nod said. "Named after you."

Three little faces peered up at me.

"After me?" I reached out a finger, and the baby Druff took it, wrapping its petals softly around the tip.

"In World Tree, children named for great members of family. Big heroes of past. Great leaders of present."

"And so you called this one Sally?"

"*Troublesome Dog* is my world now. That makes you my leader."

"I don't feel much like a leader right now."

"You great leader. All of us dead many times if not for you."

I felt my eyes prickle.

"Some of us are dead," I reminded it. "George, Alva…"

"Not dead." The petals around its face spread wide. "In my culture, when loved ones die, they return to World Tree to be reborn. Nothing ever truly lost."

I swallowed back the tears, determined not to shed

them in front of another member of the crew.

"That's a nice thought," I said. "But you didn't see the way she died. The way they both died. Torn apart…"

"Alva Clay died protecting ship and crew. George Walker died doing job."

The little Druff hopped from Nod's palm and landed on the blankets in front of me. Cautiously, it crawled up onto my lap and snuggled down. I scratched it behind the petals and it shivered with delight.

"They still died on my watch."

"So?"

"So I'm responsible."

Nod raised another face and spoke from it.

"Ship broken, I fix, Crew broken, you fix."

"I can't fix them, they're gone."

"Others here now."

"You mean Schultz and the others?"

"Times tough. Makes sense to pool resources."

"I guess so." I'd been thinking of the three people we rescued as simply survivors to be delivered to a place of safety. Now though, there were no such places. At least, not for a ship like ours. A couple of experienced new crewmembers might come in useful.

Distracted, I had stopped scratching the baby in my lap. It nuzzled its head against my hand.

"Damn you," I said. "Now you've got me thinking like a captain again."

"I have faith."

"In me?"

"Ship also has faith." Nod shuffled closer and let one of its hands rest lightly against my arm. It was a human gesture of consolation it was copying from somewhere.

"Alva Clay had faith," it said seriously. "She died defending ship and crew. She would not want you to mourn like this."

I frowned. "She wouldn't, would she?"

"What would she say?"

The frown turned to a snort of bitter laughter. "She'd tell me to get up off my ass and start acting like the captain. She'd tell me it was my turn to do my job."

"She'd be right?"

I'd been feeling hollow, as if someone had scraped out my insides with a blunt scalpel and sewn the skin closed over the resulting void. Now, I could feel a flicker of resolve—faint and frail as a candle flame, brightening with every breath. Feeding on my hurt and frustration, it would soon burn with the light of a thousand suns. And woe betide the metal lobster or marble warship that failed to scuttle from its brilliance.

"Yes," I said, clenching my fists. "Yes, she would."

Nod stared unblinking. "Then please follow her advice. For sake of whole ship." It reached petals towards the baby squirming in my lap. "And for sake of children."

CHAPTER SEVENTY-TWO

JOHNNY SCHULTZ

At 0600 ship's time, Captain Konstanz called us all together in the *Trouble Dog's* main briefing room. The auditorium contained enough seats for a hundred marines; with only five of us occupying the front row, the room felt echoingly vacant, like a classroom during the school holidays or a nightclub the morning after a party.

I sat at one end with my legs stretched out and crossed at the ankles. Lucy sat beside me, her feet swinging beneath the chair. Beyond her, Addison sat ramrod straight, waiting to hear what our situation was. Preston stood at the end of the row with a portable screen in his hand, flicking through a medical textbook, and Nod lay curled beside him like a footstool, with only one face emerging from beneath its scaly body.

Preston lowered his screen when Captain Konstanz entered the room. She looked as if she'd been sleeping in her clothes. But her face was clean and freshly scrubbed, a ratty old baseball cap held back her wet hair, and her jaw had a determined set.

"Thank you for coming," she said, taking up position at the front of the room. Her hands gripped the sides of the lectern. "Ship, are you there?"

"Of course." The *Trouble Dog*'s avatar appeared on the main screen: pale, almost androgynous-looking. For some reason, she had chosen to appear wearing a stylish white tuxedo. She had left the top button of her dress shirt open, and her red bow tie loose around her neck. She looked as if she'd just come from a formal dinner.

"Right." Konstanz drew herself up, her crumpled fatigues in stark contrast to the ship's elegance. "I thought I'd better brief you all on our situation."

She used the lectern to pull up a three-dimensional tactical projection of our surroundings. We could see our position inside the *Restless Itch*, and the positions of the two remaining knife ships.

"Okay, here it is," she said. "We're damaged and trapped. The ship has a plan to get us out of here. It's risky and not guaranteed to succeed; and even if it does, all it will do is place us directly in the sights of these two ships." She pointed to the two daggers holding station off the *Restless Itch*'s bow. "And then, even if we somehow get past them unscathed, there are a million of their brethren currently laying waste to starships across the length and breadth of the Generality. Anywhere that we went, we'd risk being blown from the sky."

Addison and Lucy were grimly silent. Only Preston spoke.

"Can't we jump away as soon as we clear the tunnel?"

Konstanz shook her head.

"We wouldn't be moving fast enough. Sudak would be on us before we could build up enough speed."

"Oh." The medic's gaze dropped to the floor.

Nobody else seemed to have anything to add. Tentatively, I raised my hand. Captain Konstanz turned to me.

"Yes, Johnny?"

"It might be crazy, but I think there's a way we can help."

Konstanz raised an eyebrow. "Go on."

"There may be a way to get you up to jump speed more quickly," I said. "But it's risky, and the *Trouble Dog* would need to be ready to come out fighting."

Beside me, Lucy clapped her hands and squealed in delight.

The captain turned to the *Trouble Dog*. "What do you think? If they can find a way to give you a boost, can you handle a short fight?"

The ship's avatar smiled. She pulled her bow tie from around her neck and began to wind the red silk around the knuckles of her right hand.

"Any fight we have is going to be *short*," she said. "But if there's a possibility we can jump away before we're completely annihilated then hell yes. Count me in."

CHAPTER SEVENTY-THREE
TROUBLE DOG

According to Lucy's information, a second tunnel ran parallel to the one in which I currently lay. In order for me to have enough space in which to turn around, I would need to break down the wall separating us from it. However, as the wall was made of solid rock, doing so would be simpler said than done. I couldn't use a torpedo, as I'd be too close to the explosion when it went off, and likely to sustain serious damage.

"Besides, I don't want to bring the whole ceiling down on top of us," I said.

"Well, we can't go out there and knock it down by hand," the captain replied. "We don't have the tools."

She was standing on the bridge. Lucy stood beside her, wrapped in a crew jacket several sizes too large for her diminutive frame.

"And anyway," the girl said, "there may still be crawfish out there."

The main screens showed different views of the tunnel. Even though it was cooling, the rock on the walls and floor still looked half-melted. Stalactites hung from the ceiling where molten drops had cooled in the process of dripping.

"I can't detect any," I said.

Lucy gave a pout. "That doesn't mean they're not out there somewhere."

I noticed that Captain Konstanz was listening to our conversation with her jaw tightened and fists clenched. I guessed she was trying not to think about what had happened to Alva Clay.

"So, if brute force won't work," she asked, "do you have any other suggestions?"

"Just one." I brought my starboard defensive cannons online and calculated firing patterns. Turrets swivelled and took aim.

The captain said, "We're still awfully close to that wall. Are you sure this is the best way?"

"It's the only option we have."

"What about damage?"

I let my avatar shrug. "A few dings and scratches from rock chips flying back at us. Maybe the odd ricochet."

"Hmm." She tapped her chin. "I think I'm going to order everybody over to the port side of the ship, just in case."

"That's probably wise."

I waited while she gave the order, and watched through my internal cameras as the rest of the crew, including Nod and its brood, made their way around the ring-shaped habitation section. When they had all reached the side farthest from the wall, I switched my attention back to the bridge.

"Should I go?" Lucy asked.

"No need," Captain Konstanz told her. "The bridge has its own armour, so you're probably as safe here as anywhere else."

"Oh, okay." The girl sat on one of the command chairs and folded her hands in her lap.

"How thick did you say this wall was?" I asked her.

"About a metre."

"Thank you." I spun the cannons up to full rotation. "Captain, if you're ready to give the order, I can proceed."

The captain's fingers were still resting against her chin. I could see her wrestling with the decision, trying to determine which course of action would prove safest—to fire on the wall or remain stranded. Eventually, she straightened the brim of her cap.

"Do it," she said.

•

All eight starboard batteries opened up at once. The tunnel flickered with light. Streams of dense metal slugs hammered the rock face, gradually chewing deeper as they pulverised the stone. As I'd predicted, chunks of broken rock rattled against my hull armour, and dust filled the tunnel, coating my upper surfaces with a thick black powder.

When the first cannon broke through to the other side of the wall, I adjusted its aim a few centimetres to the right, and set it firing again. Eventually, having repeated that process several times with all eight of them, the wall became so perforated it could no longer support its own weight, and fell, sending up even more dust.

When everything had settled, we surveyed the destruction. Where the wall had been, there was now a ragged-edged hole linking our tunnel to the one that ran parallel. Parts of the ceiling had collapsed in places.

Lucy sat forward and clapped.

"That was very good, dearie," she said, and I gave her a smile. Merchant vessels were always easy to impress.

Captain Konstanz seemed less enthralled. She gave the hole a sceptical squint, trying to judge its size in relation to my hull.

"Is it big enough?"

I bounced positioning lasers from the walls, floor and ceiling.

"It'll do." If I turned carefully, I could swing my nose into the new tunnel, and then use it to exit the *Restless Itch*.

"So we can leave?"

I checked my status levels.

"Not for a few hours. That used up more ammunition than I'd have liked. We'll have to restock."

"I'll get Nod on it right away."

"Thank you." I could feel my excitement building at the prospect of leaving this place and engaging with the enemy. I couldn't help it. At heart, I would always be a warship, and had long since accepted the fact. But no matter how itchy I might be to confront Sudak and *88,573*, I'd never be eager enough to rush into battle with half my stores of cannon ammo depleted. I had to be fully tooled up when I came face to face with those knife ships again. Having gone up against them once, I was only too aware of the damage they were capable of inflicting, and had no illusions regarding my chances. If I hoped to survive long enough to jump into the higher dimensions, I'd need to make the most of every defensive trick in my arsenal.

CHAPTER SEVENTY-FOUR

NOD

Make ammunition, they say.

Restock starboard batteries.

So I gather rocks and dust from outside.

Work hard.

Work hard, no rest.

Drag rocks up outside of hull.

Drop them into hopper at back of printer.

Printer breaks rocks.

Uses raw material to print cannon shells.

Much noise and dust. Have to wear masks.

Shells come out in batches of twenty.

Cannon shells heavy.

Take them from printer and stack in boxes, ready to slot into cannon.

Offspring help.

Preston and Captain come down and help.

New people help.

Even little girl help.

All carry armfuls of cannon shells.

All work, no complain.

No rest.

All us know survival depends on *Trouble Dog* having everything it needs to fight.

Everything it needs to keep enemy missiles away from children.

So we work without rest.

Like when preparing World Tree for oncoming storm.

Always work.

No rest.

No complaints.

To survive, work as team. As crew. As family.

Humans, ship and Druff, all together.

All important.

All work.

CHAPTER SEVENTY-FIVE

SAL KONSTANZ

In the comforting darkness of the *Trouble Dog*'s bridge, I sat on my command couch with my feet drawn up and my wrists resting loosely on my knees. Nod's words had got me this far. I'd also downed a brimming glass of gin in the galley when no one was looking. I knew it was a depressant, but I just needed the burn of it in my throat to take the edge off my grief. I had to keep functioning until we were out of this mess, and anything that kept the tears at bay had to be a good thing. On the consoles before me, status indicators shone green or amber. Weapons system readouts scrolled down peripheral screens. Star charts moved with a sedate three-dimensional rotation. I'd been terrified every moment I'd been off this ship, and now felt I was back where I belonged, alone at the heart of this gorgeously lethal machine. We were part of each other now. We may have started off on different sides of a war, but all that seemed so far away and long ago. The factions to whom we'd belonged had been swept aside, and the only thing that mattered now was our mutual survival.

The light of the main screen bathed my face, showing me the hole we'd punched between this tunnel and the next.

I cleared my throat.

"Are you ready?"

The *Trouble Dog*'s avatar appeared on the screen, overlaying the view like a newsreader standing before the scene of a natural disaster.

"I believe so," she said. She didn't look entirely sure, but I couldn't be certain whether she was putting that on for my benefit. Sometimes I had to remind myself that the avatar was a construct, and all of its expressions and body language were consciously chosen rather than unconsciously displayed. A look of uncertainty on her part could, rather than reveal a genuine timorousness, simply indicate she hadn't fully calculated the odds of success. It was a fine line, but one worth remembering. As with any other human, you could only infer so much from her appearance.

"Then let's give it a try."

No sooner were the words out of my mouth than I felt the ship quiver like an animal rousing itself from hibernation. Manoeuvring jets fired along her length. And slowly she eased backwards, withdrawing her nose from the trench it had gouged in the dead rock of the tunnel floor. Then, when her stern was almost pressed up against the barrier of fallen debris blocking the tunnel, she fired laterally. Her streamlined bow inched sideways. Pieces of loose rock rattled down from her upper surfaces. But sluggishly, she began to turn. The point of her bow passed through the ragged hole and scraped against the far wall of the new tunnel. I gripped the arms of my chair, fearing we'd be wedged sideways. Then, with a splintering of rock fragments, the ship's nose broke free and swung around, dragging her stern out and around, until she found herself entirely in the new tunnel, and facing the opposite way—back towards the hangar bay through which she'd originally entered.

Sitting there on the bridge, feeling the distant vibration of her engines, I felt a surge of overwhelming pride. The *Trouble Dog* might be dinged-up, but she was still in the game. And whatever became of us in the next few minutes and hours, at least we'd be taking the fight to our tormentors rather than waiting for death to excavate us from this sterile vault.

As the jets whined back into silence, I opened a channel to the crew lounge, where I knew everyone save Nod and its brood were now waiting. Even Lucy had left the bridge and gone down to be with her friends.

"We're in position," I told them.

Johnny Schultz acknowledged. Preston and Addison sat to his left, and Lucy sat to his right. I watched him slide a brotherly arm around her shoulders, as if she were nothing more than a real human girl.

"Okay, kid," he said to her in his studied port-hero drawl. "Time to do your stuff."

She looked up at him with an unreadable expression, her face somehow concurrently youthful and ancient.

"Right you are, dearie." She scrunched her eyes and rubbed her palms together, like a child making a birthday wish.

I looked at the main screen. The walls of the tunnel seemed to shiver. Dust fell from cracks in the ceiling, raining down on the *Trouble Dog*. I heard a fist-sized chunk of rock bounce from her hull armour.

"It's working," Schultz said.

Beside him, Lucy opened her eyes. Her smile was one of wicked glee. She said, "You'd better believe it's working."

CHAPTER SEVENTY-SIX
ONA SUDAK

Surface detonation, the ship reported. *Minimal internal damage.*

Bochnak and I were in the spherical chamber at the white ship's heart. On the forward wall, the *Restless Itch* filled the view like a black cliff. The most recent impacts presented as softly glowing blemishes. For some reason, the sight of them caused me to recall a fragment of one of the first poems I'd written in the immediate aftermath of the war. It wasn't even a good poem, just a couplet imagining past misdeeds as needle marks tattooed on the soul. Yet combined with the sight of those ember-like craters, it disturbed me in a way I couldn't properly elucidate, even to myself. I tried to shrug away the feeling, but it only tightened its grip. Every volley I launched felt like a desecration. I was shelling another race's holy site, and I found myself silently cursing Sally Konstanz for making me resort to such extreme measures.

And then all the alarms went off at once.

We're registering a huge build-up of power, the ship said, speaking directly into my brain.

"What is it?" Bochnak grabbed my sleeve. "What's going on?"

I shook him off. A penumbra of blue fire flickered into life, ringing the dark bulk of the ancient ark.

"I don't believe it. I don't fucking believe it." I hooked myself into the Fleet's sensorium, searching for hard data to confirm what I was seeing.

"What?"

Targeting lasers bounced off rock. The measurements came back.

"They did it. Christ knows how they managed it, but they got the engines online."

Bochnak gaped. "They're *moving* that thing?"

"Right at us."

He took a step back. "Shouldn't we, you know, get out of the way?"

I smiled. "Don't worry. We're backing off at the same rate it's advancing. It's a floating mountain; it's not going anywhere fast." I checked the weapons systems to make sure they were maintaining a steady lock on the hangar in which the *Trouble Dog* lurked.

"Besides," I said, "they'll be lucky if those engines don't explode. The last time those things were fired, the Crusades were still raging and America remained undiscovered."

Bochnak raised his wiry eyebrows. "And I thought I was the historian."

I gave a shrug. "I specialised in military history at the Academy."

"And now you're making it." Although his tone sounded gloomily resigned, the thought strengthened the sinews of my resolve.

"Yes," I said, "I am."

For his part, Bochnak didn't look so convinced. He had the hangdog air of the terminally put-upon. I had the impression that could he have fled back to his life of comfortable academia, he wouldn't have hesitated.

"So," he inclined his head at the slowly accelerating alien vessel, "what are we going to do about it?"

"What can we do? That thing masses at least a hundred million tons. Just imagine the inertia. We could fire every missile we had and it wouldn't make an appreciable difference. It certainly wouldn't slow her down."

"What happens if it hits us?"

"I'm confident we can move backwards faster than it can move forwards."

"And if you're wrong?"

"We move sideways."

Bochnak frowned, clearly still troubled. He reached beneath his hockey jersey, into the pocket of his jumpsuit, and produced a red handkerchief, which he used to dab his forehead.

"I don't get it," he said. "All this trouble just to destroy one ship. I mean, how much of a threat can they be?"

I turned and fixed him with a stare I'd learned on the parade ground.

"I don't know how things work where you come from, *Mr* Bochnak, but I came here to do a job and I'm not leaving until I've achieved my objective."

The old man stuffed the hankie back into his pocket and glared at me with his yellowish, vein-spidered eyes.

"And what exactly is that objective, *Captain* Sudak?"

He looked like a belligerent, wild-haired old hermit roused from his solitude. But before I could reply, the ship broke in, slamming its words directly into our minds with the force of non-verbal hammer blows.

Our primary objective was to ascertain if the enemy was involved in the wreck of the Lucy's Ghost. *This we have done. Our secondary objective remains the pacification of all combat-capable human craft, including and especially the* Trouble Dog.

Bochnak put a hand to his temple, wincing with the impact of those words. "But why?" he asked. "How can they hurt you now?"

In the past, the Trouble Dog *has linked with the Fleet. She has spoken to us directly. She has seen into our collective heart. However remote the possibility, she might have divined a physical or strategic weakness. Therefore, of all human ships, she represents the greatest threat to the accomplishment of our mission, and must be destroyed.*

Bochnak shook his head. "This isn't right," he said. "This is madness."

It is necessary.

"Defiling a sacred relic? Provoking a war in order to kill an already wounded ship?" His hands pulled at his unruly hair. "Oh yes, because that makes *perfect* sense."

He glared at the ceiling but the ship declined to reply. It had apparently said all it wanted to say. Slowly, the old man lowered his gnarled hands and looked at me.

"This is bullshit," he said. "You know that, right?"

I shook my head. The Fleet's methods might be clumsy and unorthodox, but I still believed they were sincerely trying to save humanity from itself and from the dragons that swam in the hypervoid. To stand against them on this would be to declare myself an enemy of my species. A traitor. This transition period might be painful, but it would ultimately lead to peace and security for generations to come. I couldn't let myself agree with

Bochnak. I couldn't let his liberal scruples ruin what would ultimately be the greatest thing to ever happen to the human race. I knew that somewhere in the depths of my being, securely locked away, the part of me that had once been a poet raged and wept. But I didn't need her anymore. I was a soldier now, and I had a mission, and I'd be damned if I'd let my discarded cover identity, or this ridiculous old academic, stand in my way.

I interlaced my fingers.

"Alexi," I said. "Please go to your quarters and stay there until further notice."

He blinked at me in surprise.

"You're confining me to my cabin?"

"For the time being."

"You can't do that." He looked flustered. "I mean, what's the point? There's only the two of us here."

"I'm finding your constant doubts counterproductive."

"What does that even mean? Are you afraid of a dissenting opinion?"

With my hands still woven together, I stretched out my arms until my knuckles gave a satisfying crackle.

"I'm not afraid of anything. I just think things would be better if you restricted yourself to your own personal space."

I watched his cheeks mottle with anger.

"That's crap," he blustered. "You're just scared you're wrong."

"No," I snapped, fixing him with the wintriest glare I could muster. "I'm not. But I have a mission to complete, and I'd rather be free to concentrate on it without your constant interruptions."

CHAPTER SEVENTY-SEVEN
JOHNNY SCHULTZ

I left Lucy talking to the *Trouble Dog*, and followed Addison down to the galley for coffee. I don't think either of us was under any illusions that we might die in the next hour or so. I certainly noticed the way she kept tugging her hair behind her right ear.

"Are you all right?" I picked up a cup and waited while she filled hers.

"Not really." She spoke without looking around.

"It's been a rough couple of days."

"Rough?" Now she glanced at me. "Rough doesn't even cover it. I can't even… I don't want to think about it."

"Yeah." I knew what she meant. The only way for us to keep functioning was to keep shying away from the memories of what had happened to us, and to the people we'd lost.

"Can you believe what's going on at home?" She was trying to change the subject.

"With the Fleet?" I scratched the back of my neck. "It's insane. What are they trying to achieve?"

Riley sniffed the steam rising from her cup. "I think you may have to put your fifteen-cat plan on hold for a while."

"Lucy's going to be pissed."

"Do you really think she wants to settle down and be part of a family?"

"I think she does." Lucy had been a young girl when she died. Now she had more than a century of memories of tramping around the Generality as a freighter—not to mention the part of her that had once been a millennia-old Nymtoq colony vessel. "Despite her age, she's like a child. She's learning how to be human." I put my hands in my pockets and shrugged. "And I guess kids need someone to look out for them."

Riley's forehead crinkled as she raised her eyebrows. "You want to be her *dad*?"

I scuffed a shoe against the deck. "Big brother, maybe."

She laughed. "That's… I was going to say crazy, but actually it's kind of sweet."

I felt my cheeks flush. "She saved our lives, several times. It's the least I can do."

Riley was still smiling, but there were tears in her eyes. She put her hand on my arm. "Don't mind me. I'm not laughing at you. I just never thought I'd see Johnny Schultz grow up and start acting responsibly."

"I guess we all have to do it sometime."

Her smile guttered like a dying candle. "Well, given that civilisation seems to be collapsing around us," she said quietly, "some might say you've left it a little late."

"Better late than never."

"I suppose."

She walked over to the nearest table and I followed. Like the infirmary and most of the other communal areas on the

Trouble Dog, the galley had been designed to cater to the needs of a crew of three hundred. Sitting there, surrounded by empty tables and plastic chairs, felt like sitting in a café in an out-of-season seaside resort—the only things it would have taken to complete the illusion were a set of misted-up windows and the vinegary smell of chips.

Riley placed her coffee on the tabletop and leaned back in her seat, eyes closed and palms resting on either side of her cup.

"God," she said. "How did it all unravel so quickly? I thought with the war over, things were starting to get back to normal."

"Nobody could have anticipated this."

She opened her eyes. "They had that Fleet sitting around Camrose for a year. Couldn't they have done something during that time? Quarantined them or something?"

"I don't know."

A polite cough came from the room's main screen. The *Trouble Dog*'s avatar had joined us: a skinny, androgynous-looking woman with short black hair, a white shirt and a thin black tie.

"I'm afraid things are worse than you know," she informed us. "I've been monitoring higher dimensional message traffic, and it seems the Fleet of Knives has progressed from destroying purely military targets. As of a few hours ago, all interstellar travel has been embargoed."

Riley groaned and ground the heels of her hands into her eyes. "And so we're screwed," she said. "As a species, I mean. There's no way the Generality can hold together with those *things* policing us. We'll end up as a couple of hundred insular, isolated planets living on the whim of our so-called protectors."

On the screen, the *Trouble Dog* tried to look sympathetic. "If it's any consolation," she said, "our chances of surviving the next couple of hours are vanishingly remote."

Riley gave a snort. "Thank you," she said. "That's a *colossal* help."

"You're welcome." The avatar bowed, and then shimmered away into nothingness, leaving us staring at each other. And suddenly, neither of us knew what to say. The only topic we had left was the one we least wanted to tackle. After all, what use are words when your world's falling apart?

We looked down at our hands and listened to the hum of the air-conditioning. The quiet clangs and hisses of a working starship.

After a while, Riley said, "Do you think your idea will work?"

I honestly didn't know how to answer. Lucy had been keen to give it a try, and Captain Konstanz and the *Trouble Dog* seemed to think it was worth a shot.

"I guess we'll know soon enough."

I looked at her and suddenly saw her as if through a stranger's eyes. In place of the professional, no-nonsense loadmaster from the *Lucy's Ghost*, I now saw a tough, capable survivor, and felt closer to her than to anyone else I'd ever known. I slid my hand into the middle of the table. Riley looked down at it, as if unsure what was being offered. Then, without meeting my eye, she placed her own hand over the top of mine, and gave it a hesitant squeeze.

I drank in the light shining on her cheek, the way her hair fell around her face like fine copper wire, and the glimmer of the shiny gold stud in her right eyebrow.

"I have some conditions," she said.

"Name them."

She glanced up at me. "Firstly, everything you said about growing up, I need that to be true. Not just for me, but for Lucy too."

"Okay."

"I mean it. No more hunches, no more showing off. No more 'Lucky' Johnny Schultz. Things are different now."

"I know. What else?"

She dragged her front teeth across her bottom lip. "Just promise me this is real. That it's not a result of shock or fear or post-traumatic stress. That you really want to be with me, despite everything else that's going on."

I turned my hand over so I could hold hers. We'd been through hell together, and I knew that no matter what, we were going to be together for the rest of our lives—even if the rest of our lives amounted to little more than a few minutes.

"I promise."

An alarm sounded. Riley got to her feet. "Thank you," she said. And together in silence, we walked back to the crew lounge and strapped ourselves in for the coming battle.

CHAPTER SEVENTY-EIGHT
TROUBLE DOG

The *Restless Itch* might have been slow off the blocks, but the old rock's engines were huge and powerful, and she was soon moving quickly, and increasing her speed with every second that elapsed. When she reached three quarters of the speed necessary for a dimensional transition, I began to accelerate along the tunnel that led to the hangar at her bows. Thanks to her boost, I'd be moving almost fast enough to jump as soon as I emerged into empty space, thereby minimising the time Sudak's knife ships would have to target me. With luck, I might have the accumulated velocity to be away before they even realised I'd escaped.

The crew was secure, the way ahead clear. I ramped my acceleration to the max and shot forward like a bullet in a gun barrel.

By the time I burst into clear space a few seconds later, I was moving so fast the white ships stood little chance. They were too busy trying to match their backward speed to the *Restless Itch*'s forward acceleration. I fired a brace of newly manufactured torpedoes at each of them, and they broke position, scattering to either side as they struggled to assess and react to this new threat.

Once again, I increased my thrust, pushing all my engines well past their safety tolerances.

I was already too far away and moving too quickly to have to worry about incoming missiles. And for a moment, I allowed myself to imagine I was safe. But I had forgotten the energy weapons the Fleet carried. A blinding white light stabbed from the prow of Sudak's ship, scorching the armour on my starboard side. Hull plates that could survive the photosphere of an M-class sun began to soften and melt. Then the beam switched target, panning across to hit my stern, and I felt my acceleration falter as one of my engines took a direct hit.

"Damn!"

I threw myself into a barrel roll before the deadly beam could chew any more deeply into my viscera. Inside the crew section, my inhabitants were starting to react. In the engine room, Nod whimpered in its nest. Johnny Schultz gripped the armrest of his chair. And Captain Konstanz clenched her jaw, biting back what was doubtlessly a heartfelt and venomous curse.

By this time, the second white ship had regained its composure and also fired, although my sudden change of orientation had thrown off its targeting system, and the beam crackled past my port side without inflicting damage. Nevertheless, the blow I'd just received might have already undone me.

The reduction in my engine capacity meant there would be a commensurate increase in the time I'd need to accelerate to jump speed. According to my calculations, I would require an extra thirty seconds—and at the speed those white bastards operated, thirty seconds was thirty seconds too long. For the next half a minute, I'd be a sitting duck.

I didn't even have time to apologise to the crew. By the time I'd informed them of the situation, we'd most likely be dead. So instead, I increased my mental clock speed, accelerating my thoughts until the universe around me seemed to slow almost to a standstill. If I could maximise the time I had available, I might find a way out of this—although I didn't hold out much hope. My opponents possessed weapons of devastating strength that could strike at the speed of light. Compared to them, my paltry missiles and defence batteries were of little practical use. By the time my ordnance crawled its way across the intervening distance, I'd be dead.

I ran several quick simulations without success. Then I linked to Lucy, bringing her thoughts up to the same speed as my own.

"Is there anything you can do?" I asked once I'd explained the situation.

Her little brow furrowed. "The *Itch* has bow lasers designed to deal with micrometeorites and interstellar dust grains, but I don't think they're powerful enough to do much harm to a warship."

I gave a sigh. "I was hoping you had an alien super weapon up your sleeve."

"Sorry."

"It was a desperate hope."

"Then why are you smiling?"

"I survived the Archipelago War and resigned my

commission because of my disgust at the way the war was resolved."

"So?"

"So now that disgust's about to get me killed—slain by the very ships I asked to prevent another such conflict."

"And you think that's funny?"

"I'm a heavy cruiser. I always knew I'd die in battle."

Lucy put her fists on her hips and glared. "Well, I'm scared out of my wits. There has to be a way out of this."

"I'm not sure there is." I tried to think of something to console her. "If I manoeuvre hard enough, I might be able to buy us a couple more seconds?"

"And then what?"

I shrugged.

"Then… Wait!"

Lucy jerked in surprise. "What?"

"There's something ahead." I turned my full attention to the space ahead of me. A hole was opening. Something was ripping its way through the fabric of reality. "I think it's another ship."

Could the Fleet have sent reinforcements already? If so, I'd have to radically shorten my estimate of our remaining lifespans.

I caught a glimpse of something fat and bullet-shaped silhouetted against the mists of the higher dimensions. And then it was there, directly in front of me. Bronze and shining like a reflection in a mirror.

"Hello, sister."

"*Adalwolf?*"

"Did you miss me?"

CHAPTER SEVENTY-NINE

SAL KONSTANZ

I felt an impact on one of our aft engines, and the *Trouble Dog* rolled to one side. At the same time, a ship emerged in front of us. Before I had time to register what it was it had flashed past overhead, barely missing us, and opened fire on our pursuers.

The tactical display picked up the newcomer and tagged it with a familiar icon.

"That's the *Adalwolf*?"

The *Trouble Dog*'s avatar smiled. "Yes, and this time, he's on our side."

The space between the Carnivore and the nearest marble ship glittered as high-energy weapons were fired. Although to the ships the combat probably felt prolonged and strategic, it presented to my eyes as a series of rapid flashes.

When the afterimages cleared, I saw the *Adalwolf* had sustained a livid gouge to his forward plating—but his opponent was gone, broken into a cloud of glowing slag.

"Wow."

"He never left the Conglomeration Navy," the *Trouble*

Dog explained. "So his claws were never drawn. He kept his heavy armaments."

Even as she spoke, I saw fire from the other enemy ship rake her brother's flank.

"Is Sudak still alive?"

"As far as I know."

"Then put me through to her."

•

I'd seen Ona Sudak's face on the earlier footage, but it hadn't been very good quality. Looking at her now, displayed on the large view screen in crystal clear high definition, I could see she looked thinner than I remembered from our time in the Gallery. She'd lost some weight around her face and her cheeks looked hollow, as if prison life had eaten her away from the inside.

"Hello, Captain," she said.

"Why are you trying to kill us?"

She made a dismissive gesture, as if brushing aside my question. "I can assure you, as I've already explained to your ship, that it's nothing personal."

I pulled my cap off and ran a hand through my hair. "Well I can assure you that over here, we're taking it pretty fucking personally."

She looked at me with pity. "Captain, if you agree to surrender and disarm, I will allow you to remain on board the *Restless Itch*."

"And why would you do that?"

She gave a tight smile. "For old times' sake."

"And what about the incoming Nymtoq ships?"

"You can throw yourselves on their mercy."

I curled my lip. We both knew that after the loss of their cruiser, the Nymtoq would be in no mood to stop and ask questions, or to make distinctions between one group of trespassing humans and another.

"You might as well kill us now."

"That's your choice."

"It's not really a choice, is it?"

Sudak spread her hands. "I'm sorry, but it's the best I can offer."

On the tactical display, I saw the *Adalwolf* swing around and take up station between Sudak's ship and ours. Doubtless it was having a high-speed discussion with the *Trouble Dog*—half strategy meeting and half family reunion. But as last time they'd faced each other the *Adalwolf* had been trying to kill the *Trouble Dog*, I suspected there might be a certain level of acrimony to their exchange.

However, it wasn't the *Adalwolf's* position that had caught my eye. A message light on my head-up display informed me that Nod and its brood had completed partial repairs on the damaged engine.

Sudak narrowed her eyes. "Why are you smiling?"

I leaned back in my chair and replaced my cap. While Sudak knew we had Nod on board, her assessment of the time it would take us to fix the damage she'd inflicted would be based on the presence of only one Druff mechanic. She had no way of knowing that we now had fourteen, even if thirteen of them were juniors. Which meant the repair had taken far less time than she'd been expecting.

"I have a counter proposal," I said. I gave the *Trouble Dog* the nod and she engaged the patched-together motor. Even with the inertial dampers at full power, I felt a kick as the thrust clicked up a notch. Grinning now, I gave Sudak the finger. "How about you and the rest of the Marble Armada kiss my ass."

Her face coloured. Her eyes dropped from the screen, consulting her own tactical display, obviously wondering where our sudden burst of acceleration had come from.

"You bloody idiot," she said.

I let the smile drop from my face.

"Suck it."

I broke the connection and concentrated on the readouts before me. Thanks to Johnny's idea of getting the *Restless Itch* to give us a boost, and the Druff's sterling repair work, we were almost moving quickly enough, and I felt the *Trouble Dog* begin to oscillate between the real and the unreal, dipping in and out of the void like a dolphin running before the bow of a ship. *Adalwolf* flew beside us, matching our speed and heading. Wherever we were going, it looked as if we'd have the dubious pleasure of his company.

"I'm receiving a transmission from Sudak's ship," the *Trouble Dog* informed me.

"Ignore it, I don't want to speak to her."

"It's not from Ona Sudak. It's from somebody calling themselves Alexi Bochnak."

"Who's that?"

"I have no idea."

A line of energy flashed past our bows. We were being fired upon, but Sudak's attempts to hit us were being frustrated by the fact we simply weren't there half the time.

I saw *Adalwolf* drop a cloud of mines to slow pursuit. They streamed behind him like spores. And then we made the final leap, and all I could see were ragged streamers of mist stretching away into a disquieting and inestimable formlessness.

CHAPTER EIGHTY

NOD

Storm has passed.

World Tree stands. Some branches broken but others still strong.

Thanks to Nod.

Thanks to offspring.

Worked together to save ship.

To save *Trouble Dog*, for she is our World Tree. She is place where all roads start and all roads end. The place I birthed offspring, and only home they've ever known.

A good home in which to build our nests.

A brave home.

A clever home.

A forever home.

CHAPTER EIGHTY-ONE

JOHNNY SCHULTZ

I found the engineer asleep in its nest. Its thirteen infants were curled around it, huddling close for warmth and protection. Some of them still wore their tiny tool harnesses. As I entered the chamber, the adult extended a face.

"Sleep now," it said. "Work done, now rest. Do more work later."

The pile of Druff smelled like a rock pool into which someone had emptied a bottle of mouthwash. Seaweed and peppermint. Pleasant, but odd.

"I'm not here about work," I assured it.

"Work done, tired now."

"I have a message for you."

Another head snaked from beneath its body, and it regarded me from two directions, its little black eyes unreadable.

"What message?"

"It's from the Druff engineer on the *Lucy's Ghost*. Its name was Chet. He wanted me to pass it on."

"I know Chet."

"You do?"

"We recovered Chet. Its body aboard."

I knelt beside the nest, so our eyes were on the same level.

"You did?"

"Chet dead."

"It wanted me to tell you the white ships are cousins."

"Chet told me, before it died."

"It said it was very important."

Nod moved its faces from side to side—a sign of puzzlement I remembered from my time with Chet. "Meaning unclear. Did it say more?"

I thought back. "No, that was it. Just those four words. White ships are cousins."

"Hum." The creature considered this. Then it opened and closed its fingers—a clear sign of amusement. "Chet always was strange. Always way out on own branch."

It was apparent the message meant nothing to Nod. I sighed and climbed back to my feet.

"Anyway, I promised I'd pass it on, and I have."

"Thank you, Schultz."

"You're welcome."

I started to leave.

Behind me, Nod asked, "Did you love Chet?"

I paused at the door. "I guess so."

"You tried to save him?"

"I did."

The fingers around the edges of its faces opened and closed in a slow blink.

"Then thank you for that, too."

•

I went to sit in the *Trouble Dog*'s crew lounge, where I considered the wash of stars on the wall display. The idea of ships fighting and dying around those tiny diamond-like points seemed unintuitive and absurd. From here, the night sky appeared as serene and constant as it had to our forebears on the plains of Africa.

Addison came and sat in the couch beside me, and became similarly transfixed. She had pinned back her hair, and the soft cabin light caught the gold stud in her right eyebrow. Just looking at her, I knew I would keep my promise. I guess when the world falls apart, it throws a lot of things into perspective, and you realise what really matters. So, after today, there would be no more Lucky Johnny Schultz. I couldn't go on pretending to be a trading captain now I'd lost my ship to an inter-dimensional horror, and most of my crew to the ravenous parasites that had fallen from the monster's back. And with those creatures on one side of us and the Fleet of Knives on the other, I knew there'd be no room in the middle for a freewheeling rascal to operate. The world had changed and the apocalypse was upon us. I could give in to the trauma I'd suffered, curl up in a ball and wait to die, or I could find a way to fight back. For most of my life, my own happiness and survival had been my top priorities; but now it was time to stand up and be counted as a member of the human race. Now it was time to do something useful, if only to avenge my fallen crew. Sometimes, being an adult meant more than taking responsibility for your own actions; it meant taking responsibility for your friends, your family, and even your entire species.

From now on, I wanted John Schultz to be a different

man. But at the same time, I bitterly resented the necessity for change. Up until a few days ago, I'd been having fun playing fast and loose. In contrast, being an adult sucked in so, so many varied and fearful ways. But if the *Trouble Dog* could change its spots and find a new purpose in life, so could I.

I mean, how hard could it be?

CHAPTER EIGHTY-TWO

SAL KONSTANZ

In the evening, we gathered in the crew lounge. Schultz and Addison sat close to each other, their fingers occasionally brushing. Lucy sat on Schultz's other side, with her legs curled under her and her head resting on his shoulder. All three sported a variety of cuts and bruises, and their eyes held that faraway look that I'd seen in so many rescued survivors.

Preston occupied the next chair along, looking tired and uncomfortable. Nod and its posse had moved up from the engine room and were now asleep at the back of the room, curled up like a set of footstools.

"The good news is we got away," I said. "The bad news is that I have no idea where we should be going." I had been slumped in my chair since we made the leap into the higher dimensions, wracking my brain for a safe destination—somewhere we could refuel and resupply without drawing the ire of either the Nymtoq or the Fleet of Knives.

Schultz raised his hand.

"If we can't go back, can we go further out, into the Multiplicity? They can't follow us there."

"You better hope they can't," Addison said.

I quieted them down.

"As I was trying to say, *I* have no idea, but the ship informs me it might."

I stepped aside to allow everyone a clear view of the main screen.

"I have been reviewing the message we received just before we jumped," the *Trouble Dog*'s avatar said. She had changed her attire again. Now she appeared to be wearing an old-fashioned pressure suit made of bulky white material, with mission patches sewn onto the sleeves and a thick metal neck ring. She wasn't wearing a helmet, but still looked the very image of a traditional space explorer.

"It was a data file," she continued. "A set of notes containing everything the Fleet of Knives knows about the creatures that attacked the *Lucy's Ghost*."

"And this was sent by this Bochnak person?" I asked.

"From the notes, he appears to be an historian who was unlucky enough to have been stranded aboard when the Fleet's attack began."

"What does he say about the creatures?"

The main screen cleared and displayed the image of a creature that looked as if it had been trawled from the depths of Hell. It had a long, powerful body, ragged outspread wings that looked like banners cut from the very cloth of night, and a mouth lined with row after row of serrated diamond teeth. It resembled a lamprey crossed with the half-rotted skeleton of a dead vulture.

"Bochnak refers to them as dragons," the ship said.

"Although they bear only a passing similarity to the creatures of human legend."

Despite my distaste, I leaned forward for a better look.

"And how large are they?"

"About the same size as I am."

"Holy crap."

"You saw the bite one of them took out of the *Lucy's Ghost*," Addison said. "Its teeth went through her hull plating like it was nothing."

Preston whistled. "How do we defend against something like that?"

"I don't know that we can," the *Trouble Dog* said. "I suspect our best strategy would be to try to avoid them altogether."

"And how are we supposed to do that?"

The avatar pulled up a star map.

"We're here," she said. "Now Bochnak's data suggests this region over here is relatively free of these creatures. In fact they seem to avoid it." A highlight appeared over the area of space containing the Intrusion.

"But that's within the borders of the Generality," I reminded her. "Won't we run into trouble with the Fleet?"

She smiled infuriatingly. "That's the curious part." Her tone was light and confident. "It seems the white ships are also avoiding it."

"Maybe they know something we don't?" Schultz murmured.

Addison dug him in the ribs with her elbow. "Hey! I'm from the edge of the Intrusion, remember?" She looked at me. "I was born there," she said. "If you can get us there in one piece, I'll be able to help you find a hiding place."

Preston coughed. "That's all very well." He gestured at

the picture of the dragon. "But what do we do if we run across one of these things before we get there?"

"We'll just have to hope we don't." I glanced at the avatar. "Right?"

For the first time, the *Trouble Dog* let herself look uncomfortable.

"Something about the dragons renders them invisible to artificial instruments," she said. "I have no idea how that might work, but apparently it does. We could be surrounded by a horde of them right now, and I'd have no idea until they struck."

Preston sucked in a breath. Addison looked around at the walls, as if expecting diamond fangs to pierce the bulkhead at any moment.

"What can we do?" Schultz asked. "Can we keep lookout?"

The avatar held up a palm to stop him. "You can't look in every direction at once," she said. "And it's well documented that humans who stare too long into the void start hallucinating."

I had the feeling she was edging towards something. I tried to keep the impatience from my voice.

"Well, what do you suggest?"

"I think I'm going to need an eye."

"An *eye*?" I wasn't quite sure what she meant.

"A real human eye," she said. "Ideally with the optic nerve still attached."

I gave her an incredulous stare.

"And where do you propose acquiring one of those?" I couldn't believe she was talking literally. "It might have escaped your attention, but we're a long way from the nearest hospital."

The avatar's face lost all expression. "We'll have to ask for a volunteer among the crew."

Addison leapt to her feet. "You want one of us to *donate an eye?*"

The *Trouble Dog* gave the slightest of nods. "I wouldn't ask if it weren't a matter of survival."

I felt a sinking feeling in my stomach. Alva Clay had sacrificed her life for the survival of the crew. Now all the ship was asking from us was an eye. I pictured Clay and imagined what she'd say, and immediately knew what I had to do.

"You don't have to ask for a volunteer," I said, speaking before I could change my mind. "I'll do it. You can have one of mine."

Schultz stiffened. "Captain, you can't!"

"Oh, shut up. Of course I can."

"What about Nod? He has twelve eyes."

"It would be easier to integrate a human visual cortex," the *Trouble Dog* said. "Seeing that the organic parts of my brain are human, and Druff biochemistry is somewhat different in several inconvenient respects."

I sighed. "Besides, the only other member of our official crew is Preston, and he'll need to be the one to perform the… extraction."

Schultz tapped his chest. "What about me?"

"No, this is something I can't ask anyone else to do. As captain, it's my responsibility."

"Thank you," the *Dog* said.

I shrugged away her thanks. "When do you need it?"

"Right away."

The sinking feeling became a cold, deep emptiness that seemed to stretch from the pit of my stomach to the base of my windpipe. I rose unsteadily to my feet and straightened my cap. My tongue felt dry. At that moment, I would have given anything to have Alva beside me, urging me on with her bravery and sarcasm. I coughed to clear my throat.

"Okay, let's do this quickly," I said. "Before I chicken out."

CHAPTER EIGHTY-THREE

TROUBLE DOG

The higher dimensions echoed with distress calls. All over the Generality, ships were fleeing the Fleet of Knives. Merchants, travellers, diplomats. I ached to tell them what I had learned. They deserved sanctuary as much as I did. But broadcasting my destination would also alert the Fleet, and jeopardise the safety of my passengers and crew. The best I could do was broadcast Bochnak's data and hope a few of them would be able to figure it out and come to the same conclusions I had. The more ships that reached safety, the more options we'd have when it came time to discuss how we might fight back against the Fleet's occupation of the Generality.

In the meantime, I scanned the surrounding mists. Even though I knew it was futile, I couldn't help it. I felt sightless and vulnerable. Knowing something undetectable lurked out there filled me with a prickly dread. I could be struck at any instant, and not see my attacker until the moment of impact—and even then, all I'd actually *see* would be the damage they inflicted. The sooner I hooked the captain's eye into my sensor array, connecting it to the organic tissue at the heart of my processors, the happier I'd be.

Right now, Konstanz lay sedated on a bed in the infirmary while Preston readied the instruments he would need to remove her right eye. The operation would be long and difficult, as he needed to keep the optic nerve intact. But I would be looking over his shoulder, offering my advice. And he really had come a long way in his studies over the past year. Even if his hands were shaking now, I was confident I would be able to successfully guide him through the procedure.

In the meantime, the *Adalwolf* and I were crossing Nymtoq space, heading for refuge on the far side of their territory, in the region of the galaxy controlled by the Hoppers—the benevolent, cricket-like race that had taken the captain's lover on their expedition to Andromeda.

As we flew, *Adalwolf* and I talked. We were the only two surviving members of our pack, and pack loyalty runs strongly in Carnivores. It is literally bred into us. And so, although we'd fought, I was delighted to have him with me. I felt as if I'd regained a little part of myself that had been missing since I resigned from the navy. We talked of our dead and missing siblings, killed during the war, and I forgave him for his misguided actions at the Gallery—just as he forgave me for killing our sister, *Fenrir*.

We hoped the Hoppers would allow us to repair our damage and refuel our engines. From there, we could plot a circuitous course around the edge of the Generality, leaping from one alien province to another, until we finally reached the Intrusion.

What we would find when we reached that anomaly, I didn't know. But if both the dragons and the knife ships were afraid of it, I hoped it would make an ideal gathering place for the last human starships—a refuge where we could hide until we figured out what our next step was going to be.

The journey to get there would be lengthy and filled with peril, but I knew we were capable of making it.

Until then, all we could do was mourn our losses and turn our faces to the stars. No matter how upset and weary we might be, we were, as Alva Clay had once observed, like sharks—we had to keep moving forwards lest we died.

ACKNOWLEDGEMENTS

Special thanks are due to Adrian Tchaikovsky, who suggested the title of this book when I was stuck for one. He's one of the best writers we have; please go and check out some of his novels.

I'd also like to thank my agent, Alexander Cochran at C+W; my editor, Cath Trechman at Titan Books; my copy editor, Hayley Shepherd; and my friends and family, for everything they've done to support and encourage me during the writing of this novel.

ABOUT THE AUTHOR

Gareth L. Powell lives and works in North Somerset. His alternate history thriller *Ack-Ack Macaque* won the 2013 BSFA Award for Best Novel, spawned two sequels, and was shortlisted in the Best Translated Novel category for the 2016 Seiun Awards in Japan.

Gareth's short fiction has appeared in a host of magazines and anthologies, including *Interzone, Solaris Rising 3*, and *The Year's Best Science Fiction*, and his story "Ride The Blue Horse" made the shortlist for the 2015 BSFA Award.

In addition to his fiction, Gareth has written film scripts for corporate training videos, penned a strip for the long-running British comic *2000 AD*, composed song lyrics for an indie electro band, and written articles and reviews for *The Irish Times, Acoustic Magazine*, and *SFX*.

He studied creative writing under Helen Dunmore at the University of Glamorgan, and is now a popular panellist and speaker at literary events and conventions around the UK. He has run workshops and given guest lectures at a number of universities, libraries and conferences, is a frequent guest on local radio, and has appeared on the BBC Radio 4 *Today* programme.

Gareth lives near Bristol with his wife, daughters, and cats. He can be found online at: www.garethlpowell.com

THE RIG

ROGER LEVY

Humanity has spread across the depths of space but is connected by AfterLife – a vote made by every member of humanity on the worth of a life. Bale, a disillusioned policeman on the planet Bleak, is brutally attacked, leading writer Raisa on to a story spanning centuries of corruption. On Gehenna, the last religious planet, a hyper-intelligent boy, Alef, meets psychopath Pellon Hoq, and so begins a rivalry and friendship to last an epoch.

"Levy is a writer of great talent and originality."
SF Site

"Levy's writing is well-measured and thoughtful, multi-faceted and often totally gripping."
Strange Horizons

CLADE

JAMES BRADLEY

On a beach in Antarctica, scientist Adam Leith marks the passage of the summer solstice. Back in Sydney his partner Ellie waits for the results of her latest round of IVF treatment. That result, when it comes, will change both their lives and propel them into a future neither could have predicted. In a collapsing England, Adam will battle to survive an apocalyptic storm. Against a backdrop of growing civil unrest at home, Ellie will discover a strange affinity with beekeeping. In the aftermath of a pandemic, a young man finds solace in building virtual recreations of the dead. And new connections will be formed from the most unlikely beginnings.

"A beautifully written meditation on climate collapse."
New Scientist

"An elegantly bleak vision of a climate-change future…
urgent, powerful stuff."
The Guardian

NEW POMPEII

DANIEL GODFREY

In the near future, energy giant Novus Particles develops
the technology to transport objects and people from
the deep past to the present. Their biggest secret: New
Pompeii. A replica of the city hidden deep in central Asia,
filled with Romans pulled through time a split second
before the volcano erupted. Historian Nick Houghton
doesn't know why he's been chosen to be the company's
historical advisor. He's just excited to be there. Until
he starts to wonder what happened to his predecessor.
Until he realises that NovusPart have more secrets than
even the conspiracy theorists suspect, and that they have
underestimated their captives.

"Tremendously gripping."
Financial Times (Books of the Year)

"Irresistibly entertaining."
Barnes & Noble

TITANBOOKS.COM

THE HIGH GROUND

MELINDA SNODGRASS

The Emperor's daughter Mercedes is the first woman
admitted to The High Ground, the elite training academy
of the Solar League's Star Command, and she must
graduate if she is to have any hope of taking the throne.
Her classmate Thracius has more modest goals—to defy
his humble beginnings and rise to the rank of captain. But
in a system rocked by political division, where women
are governed by their husbands, the poor are kept in their
place by a rigid class system, and the alien races have been
subjugated, there are many who want them to fail. The
cadets will be tested as they never thought possible…

"Snodgrass just keeps on getting better."
George R.R. Martin

"Entertaining and briskly paced."
Publishers Weekly

TITANBOOKS.COM

For more fantastic fiction, author events, exclusive
excerpts, competitions, limited editions and more

VISIT OUR WEBSITE
titanbooks.com

LIKE US ON FACEBOOK
facebook.com/titanbooks

FOLLOW US ON TWITTER
@TitanBooks

EMAIL US
readerfeedback@titanemail.com